Cry of the Phoenix

A novel
by
Jane Dater

First Edition

Printed in the United States of America

For my mother,
for always believing in me

Acknowledgments

I would like to thank the people who helped make this book a reality. S.R. served as midwife to the concept and edited countless revisions. Graham and Theresa, guardians of the real Skokholm Island, served as gracious hosts during my two trips to the island for research. I would like to thank Toni Harris, from the El Paso Holocaust Museum, for her reading of an earlier draft and helpful suggestions. John Hansen, with both his legal expertise and knowledge of history, was a valuable resource. A special thanks to Nancy Neal and my daughter Julie for their thoughtful critiques of the manuscript at various stages, as well as to Kathy McIntosh, Susan Murphy, and Peggy Staggs, who sat through endless readings of my original first chapter, so long ago. Patricia Hopper served as artistic advisor for the cover's design. And finally, I owe a huge debt to my husband, Phil, for his unfailing support and encouragement throughout this entire project.

I would also like to acknowledge the wonderful books by Ronald Lockley that drew me to the island—*Letters from Skokholm*, *The Island*, and *Dream Island*. Other books that were invaluable were first person accounts such as *Alicia:*

My Story by Alicia Appleman-Jurman; *The Survivor of the Holocaust* by Jack Eisner; *Playing for Time* by Fania Fenelon; *The Journey* by Ida Fink; *Rena's Promise: A Story of Sisters in Auschwitz* by Rena Kornreich Gelissen; *Auschwitz: A Doctor's Eyewitness Account* by Dr. Miklos Nyiszli; *And I Am Afraid in My Dreams* by Wanda Pottawska; *Memoirs of a Warsaw Ghetto Fighter: The Past Within Me* by Simha Rotem; and *The Cage* by Ruth Minsky Sender. I am also indebted to the works of Simon Wiesenthal, specifically *The Murderers Among Us* and *Justice Not Vengeance.*

Two additional sources of inspiration were Linda Atkinson's *In Kindling Flame: The Story of Hannah Senesh* and Peter Malkin's *Eichmann in My Hands.* Other valuable resources were *Eichmann in Jerusalem: A Report on the Banality of Evil* by Hannah Arendt; *The Warsaw Ghetto: A Christian's Testimony* by Wladyslaw Bartoszewski; *A Nightmare in History: The Holocaust 1933-1945* by Miriam Chaikin; *Auschwitz and After* by Charlotte Delbo; *To Pray as a Jew* by Rabbi Hayim Halevy Donin; *Treblinka* by Jean Francois-Steiner; *The House on Garibaldi Street* by Isser Harel; *The Wiesenthal File* by Alan Levy; *Nuremberg: Infamy on Trial* by Joseph E. Persico; *Prosecuting Nazi War Criminals* by Alan S. Rosenblum; *The Law and the People: An Outline of the Legal System of England and Wales* by N. R. Tillett; *War Crimes, War Criminals and War Crimes Trials* by Norman E. Tutorow; and *A Surplus of Memory: Chronicle of the Warsaw Ghetto Uprising* by Yitzhak Zuckerman.

All correspondence should be addressed to:

Moose Lake Publishing LLC
223 Sugar Hill Road
Harmony, Maine 04942

Phone: 207-683-2959
Fax: 207-683-2172
E-Mail: http://www.smallarmsreview.com

"Life shrinks or expands
in proportion to one's courage."
—Anais Nin

SCOTLAND
Atlantic Ocean
North Sea
Irish
Sea
IRELAND
ENGLAND
WALES
London
Skokholm Island
English Channel
GREAT BRITAIN

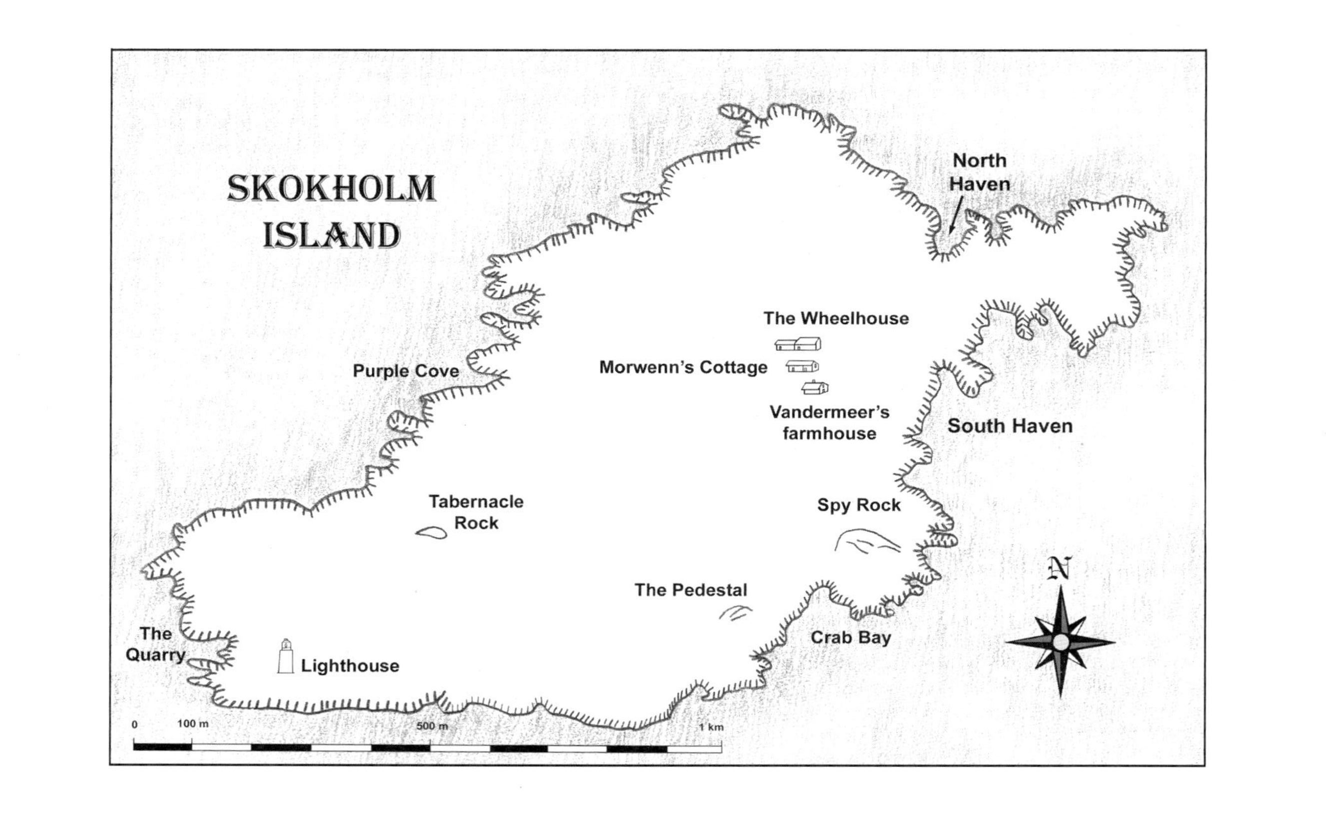
SKOKHOLM
ISLAND
North
Haven
The Wheelhouse
Morwenn's Cottage
Vandermeer's
farmhouse
South Haven
Purple Cove
Tabernacle
Rock
Spy Rock
The Pedestal
Crab Bay
The
Quarry
Lighthouse
N
0
100 m
500 m
1 km

KATYA DENYS

From the moment I realized Janisch might still be alive, there was no turning back. Some say I walked into the tiger's cage, knowing full well what the beast was capable of. Some say I've ruined my life, as if my twenty-six years on this earth had been perfect until that one night last week. Some even say I am guilty of murder. I'm not sure anyone can judge me without knowing the whole story.

It's been only eight weeks since I found the letter from Robert and the sketch he'd made of Emil Janisch. Eight weeks, and my life has turned one more time. Every morning when I wake up in this Welsh prison, it feels strange to be charged with Janisch's murder, when he's the one who killed so many. If things had turned out differently, I would have been a witness at his trial.

My cell has a narrow cot, hung from the wall, with a lumpy thin mattress, a flat pillow with a torn case, and a shabby blanket of green wool. I'm the only prisoner on the women's ward, so it's very quiet. There's a small window but it's up near the ceiling, so I can't see anything except a bit of sky and the moon for a few hours at night if it's not cloudy. Next to the cot is a sink—it's quite small, made of metal—and there's just a sliver of some brown soap that smells like lye. The toilet has no seat. When I lie down and look up at the ceiling, I find shapes in the peeling paint—a horse's head or the face of a leering old man. Compared to Auschwitz, this is heaven.

On the morning I found Robert's letter, it had been snowing in London for three days. It was so white, so quiet that day, as if the universe were holding its breath. All the cars parked along Finchley Street had several inches of snow on their roofs, and everything was muffled—footsteps, voices, traffic.

I remember standing at the window of my office with my fingertips on the cool glass of the panes. The world had lost its color, all life sucked out of the sky until it was flat and grey, and everything else was a blur of white.

I turned round from the window to face the chaos of my office, where half-filled cardboard boxes covered most of the floor. I sat down at my desk, which was pulled back six feet from the window because of the cold air that seeped through gaps in the casing. I finally pulled a stack of folders from my desk and held them in my lap, as if the intention of sorting through them would get the job done. In three hours, all I'd accomplished was to fill two more boxes with file folders.

Chaos made me jumpy and irritable, but I couldn't bring myself to seal the cartons. This had been my life's work for three years, my reason for living—these files of survivor testimony, these typewritten accounts of dates and places of massacres and executions, names of perpetrators and victims.

I had typed every word of these pages from my interview notes. As survivors sat in the chair next to my desk and told their stories, I tried to insulate myself from their pain. My own stories were inside, in a secret place that I rarely visited. I would sit up perfectly straight, with my feet crossed at the ankles and my notebook in my lap, and I would look into people's eyes, knowing that whatever they told me couldn't be any worse than what I already knew. "Tell me what happened then," I would say automatically, but I don't think I was unkind. I brought them mugs of hot tea and tissues when they cried. But I knew, just as I had known in the camps, that to allow myself to feel anything during the interviews would be foolish. Only later, after they'd left, would I let myself cry if I needed to, and then I would wipe the tears away before anyone could see.

I remember thinking that so little had come from our efforts—a few convictions, which might well be overturned in the future. We were sending all the files to a man in Israel, Benzion Dinur, who would probably put them in storehouses like mass graves. I looked out the window again, where the sky, for weeks in a row, had turned from the grey of daylight to the blackness of night, with no hint of blue in between. Perhaps, when our work was done, I would become an artist and splash riots of color on canvasses of pristine white. Perhaps it would help me get through days like this.

I touched the smooth glass of the banker's lamp, perfect except for a small chip in the rim. A month ago, before Aaron's decision to close the office, I'd found the lamp and the desk blotter with maroon leather corners at a jumble sale, and I thought they would brighten things up a bit. The walls of my office were bare, except for the clock and calendar over the file cabinets and the map of Great Britain just above the radiator. My desk was the only thing tidy in the whole room; I could always concentrate better when the surface was clear. Normally, the whole office was in order, but now, stacks of manila folders cluttered the tops of all the file cabinets that ran along the wall, and whenever I left my desk, I had to walk carefully because there were so many boxes on the floor.

A staccato burst from a typewriter somewhere down the hall brought me out of my trance. I opened the top folder and began to stack the pages and clip photographs to the inside cover, as I'd been doing for the past six days, refusing to read the words. Like Aaron, I would keep these people and their stories at a distance. I closed this folder and leaned down to place it with the others in the box nearest my desk.

I rubbed my hands together and blew on them, but they were still like ice when I touched my face. I thought about a hot bath—it would be so lovely to submerge in hot water with a glass of wine and my new Beethoven album on the record player. Leaning forward to wrap my hands round the mug of tea on my desk, I found it had already gone cold because the room was freezing. The radiator hadn't worked since February, and I'd left my coat on, even though I was wearing a wool dress. What did it matter? In a few days, Aaron and I and all the boxes would be gone—everything would be stripped bare.

Outside, the snow fell in sheets blown off-course by the wind. Inside the second folder, which had no label, I found a pencil sketch of a man's face that made time stand still. He was dead—how could anyone have drawn him? But here was a ghost created by someone's pencil—a face with the same wide forehead as Emil Janisch, the short dark hair, those eyes so deeply set under the brow, the same thin lips. I remembered the day in Auschwitz when we'd heard rumors about Janisch's assassination, and then we never saw him again. Where had this drawing come from, and how long had it been in the file? Underneath it, I found a handwritten letter on lined notebook paper—something about a reclusive man on an island who claimed to be Dutch but had an Iron Cross in his desk. Could it possibly be Emil Janisch? I looked at the sketch again, and when I covered the lower half of the face and looked just at the eyes, it was him. My chest and throat were tight, and I wanted to lash out at something. I wanted to rip that paper into shreds, but I knew I would not.

I walked to the window, and through the snow, I saw another grey scene, a landscape from a different place and time, where columns of prisoners shivered in the baggy trousers and jackets of dead Russian soldiers and felt their toes grow numb inside the wooden clogs meant for shoes. SS Captain Emil Janisch strutted, warm and well fed, in his trim uniform with tall black boots. Another image broke through—my sister falling to the ground in slow motion, the red rose in bloom on her chest, and I could not scream.

I felt as if my knees might give out, so I collapsed

into my chair to read the letter one more time.

22 March, 1953

Dear Grandfather,

I have found something that has caused me a great deal of concern. I am not proud of the way in which I made this discovery, but I hope you will forgive me.

The man to whom you sold the island, Mattheu Vandermeer, has an Iron Cross—not something that he displays with pride, as one would showcase a medal of honor or a collector's item, but something that he hides away in the back of a desk drawer. As far as I know, and correct me if I'm wrong, these medals were awarded only to Germans. Vandermeer claims to be Dutch and says he was a minister in the Dutch Reformed church of Amsterdam during the war. This is not something with which I can confront him, considering how I came to find the medal. But that's another story.

Even before I found the Iron Cross, I wondered why a minister would choose to live in isolation as he does. This path of austerity he has chosen does not make sense to me. I am more like you than I knew; I also love a mystery.

In that spirit, I have sent you this sketch that I made from memory. Vandermeer knows nothing about this, of course. After I took a photograph of him, my camera went missing. He is about five foot eleven and weighs close on 170 pounds. I think his hair must have been medium brown a few years ago; now it's lightened quite a bit by the sun. Piercing blue eyes, but very deep-set. A small scar over the left eyebrow.

With your connections, I thought you might have an interest in researching Vandermeer's past. It also seems natural to know the merit of a man who now lives in the place I once thought would be mine. Address all correspondence to Thomas Weaver, General Delivery, Marloes. I'll explain about *that* later.

As always, Robert

Who was this Robert? And why did a man named Mattheu Vandermeer have an Iron Cross if he was Dutch? I leaned back, tilting my head up to look at the ceiling, and the swirls of the textured pattern made me dizzy as I remembered Janisch's face and the Iron Cross at the neck of his uniform. Why a minister would live in such an isolated place, I didn't know, but Emil Janisch would do it, with contempt for the whole world, believing with his natural arrogance that he need answer to no one but himself.

I put the stack of folders on my desk, got up from my chair and watched the endless chains of snowflakes that threatened to blot out the whole of London. If only I could get rid of Emil Janisch's memory as easily. Instead, I turned to the file cabinets and pulled open the second drawer of the middle one, where I knew his file would be. It was only an inch thick, not as full as the others were. I put the folder on my chair and stacked the ones from my desk into a pile on the floor.

As I picked up his file again, my heart beat like a war drum. I dropped the folder on the desk and shoved my hands into my coat pockets. How much pain could this still inflict on me? Even though I thought Janisch was shot at Auschwitz, we'd maintained a file on him because there was no proof of his death. I needed to escape from that room full of ghosts, so I tried to see the white trim, now blurred against a backdrop of more white, on mullioned windows across the street. I massaged the back of my neck. My stomach burned, and my shoulders were tight with the memory of camp guards who grabbed or pushed if I didn't move fast enough, or just because I was there.

I knew that to open Janisch's file would resurrect him. Could I handle any more memories? As hard as I tried to forget him, Emil Janisch had played the leading role in my nightmares for so long. I felt my life turning one more time, and I counted the years of my existence—twelve of childhood happiness, six of hell in varying degrees, and the last eight—how does one describe any years of life after Auschwitz? Is "life," in the fullest sense, even possible after experiencing so much that was worse than death? I felt myself being pulled into the cave, that dark place where memories wrap round my head like a shroud, and I can neither see nor breathe.

A subtle tremor took hold of my fingers as I reached out to open the file, to page through documents in search of the photograph of Janisch with Rudolf Garner. I had always believed that Janisch set up the shot to make himself look good in comparison. Garner was a fat, dark little weasel, while Janisch was at least four inches taller, and his pride in his obviously "superior" physique showed in his posture and the arrogance of his expression. In the background, there were wooden buildings—the barracks in Birkenau.

I held the photograph closer to study Janisch's face, then picked up the sketch and held the two side by side. I had always avoided photographs of Janisch, but because of the sketch, I found the courage to look directly into that picture. I compared face shapes, the placement of eyes in relation to nose, the widths of two mouths. My hands no longer shook, as I glanced from one face to the other, but in the back of my throat there was a sharp, bitter taste. I willed the face in the sketch to be Janisch—surely, God would grant me this.

I dropped the sketch and the photograph on the desk and stood up again, unable to concentrate. I should leave it alone. I should put the sketch and the letter back into their folder and bury them at the bottom of a box. I could tell Aaron I was sick, go home, get drunk out of my mind, and forget what I had just seen. Remembering could only lead to more pain.

Sometimes at night, I lie very still, cocooned in blankets, my mind empty and at peace. But then a face will come—someone from the past—my brother Patryk or one of my cousins or an old friend from school. I don't think about the face—I see only its physical contours. I hold it at a distance; I don't let it have a name. I keep holding it back as long as I can, but I am always confronted, in the end, by the fact that all these people are lost, and I will never see them again. My ghosts stay in the dark tunnel of my mind when I am balanced, but when I am not, they overwhelm me. Then I have to count them, chanting their names and their ties to me like a prayer, and I have to ease the sharp pain under my breastbone with wine.

With great effort, I drew my mind back to the present, putting the papers back into the file, with the sketch and the letter on top. As I walked to Aaron Levy's office, down the short stretch of linoleum where my footsteps echoed, I couldn't help thinking of Rebekah, and I had to tell myself to keep breathing.

Aaron's door was open, and he sat in his chair, which was swiveled to the right. He seemed to be staring at the Israeli flag on the wall, but I couldn't be sure. Maybe he was having as much trouble letting go of our work as I was. Smoke spiraled into the air from a forgotten cigarette in his ashtray. As I raised my hand to knock on the doorframe, Aaron turned toward me in his chair, and although he smiled, he seemed distracted, his eyes deeply shadowed and not quite focused. With a wave of his hand, he motioned me in.

He glanced at my coat and shook his head. "I'm sorry about the heat, or rather, the lack of it." His eyes narrowed. "You look like you've seen a ghost, Katya. Are you all right?"

"I have seen a ghost." It was better this way—to talk it out with Aaron, to get his opinion. Without being invited, I slid into the chair in front of his desk and tossed the folder toward him. "No, I'm not all right. Take a look at this." In the weak light from the window, Aaron suddenly looked older than his fifty years, with those shadows under his eyes and thinning hair that had gone silver. He put on reading glasses and picked up the sketch. "I remember this. It was sent by William Kensley's grandson. I filed it away. Nothing to go on—not even a good photograph."

"I think it might be Emil Janisch."

Aaron sighed and rubbed his forehead, running his fingertips along the creases. "I thought you told me

Janisch was dead."

I ignored his remark. "Why was that folder with my interview records?"

"Why are you so interested in this, if he's dead?" Aaron flicked a piece of lint from the sleeve of his grey pinstriped suit.

"No one ever saw his body—his death was a rumor. Now I think he may have been transferred, for his own safety."

Aaron put his glasses back on and read the letter. He held the sketch beside the photo. "I don't know." He took off his glasses, tossing them on the desk, and looked up at me, with the quick half-smile I knew he didn't mean.

I didn't blame him for wanting to quit. He'd dedicated his life to recording Nazi atrocities, but it had begun to seem futile. "My gut instinct tells me there may be something to this." I tried to keep my voice light as I said to him, "Where is the island mentioned in the letter?

Aaron looked at me for a long time, studying my face, until I began to believe he was inside my mind, probing my thoughts, turning them over like shells on the beach. Finally, he said to me, "Can you be objective where Emil Janisch is concerned?"

To show how nonchalant I could be, I stuck the fingers of my left hand, like a comb, into the tight waves of my hair, and pulled them through. My voice was level and calm as I said, "I would hope so."

"Robert went back to the island of Skokholm for a visit. He and William had lived there before the war; actually, I think Robert grew up there. It's a very small place, just off the coast of Wales." Aaron straightened the papers in Janisch's file. "You know who William Kensley is—the owner of *The London Daily Times*— and also my friend." Aaron closed the file and took a cigarette from the silver case on his desk. "Anyway, Robert goes to the island—God only knows how he got hold of the Iron Cross. All of a sudden, Robert gets suspicious of Vandermeer and writes to his grandfather." Aaron lit the cigarette, inhaled deeply and drummed on Janisch's file with the fingers of his left hand. "For years, I've begged for funding, and now there's nothing left. I don't have the energy for a wealthy dilettante who could be playing spy games."

Aaron stood up, and his voice was louder than before as he said to me, "I would advise you to forget this whole thing. William rang me up; he only sent the letter and sketch to us to placate Robert." Aaron hesitated. "It seems the young man has been somewhat of a flake in the past." I heard in Aaron's voice what he was too polite to say—that he felt no need to placate anyone.

As I stared past him, and the hands of the clock ticked their way, second by second, round the white face, I struggled to organize my thoughts. I once swore that I would walk to the edge of the earth to find Janisch. I didn't care if Robert Kensley was the biggest flake in the world. The ghost of Emil Janisch had come back, and there was no way to ignore it. "Do you remember," I finally said to Aaron, "how you told me that we are markers for the dead—that our testimony against men like Janisch keeps our loved ones from being forgotten? That's why we're here, why we work day after day, year after year, to preserve those words—the truth the Nazis tried so hard to conceal."

"Yes, of course."

"I am Rebekah's marker, and Justyna's and Klara's and Mala's and everyone else I saw him murder in Auschwitz. And he would have signed the death warrants for thousands more."

"We have no more funds, Katya."

I sighed and held my arms across my stomach, which felt like it was on fire. "I need to know for sure this man isn't Janisch—just for my own peace of mind. It doesn't have to go any farther."

Aaron slumped into his chair and put his glasses back on, picking up the file. It felt like a small victory—at least he was looking at it a second time. As he bent his head to study the papers, I shifted my weight in the chair and put my palms over my eyes to cool the scratchy dry feeling from too much reading in bad light. The dull pain inside my head threatened to become a headache later on. I massaged my forehead and listened, as Aaron slowly turned the pages of the file, the turn of each page loud to me. I stared at the Israeli flag to my left and found myself rubbing at the fabric of my coat, over the tattoo on my forearm.

"Katya," I heard him say, and his voice was soft. Taking off his glasses, he closed the file, and as he handed it back to me, I knew the situation was hopeless. "I'm sorry. There's little to come and go on, certainly nothing to warrant an investigation. Send Janisch's file with the others." I knew I had made an impossible request.

"But what if this is really him?" I wanted to say, but instead I opened the file folder and stared at the drawing again, at the eyes that could freeze grown men, even Germans, with their coldness. I remember those eyes, an old woman had told me. His eyes were terrible. "Aaron, the man was. . . " How could I even describe him with words? "He was the dark corner in our nightmares in the worst of the camps—the monster that has no words to define it." I felt my knees give way and sank back into the chair. "And that's only what I knew about." I watched his face for some kind of emotion, but he kept his expression completely neutral. When it came to hiding our feelings, Aaron and I were masters at it—a skill developed for survival.

"You have a pencil sketch of a man who owns an Iron Cross." Aaron lit another cigarette with great care and inhaled, blowing the smoke toward the ceiling. "Some people collect things like that, and there's the real possibility this grandson of Kensley's is dead wrong. Many of the old Gothic crosses look a lot like the Iron Cross." He paused, as if he hoped I would not be able to say "yes" to his next question. "Is the resemblance so strong?"

"I doubt if I'll sleep tonight."

He sighed and closed his eyes for a moment. I was pushing, but I couldn't help it. When he spoke, Aaron's voice was still soft, his words measured, but he seemed drained of all energy. "So, Katya, what do you want me to do?"

I felt my nails dig into the palms of my hands. "Please, I've never asked you for much. Help me with this." I tapped the folder on his desk.

"Look round you." Aaron gestured at the stacks of folders, at his own half-filled boxes on the floor. "We have to wind this down—it's over."

"Not for me, it isn't." I stood up slowly, avoiding his eyes, and turned away from him. Holding the file like a shield across my chest, I could feel Aaron's eyes on the back of my neck. I stared at the white paint in the hallway, faded and peeling. As usual, Aaron had all the answers—did he think he was better than everyone else? I turned back toward him, aware of the burning patches under my eyes that flared when I got angry. "You're the one who got me involved in all this." I waved my hand across the room in a broad gesture to include all the files in Aaron's office, as well as the flag on his wall. "You were the one who told me we couldn't forget the victims, couldn't just go on blindly with our lives." I lowered my voice, trying to calm down. "We have to bring these murderers to justice, you said to me. We have to make them accountable." I slammed the file down on the stack of folders. "Aaron, I need to know if the most sadistic Nazi who ever lived is out on that island—it can't be that far from here." I leaned forward, over the clutter of Aaron's desk, to look him in the eyes. I had nothing to lose. "What if Janisch is living in this little paradise when he should be burning in his own private hell?" I crossed my arms. The muscles in the back of my neck were rock-hard. "Aaron, the man killed because he wanted to. He wasn't doing his duty to the Fatherland; that's only a convenient excuse. Emil Janisch took great pleasure in the act of killing." I felt drained, and I said to him, almost in a whisper, "The only duty he felt was to gratify his sick urges."

Aaron sat back in his chair and tilted his head as if

to inspect the ceiling. I hated the fact that he could look at the situation so calmly, because he was not in Auschwitz long enough to have experienced Janisch. And yet I knew, because I knew Aaron so well, that it would make no difference. He had disengaged himself emotionally from this work, even though it had been his life since the end of the war.

"Who do you think would give us an indictment?" he said. "West Germany? Poland? . . . West Germany's trying to buy us off. Chancellor Adenauer has just offered $822 million in reparations to the Jews of the world."

With a wave of my hand, I dismissed the thought that Germans could buy an easement for their collective conscience. I slumped into the chair. "I would think Poland would love to get its hands on him." Talking this way, dealing with the black and white of reason calmed me, and I saw that my hands no longer shook.

"You and I both know it would be an automatic death sentence if we gave him up to the Communists. Besides, how would we get him extradited?"

I shrugged my shoulders to try and ease the tension in them. "An automatic death sentence sounds like a good idea to me. If anyone deserves it, he does." I was more convinced by the moment that the man in the sketch was Janisch. Suddenly it occurred to me that it didn't matter who extradited him—I simply needed to know that his idyllic, anonymous life would no longer be possible.

"This is not the right time, Katya." Aaron stood up and crushed out his cigarette. "I'm sorry. I wish I could back you on this, but even if we weren't shutting down here, we'd have trouble with extradition from Britain. Perhaps a time will come when this investigation will have a chance." Aaron gestured at the stacks of files. "Isn't this why we're sending all this to Dinur?"

"You've become a different person," I said to Aaron. "The man I met in Israel four years ago wouldn't have given up so easily."

He walked to the window and stood there a long time. I wondered what he was thinking. My stance, until that day, had been slightly deferential—I'd never asserted myself with Aaron very much. Turning back to me, Aaron said, "Let's suppose this man is Janisch, and we get an indictment, and finally everything falls into place like magic." He snapped his fingers. "We bring him to trial in West Germany. Then the magic stops. With the political climate there, he is acquitted. Janisch is *exonerated*, not condemned, in the eyes of the world. What would that accomplish?" Aaron leaned against his desk. "How would you feel on that day, Katya?"

I pictured Janisch standing up to hear the sentence, smiling that arrogant smile as he heard the words "not guilty." My throat was as dry as if I'd swallowed sawdust. I said to Aaron, "I once heard you say you'd fight for the right of the Devil himself to stand trial." I tried to imagine what kind of life Janisch might be living—what was he doing at this very moment? Why was he still breathing the air of this earth?

Aaron flipped open his lighter and stared at the blue-orange flame. "I made that statement before John McCloy started reviewing the sentences of convicted Nazis." Snapping the lighter shut, Aaron tossed it on the desk.

"What good is a system of justice, when the American High Commissioner hands out pardons like Communion wafers?"

"Ah, yes," I said, and I knew my voice would sound bitter, "McCloy is bending over backwards to support the new Germany."

For a moment, Aaron seemed preoccupied by something outside the window. He had believed the world after the camps would be a better place. So many times, during a late supper, he had shared his dream about a universe of reason and compassion, where other nations watched and listened and learned from the prosecution of war criminals, so such atrocities would never recur. Instead, after Nuremberg, we watched as various governments protected Nazi murderers from arrest or prosecution. Those Nazis actually brought to trial for their crimes were acquitted or given sentences that were later revoked.

Now Aaron stepped toward me and said in a soft voice, "We have to be realistic, Katya. If this man really is Janisch, and it's still a very big 'if,' I doubt there's anyone even willing to try him now." He sat down at his desk again, putting on his glasses. "I can't argue about this any more. My priority is to get these documents safely to Israel."

"Why?" I said, and I felt my face grow warm again. "They're just papers. How do you know they won't be hidden away somewhere and never used or even seen again?" I stood up, thinking about Rebekah, about what I owed to her. "I can't let Janisch slip through my fingers!"

"Have you thought this through?" He ripped off his

reading glasses and threw them on the desk. "You're so strong-willed, never stopping to consider all the angles. If you can identify him, then what? There's no extradition treaty with Poland. To whom can we turn?"

"We could find a way," I said, unwilling to hear any more of Aaron's doubts.

"I can't help you. These documents have to take priority, and this Emil Janisch thing is probably a wild goose chase."

"I don't think it is." I looked over at the blue and white of the Israeli flag. "I want to find Janisch as badly as you want Eichmann." I remembered Dieter Wisliceny's testimony about Eichmann at Nuremberg—Eichmann saying he would leap laughing into his grave because the feeling that he had five million people on his conscience would be for him a source of extraordinary satisfaction. No matter what Aaron said about the failure of justice, I knew his lifelong dream was to see Adolf Eichmann on trial—a victory for all Jews—but there had been no word of him for years.

Without looking at Aaron, I picked up the folder from his desk and walked back to my office, as an idea shaped itself in my mind. I made my way carefully round cardboard boxes and stood in front of the map that hung to the left of my desk, and with one finger, I traced the path from London to the western edge of Wales. In the bottom left-hand drawer, there was an atlas that showed Wales in greater detail, with the island of Skokholm as a small dot just off the southwestern coast. Five or six hours on the train, and I could be there.

An image in my mind had started when I found the

letter—Emil Janisch kneeling on the edge of a pit he had dug with his own hands, his black boots ruined in mud, begging me for compassion. I added details—a bright sunny day, a day too beautiful to die in a black pit, the look of shock on his face as I aimed the gun at his chest. But as I pulled the trigger, even in my own fantasy, I grew smaller. He towered over me, laughing, mocking me, saying, "Is this the best you can do? No wonder the Jews will not survive. They are too weak." I saw myself, small and unable to pull the trigger, as he kept on laughing.

Feeling as helpless as in the camps, I jerked out of the scene, my heart pounding—out of control—my breath shallow. I took the one-page physical description from Janisch's file, folded it three times and slipped it into the right-hand pocket of my coat. I closed my door and walked down the hall past Aaron Levy's office, but he didn't look up. I remember thinking how much I loved him, as if he were my father, but I would have to pull away from him now, because of what I had to do.

ROBERT KENSLEY

What would I do differently, knowing how things have turned out, if I could reverse the clock to the moment I found the Iron Cross? I've asked myself that question so many times in the last few days. The only reason I was looking in Vandermeer's desk was that my camera had gone missing, and Vandermeer was the only one who could have taken it. There were only three of us on the island at the time—Vandermeer, his housekeeper Morwenn Madoc, and myself. Vandermeer acted so rum when I took a snapshot of him, and the camera disappeared the next day.

We were having a silly conversation about birds, but it was the one thing we had in common, apart from a deep-seated love for the island itself. Vandermeer seemed to enjoy my contributions to the bird census, and it was clear he enjoyed sharing observations with a fellow bird fancier. His usual demeanor was cool and reserved, but when he talked about the birds on the island, his face became animated. The man's passion for the creatures was obvious.

"What makes the puffins come in?" I asked him, as we walked near Crab Bay.

He wore a black windbreaker, and his long sun-bleached hair blew across his face. "It depends on the time of the month. They're not all fully on yet—they will be next week."

I walked partway down the slope, stepping carefully to avoid the rabbit burrows. Slightly below us, groups of puffins toddled about, came in and out of rabbit burrows, and landed on the slope, with the afternoon sun glinting on their black feathers. It was a flurry of activity. "I watched the Canada geese today with their goslings."

"Has the other pair been out," Vandermeer said, "with their one gosling?"

"For a short while. It would be interesting to see how it grows up, as an only child. Oh, and I saw the moor hen." I looked down at Crab Bay below us, as I inhaled the rich fragrance of sea air. I knelt down, took out my camera, and began taking snaps of the puffins.

"Are there two of them?" Vandermeer asked.

"Actually I think there may be six." I turned slightly and took a photograph of him. "Smile," I said.

Vandermeer turned away abruptly, as if by reflex. "I have to go back to the house," he said. "No need for you to come."

I didn't think much about Vandermeer's reaction at the time. It wasn't until my camera disappeared that I became suspicious. Unfortunately, the roll of film with Vandermeer's picture on it was in the camera, so that was lost as well. With limited access to the island, there was no way the camera could have been nicked by a stranger. That left only Morwenn and Vandermeer. I checked with Morwenn—no, she hadn't seen the camera, and she'd have no reason to take it.

When Vandermeer was out setting lobster pots in Crab Bay, I decided to see over his house, knowing he would be gone at least an hour and a half. I walked between Morwenn's house and the small building where I was staying, knowing that Morwenn would be in the Wheelhouse kitchen and could not see me.

The ocean was a darker blue that day, but the sky was light and frivolous, with clouds like feather boas. I lifted the latch and pushed open the heavy farmhouse door. The first thing I saw, as I knew I would, was the closed door of the bedroom that had been mine so many years ago. Afraid that it might have been changed in some way, I preferred to keep my memories of it intact by not going in.

As I walked through the entry hall lined with in-built bookshelves, two books, side by side, caught my eye because of the author's name on their spines—Mattheu Vandermeer. The titles were less than inspiring: *Migratory Habits of the Manx Shearwater* and *A Natural History of Mallards on the Pembrokeshire Coast*, but that's the sort of thing he wrote. Another latch and another heavy door. The latches had been more of a challenge when I was younger and smaller. The living room hadn't changed much, although the wooden couches and chairs that my grandfather had left behind now had new cushions, probably stitched by Morwenn.

On the left-hand wall, above the chimney breast,

hung a watercolour of the rocky inlet known as Purple Cove, on the western part of the island. The painting had been there as long as I could remember, painted, as I recall, by an artist friend of my grandfather's who came to visit us quite often. Visible through the small eastern window was the walled garden that I had loved and which held my earliest and fondest memories. Yellow flag irises stood beside the marshy pond, just as I remembered, and tall grasses still waved in the wind. On the right-hand wall of the room, in the corner, was a shelf with more books.

I stood in front of Vandermeer's bedroom, which had been my grandfather's when we lived on the island. I listened for the sound of footsteps outside, but heard nothing, so I pushed open the heavy door and stepped into the room, with the eerie feeling that even less had changed there than in the living room. It was as if no time had passed, even though I had not been in that room for close on fourteen years. The whitewashed walls and the unvarnished wooden floor were exactly the same. My grandfather's magnificent desk, which had been too heavy to move back to London, still took up half the long wall, mahogany wood dark against the whiteness. Grandfather had built it over the course of two years, bringing the wood over from the mainland a few pieces at a time. The top was inlaid with narrow strips of light oak round the border, with small squares of ash at four-inch intervals. I had watched every step of the process and had even been allowed to help sand the wood.

The other furniture in the long, narrow room consisted of a simple bed with a slatted headboard, a plain nightstand, and a washbasin, all built, according to Vandermeer, in the space of two weeks. I noticed with some satisfaction that Vandermeer's craftsmanship was inferior to that of my grandfather. All three pieces were of pine, inadequately sanded and crudely joined. A small recessed shelf near the bed held Vandermeer's violin in its case, with nothing hidden in its compartments except rosin for the bow. The only light sources were a propane lamp and the light from two small windows, one near the bed and the other at the far end of the room over the washbasin.

Sitting down in Vandermeer's straight-backed wooden chair, I ran my fingertips along the design of the desk's inlaid top, as I had done so many times as a child, still in awe of my grandfather's skill. I had spent so many hours at that desk. It was always a special treat to be allowed to draw there, on a sketching block, while Grandfather read in the armchair under the window.

I pulled out the right-hand middle drawer, where the drawing paper used to be kept, and the familiar tablet, of course, was gone. Now it held Vandermeer's things: a map of the British Isles, several keys, and a leather-bound pocket diary, which I wanted to open but did not. Instead I slid the drawer shut and reminded myself that I needed to find that camera.

In the drawer below were two ledgers, most likely household accounts, and at the very back of the drawer was a folded piece of black velvet. I touched the soft fabric, so lush and so extravagant. It seemed out of place in the midst of Vandermeer's austerity.

I put the small bundle on top of the desk and unfolded

it carefully to find a small, symmetrical cross in black metal outlined with white. An Iron Cross. I stared at the medal—what was he doing with it? I held it in the palm of my hand for a few minutes, and in spite of myself, I began to imagine the Reverend Mattheu Vandermeer with short hair in a Nazi uniform, clean-shaven, needing someplace to hide from the world, someplace at the back of beyond. No visitors, very little contact with the mainlanders, a reluctance to having his photograph taken. It began to add up, and I felt chilled. I wrapped the medal up in the black velvet, arranging the folds carefully. As I tried to stroll casually out of Vandermeer's bedroom, I prayed that he was still out on the bay. Once out of the house and feeling more secure, I sat down on the bench next to a low stone wall and began to examine the possibilities. What if Vandermeer was wanted for prosecution? What I desired most—what I had almost given up hope of obtaining—was Skokholm Island. Perhaps it was not so hopeless after all.

I got up and walked toward the Wheelhouse, as my mind jumped back and forth. Iron Crosses were awarded to German soldiers; I couldn't see why a Dutch minister would have one. What if Mattheu Vandermeer wasn't who he said he was? What if he was not a Dutch minister at all? I stopped and turned over a rabbit carcass with the toe of my boot. What if he was really a former Nazi, and he'd been hiding out on the island to escape prosecution for war crimes? He claimed to be a minister of the Dutch Reformed church, but he was living with the seagulls and the rabbits. Where was his congregation?

Surely, there was a logical explanation. Mattheu

Vandermeer led a simple life and kept himself to himself, but that was no crime. I wanted to stay on the island, and I didn't want to muck things up for myself, but I couldn't ignore the Iron Cross and Mattheu Vandermeer's seclusion and his strange reaction to being photographed.

HER MAJESTY'S PRISON

When it was time, the guard took me up the narrow stairs, cupping his hand under my elbow. He told me to sit in the chair at the front of the prisoners' dock, and he seated himself at a small table to my left. I sat back in my wooden chair with my feet in their navy-blue pumps resting flat on the floor. Mark Wickham, my barrister, had explained the procedure that would follow. I had gone into emotional shutdown—it was easier to watch this as if it were happening to someone else.

Judge Mulholland entered from a side door. He wore a gray bench wig, black robe, and white jabot, and the court clerk announced, "All rise. All persons having business with this court draw near and be heard." The judge folded his considerable height into the carved chair, and I thought that his face, in spite of the bushy eyebrows, looked tired and pinched.

Everyone sat down, except for the prosecutor who stood facing the judge. "The defendant, Katya Alina Denys, is charged with one count of murder, in the death of

Mattheu Vandermeer on the 21st of May, 1953, on the island of Skokholm."

I was asked to rise, and I stood up, gripping the rail of the prisoners' dock. Judge Mulholland looked at me for a few moments. "The charge against you is that of murder. Do you understand this charge?

I knew he was required to say this, but it made me feel like I didn't have all my chairs at home. I tried to sound intelligent, nonchalant, and calm. "Yes, M'lord."

"Are you aware that a conviction for murder could result in a sentence of death?"

I straightened my shoulders and took a deep breath. "Yes, M'lord."

"Do you read, write, and understand the English language?"

"Yes, M'lord."

"How do you plead?"

I let Mark Wickham speak for me, as I had been instructed.

"Not guilty, M'lord," he said.

Standing there, accused of murder, with the possibility of the gallows in my future, I couldn't help remembering Chanele. I was standing in line during roll call in Auschwitz with the wind blowing through the thin cotton of my uniform. It was so cold. I stood with the others as we always did, twice a day, to be counted endlessly. That evening was different; there was to be a public execution, ordered by Emil Janisch, the under-Commandant. My sister, Rebekah, shivered beside me in our row of five women, and the guard watched from his tower, protected from the wind while he counted. SS officers, Emil Janisch among them, strolled on the periphery of the gathered women. My left leg had gone numb from the cold, and I worked it back and forth as unobtrusively as I could, not wishing to draw attention to myself.

I could not take my eyes off the gallows, built just outside the kitchen in the place where we had roll call, so that all of us would be forced to watch the hanging of one of our own. Chanele had been favored by the Nazis and given special privileges because of her beauty. She was allowed to keep her hair and retained a certain degree of freedom. We didn't resent this, because she was our hope. When she escaped with her Polish boyfriend, we secretly rejoiced, whispering among ourselves about where Chanele and Yurek might have gone and what they would see and eat, where they would sleep, and how they could avoid capture.

One day, weeks later, they were dragged back into camp and sentenced to be executed at the same time—Yurek in the men's camp and Chanele in ours. Chanele now stood on the platform, a smile of defiance on her lips, still beautiful in spite of her newly-shaven head. The bloodstains on her dress told us she'd been tortured, but I knew she had not betrayed those who helped her escape. As Emil Janisch read her death sentence, Chanele lifted her chin and smiled.

The SS man, Dengler, started to put the noose round her neck. She pulled out a razor from the folds of her loose dress and slit both her wrists before Dengler could grab her hands. He tried to stop the bleeding, but she clawed at his face. When he knocked her down and started kicking her in the ribs, I had to close my eyes, and I heard Dengler cursing Chanele as he kicked her, but Chanele never screamed or even groaned—she wouldn't give him that satisfaction. Emil Janisch called out for the guards to bring a cart, and I saw them lift Chanele into it. She was limp, with blood trickling from her nose, but she was still breathing. "Take her to the crematorium," Janisch had said. I prayed, and I know we all did, that Chanele would die before she got there. Later we heard, through the camp grapevine, that a guard had shot her before she entered the flames. Our causes for celebration in those days were small and strange, but we were living in a world turned upside down.

* * *

From the defendants' box, I was taken down the stairs to the holding cell and then driven to the prison a short distance away, a grim two-story fortress of brown stone walls blackened by time, with white iron bars on the windows. We drove through the gates, and I heard them clang shut behind me. A stone-faced woman in a navy-blue uniform escorted me from the police car to my cell.

Even though it's my future at stake, I think Robert's taking this harder than I am. He came to see me this afternoon, and he looks ghastly, as if he's not been sleeping, but he swears he has. He brought me some Gerber daisies, which was a lovely thing to do, but I could see how disappointed he was when he saw the flowers from Mark Wickham. I told him Mark was just trying to make me feel comfortable, and I put Robert's daisies in with Mark's carnations, to put them on an equal footing. In just a few days, I've gotten pretty good at using my left hand. I hope I can get the cast off my right arm soon.

"It's not very fancy," I said, gesturing at my cell and its furnishings, "but make yourself at home." As I sat down again on the bunk, I remembered how Robert had used the same words to welcome me to his small room on the island. It seemed so long ago.

As Robert sat down next to me, he looked uneasy. "How close can I sit to you?" he said. "Do they have rules about this?" Sometimes, he reminds me of a little boy.

He looked at his hands, ran a thumb along the back of his index finger. "I went to the Dolphin House yesterday afternoon to see you, but Mr. Welby said you'd been taken up, that they'd brought you here to Carmarthen." He turned toward me. "I should never have sent that letter to my grandfather. If I'd not gone rummaging through Vandermeer's things, I'd never have found the Iron Cross, and you'd still be in London."

"I don't have any regrets, Robert." I looked round my cell. "This is all so unreal, it doesn't bother me. He's dead; I'm alive. There has to be some justice in that."

Robert avoided my eyes. "How do you think it might have turned out, if I'd been there for you?"

I studied my thumbnail, ran a fingertip along a rough edge on the side. "I didn't want you there," I said quietly. "I didn't want you involved."

"Why not?" From the tone of his voice, I knew I had offended him.

"If anything went wrong, like it did, you couldn't be blamed." I reached out to touch his hand. "It was my idea to come to Skokholm. I could have left it alone."

He searched my face, as if looking for redemption.

"Are you saying that if you could do it all over again, you would still have come?"

"Yes."

"He almost killed you. Was it worth that? Was it worth this?" He stared at my tiny sink with no mirror, my wretched toilet.

"Absolutely."

"But what about your freedom? You're stuck here for God knows how long."

I smiled. "I'm free, Robert. Emil Janisch has been dead for nine days, and I haven't had a single nightmare the whole time. I'm as pure as new snow on the mountaintop."

I leaned my head back against the wall and closed my eyes, and I knew he was watching me. I imagined that he was wondering how I could be so calm.

The decision to pursue Janisch was mine, and mine alone, and now I was paying the piper, so to speak. But it was my decision and my action—not something that was done to me. I was no longer a victim.

On the day I found Robert's letter, I'd left the office early, with the page from Janisch's file carefully folded in my coat pocket, my collar turned up toward my face and a wool scarf wrapped tightly round my head. Cold stung my eyes as I watched my breath frost in the sharp air of Finchley Road. Against streetlights, shimmering chains of snowflakes gleamed in the early darkness. I looked back at the red brick building where Aaron's light still burned at the window, his silhouette hunched over his precious documents. I loved him deeply, but I also felt he had betrayed me.

I looked into the future, to when I would be his age, and I vowed to be more than a keeper of documents. My life and the deaths of so many had to count for something. All of the faces, the stories, now I was burying them, too, leaving them in the unmarked graves of sealed cardboard boxes. The only thing that let me know I existed was my pain. What if, without the proof of my pain—the faces, the stories—I had nothing to sustain me and simply disappeared? I could become more and more translucent, and one day I would be visible only to myself, and then I would be gone.

Careful of my footing on the icy sidewalk, I heard the crunch of snow under my boots. Like something final, the darkness closed round me, and I began to walk faster. I told myself I mustn't think about Janisch, but I had already gone there, and memories are always more dangerous in the dark. My mind skidded, out of control, into thoughts of Auschwitz and Emil Janisch and his dark sable German shepherd, trained to kill. I tried to run, but my boots sank into deep snow.

As I climbed the steps to the courtyard, I shook my head to bring myself back into the moment, where I was shaking so badly I couldn't fit the key into the lock. I stood outside my flat, so grateful to be home, but shivering violently, with fingers unable to hold the key still. The harsh wind blew a shrill whistle in my ears, and my eyes watered from the cold. With my left hand, I steadied the right and was able to turn the key in the lock. I entered the house and left my coat and scarf on a hook in the entry, where they dripped onto the floor tiles. I pulled off my wet boots and the socks that were also damp.

Walking slowly through my small living room, I tried to focus on my surroundings and to absorb the emptiness, the serenity, of the white walls. On the beige sofa were pillows in deep forest green and gold—the only colors I had allowed myself. With a green pillow clutched to my chest, I stood, breathing deeply, with the roughness of jute carpet beneath my feet. I tried to think of nothing but the soft pillow and the rough fibers under my toes. I tossed the pillow back on the sofa and moved to my desk, where I picked up the palm-sized black stone that I used as a paperweight. It was cool and heavy, dense with reality, and the roundness of it soothed me. I enjoyed my solitude. I took refuge in that calm place where I didn't have to justify my thoughts to anyone. But now, thanks to a face sketched on a sheet of white paper, Emil Janisch had again invaded my world.

In the kitchen, I got down a half-empty bottle of brandy from the metal cabinet above the sink, and I poured an inch of the amber liquid into a juice glass. Entering the blue-tiled bathroom, I flipped on the light, a bare bulb in a ceiling socket. The water was scalding hot on my numbed fingers. I left my clothing—a jumble of damp wool— on the floor and slid my body into the hot water as the tub filled.

Then I leaned my head back, studying the maze of painted vines and tendrils on the ceiling—the artwork of the previous tenant. I reached out for my drink and took a sip. Holding it in my mouth, I finally swallowed, feeling my muscles loosen as the brandy crashed into my brain. I slid down in the water until it dampened the ends of my hair. On my arm, the numbers were upside down, tattooed in blue: 48275. I had rubbed at them for years, those numbers burned into pale skin with Nazi ink.

From shoulder to shoulder, I ran the soft washcloth over my skin, hot water running in small rivulets toward my breasts, remembering the filth in the concentration camp and the smell of unwashed bodies, including my own, and the bites from lice that itched so badly I scratched my scalp into bleeding sores. I had adjusted to the hunger after only a few weeks, although others had been obsessed with the idea of food. My stomach became smaller, and I grew used to the light-headedness and fatigue of starvation. Camp food was not worth eating, nothing more than a foul broth with bits of debris that could sometimes be identified as potato or vegetable. But in the camps I did not taste or feel the food in my mouth. I ate only to stay strong and to protect Rebekah.

Even now, food has so little meaning to me. I don't cook. After all these years, I still eat only to survive. I looked down at my arms, floating on top of the bath water. My hipbones are still visible under my skin, and my breasts are more like those of an adolescent than a woman of twenty-six. People say I am too thin, that I need to put "meat on my bones." They should have seen me in Auschwitz; I was nothing but bones.

I took two more sips of the brandy and let my arms float in the warm water for several more minutes, smiling to myself as I realized I was slightly drunk. Aaron would not approve. So what? After convincing me to uproot myself from Israel to come to London, now he's pulling the rug out from under me. I swirled the last bit of brandy in the bottom of my glass.

The bath water had gone cold. I crawled out of the tub, feeling a dull ache in the top of my head. My arms and legs quivered with fatigue as I dried off and put on a white terrycloth robe and a pair of wool socks. I walked heavy-footed into the living room, gazing at the walls bare of photographs or any kind of art. What should I hang on these walls? There are no pictures left of any of my family. How could any paintings replace those precious photos, and how could anyone else replace them in my life?

Dropping into the softness of my couch, I closed my eyes and saw Rebekah's face. People have told me I couldn't possibly remember things that happened when I was three years old, but I do remember the day Rebekah was born. My father told me to sit down on the big sofa in our living room, and then he handed me the baby, wrapped snugly in a soft flannel blanket. To this day, I still remember how heavy her head felt in the crook of my arm and how her face was so red from crying. Surely, this scrawny little thing would not replace me in Papa's heart. The baby, who had not yet been named, opened her eyes and looked right at me. I said to Papa, "I think she knows I'm her sister."

I got up slowly and walked across the jute carpet to my small writing desk. On blue stationery, I began a letter to Robert Kensley, being careful to address the envelope to the name mentioned in his letter—his unexplained alias.

ROBERT'S FOLLY

I was devastated when I found out my grandfather had sold the island. Right after the war, I was finishing my last year of boarding school, at the Millbrook Academy in Connecticut. One day, I received a letter from him and he mentioned that he'd sold Skokholm, because he knew he'd never be able to go back there, because of his injuries.

"Not a word to me beforehand," I'd said to my roommate at Millbrook, as I crumpled the letter into a ball and threw it across the room. "What do you think of this idea, Robert? What would you think of my selling your birthright out from under you? Would you mind terribly?" My roommate had never seen me this angry, and he watched with his mouth practically hanging open. "You'd think the friggin' bomb had scrambled his brains as well as blowing off his leg."

I packed a bag and caught a ride with a friend to New York, where I booked a flight back to London with the money in my savings account. When I arrived by taxi at my grandfather's Georgian home near Queen Victoria Street, I found him sitting in a wheelchair with a blanket draped over his lap, even though it was warm outside, so that no one could tell the leg was missing. His face had an unhealthy pallor, and his hair had gone completely white since I'd last seen him. Holding a glass of what looked like bourbon, his hand shook uncontrollably. "What in God's name are you doing here, Robert? You haven't been sent down, have you?"

"No, sir, I'm still in good standing at the academy. I wanted to talk to you about Skokholm."

He frowned. "Sit down, son. You make me nervous just hovering there."

I moved a large tapestry pillow and sat down on the sofa facing my grandfather. "Did you ever consider that I might want to go back and live on Skokholm some day?"

"Live on Skokholm?"

"You lived there for nine years," I said.

"Yes, but that was different. I was fifty years old and had already achieved some measure of success. I had resources to fall back on. What did you plan to do on Skokholm, anyway? Raise parsnips and gather gulls' eggs?"

I felt my jaw clench. "You seemed happy there," I said. "Happier than you've ever been in London."

He set down his empty glass on a side table and looked at me with somewhat less of a scowl than he'd had before. "Don't you know it's impossible to recreate the happiness of the past?"

I ignored this and continued. "I had a plan, sir, to raise Chinchilla rabbits and sell their pelts. A good pelt brings about four pounds in today's market, and the island would support close on ten thousand of them. And selling the meat as well would fetch another good sum."

"You're serious, aren't you?"

"I am." I crossed my arms and looked down, rubbing my forehead. I tried to keep the accusation out of my voice when I said, "Why did you sell the island?"

He shifted his weight in the wheelchair, and his face showed the discomfort this caused him. "Robert," he said, and his voice was hoarse. "I've been in constant, excruciating pain since the night of the bombing, because my back was injured as well as my leg. I knew there was no way I could ever climb those cliffs at Skokholm or even handle the boat. Hell, I can't even walk properly. And I'd never be able to tolerate the dampness or the cold there."

"Did you even think of me when you sold it? I always thought that one day Skokholm would pass to me, and it's the only thing that's kept me going all these years, knowing some day I'd go back there."

William leaned forward. "I'm sorry, Robert. I truly am. I'd no idea you still wanted to live on Skokholm because you never mentioned it." His gaze traveled round the room. "Skokholm seems so far in the past; we've not even been there in seven years."

I stood up and looked round his living room. The furnishings were ponderous and ornate—carved and gilded in the Victorian style, the furniture and windows clothed in heavy brocades and dark-colored velvets. Having been away in America for so long, this was the first time I had seen this newest flat. "Skokholm is the only home I've ever had, the only way of living that feels right to me." I gestured at the room, which seemed opulent to me. "This is not my home. I've never even been here before."

He coughed violently. "I thought you'd be like me," he said, "champing at the bit and anxious to make a name for yourself. I guess I was wrong."

I rubbed my hands together, suddenly very cold.

"I'm sorry, son. There's no way to undo the sale. Mattheu Vandermeer now owns the island, free and clear."

At that moment, I hated Mattheu Vandermeer, a man I had never met. My grandfather was too broken and ill to bear any blame, even though he was the one who had ripped my dreams so carelessly, tossing my life away like scrap paper into the dustbin.

* * *

For years, as I drifted across the British Isles, unable to hold a job for more than a few months or to commit to a relationship with a woman, I had this recurring dream. I would see the island in the distance, and I would be in the water, swimming toward it. I'm crying because it's been so long since I've been there, and the gulls are swirling overhead, and the water I'm swimming in is the deepest turquoise imaginable. I swim until my muscles cramp, and I don't think I can go any further, but the island is still ahead of me—out of reach. I can see in my mind the way the buildings stand out against the sky—white against blue—and how the sun hangs every evening, like a golden ball over the ocean. In my dream, I stop swimming, tread water for a minute or two, then I just stop. I sink under the waves. I'm not breathing, but

I don't need to. Somehow, I'm not myself, and I've never felt this happy before. I rise from the water, hover in the air beating my wings—what am I?—and then sail high above the island. I land without grace on a slope as green as emeralds. When I follow the call of my mate into an underground burrow, I realize I have become a shearwater.

* * *

I had thought it was a stroke of good fortune to meet Thomas Weaver that night in the pub. I'd wanted to go back to Skokholm so badly, but it seemed close on impossible, as long as Mattheu Vandermeer refused to allow visitors. I'd found work on a fishing boat out of Milford Haven, but I spent most of my time on Marloes Beach, looking out across the water to Skokholm, which was four miles away.

The pub was crowded that evening, as on most evenings, with a congenial mixture of local farmers and fishermen. With my back to the fireplace, I sat at a large table, drinking stout with three of my fellow fishermen and two farmers. Rain drummed on the roof.

"Have ye seen the dead coneys all round, then?" said one of the farmers. His voice was relaxed and happy—the result of three pints of stout.

"Aye, and there's the sick uns, too," said the other. "They stagger about like us when we've 'ad too much o' this good ale." Everyone laughed. "I think they go blind, too," he added, in a more serious voice.

"Their heads swell up somethin' awful," said the first farmer. "They look like a work of the Devil hisself."

"I've heard it's called the 'myxy,' " I said. "You farmers

should be happy, since you've fewer rabbits to eat up your crops."

One of the fishermen set down his mug. "Aye, but those of us who likes to nip up a coney ever' now and then for the stewpot, we're not so joyful." More laughter.

A small man, odd-looking with protruding ears and black horn-rimmed glasses appeared at our table. I hadn't seen him come in. "Excuse me," he said, "but I couldn't help overhearing your conversation." He dug in his coat pocket and pulled out a folded piece of paper, which he held up, as if to validate himself. "I've been commissioned by Her Majesty's government to study the rabbit population on Skokholm Island. It seems to be the last remaining enclave of wild rabbits untouched by the myxomatosis epidemic."

"Really," I said to him, as I pulled out the empty chair to my left. "Here, why don't you join us, Mr. . . what did you say your name was?"

"Weaver. Thomas Weaver." The little man grinned and flushed slightly as he sat down.

I studied Thomas Weaver's face as he greeted the others at the table. God in Heaven, this could be my chance. "Brian," I said, "bring Mr. Weaver a drink, would you? What will you have, Thomas?"

"A milk stout, please."

"It's so good to meet you, Thomas," I said, shaking his hand, as cold and stiff as a dead fish. "I'm Robert Kensley, that's Brian Carne over there, Kevin Prosser and his brother Dylan, and the notorious Mulligan brothers. Now, for whom do you work, exactly?"

"I'm with the British Wildlife Society. There's been a

concern that this epidemic will wipe out the entire wild rabbit population. The Society wants a study made of wild rabbit behavior so we can determine how the epidemic is being spread."

I made a mental note. British Wildlife Society. "Are you an expert on rabbits, then?"

He straightened up in his chair, puffed out his chest a little. "I've a Master's degree in biology, currently working on my doctoral dissertation."

"Tell me everything you know about myxomatosis," I said, trying to keep a straight face. I wanted to stand up and shout with joy.

Thomas Weaver took a sip of his lager and smiled at me with teeth that were large and uneven. "It's a lethal disease—no cure for it. Once a rabbit's been infected, the course of the disease is fairly predictable. Swelling of the head, and especially the eyes, resulting in blindness. The poor beggars can't find their burrows, so they scramble in pathetic circles, crashing into things."

"Lord," I said, "it sounds dreadful." How can I talk him out of this trip to Skokholm? Booze, more booze.

Thomas finished his milk stout, and I motioned to Brian to bring another. Thomas leaned toward me and lowered his voice. "It may not be quite as bad as it sounds. I've heard they'll still try to mate up until just a few hours before they die."

"That's lovely," I said, anxious to change the subject. "You know, Thomas, I've heard that the owner of the island is not a very friendly sort. How in the world did you get permission to study the rabbits on Skokholm? I've heard he's absolutely on pins about his nesting birds."

"Quite a simple matter, really," Thomas said. "Mattheu Vandermeer is an amateur naturalist and has been corresponding with a member of the Society for several years. He gave his permission quite readily once he was made aware of my qualifications. He will allow me to stay on the island as long as the study requires, and I'll do odd jobs about the place to pay for room and board."

"Splendid," I said to him. I can pull it off—I know I can. "There's just one problem."

Thomas Weaver set down his mug. I lowered my voice to a whisper and leaned toward him. "Do you really know anything about this Vandermeer fellow?"

"I've corresponded with him."

"But you've never met him."

"No."

"Then I feel obligated to tell you this."

"What?" asked Thomas, frowning.

"You've no idea what you might be getting yourself into." It was difficult for me to keep a straight face, but I silently blessed my prep school drama teacher, Mr. Evans, who had encouraged me to polish my acting skills.

"What d'you mean?" Thomas Weaver's eyes widened behind the thick glasses. He was falling for it.

"Oh, he's a wrong 'un, that Vandermeer. I can feel it whenever he walks past, which is not very often, because he mostly hides out on that island of his." I leaned back in my chair, stretching out my legs. I tilted my head toward Thomas. "They've not been able to pin a thing on him." I paused for dramatic effect. "Never found the body."

"What body? What are you talking about?" Thomas's

voice was rising even higher than his normal tenor, and his pudgy face was flushed. I didn't want to give him a heart attack, but now was the time to move in for the kill.

"Keep your voice down, Weaver. It's dangerous even to discuss this. Why, if he thought you were the least bit suspicious of him . . ."

Thomas, staring straight ahead, wouldn't look at me. His words came through clenched teeth. "To what body are you referring?"

"Couple of lads from here on the mainland went out to Skokholm to work for Vandermeer when he was remodeling the farmhouse. Only one of them came back. Said he couldn't prove what happened but he knew in his gut that Vandermeer had a hand in it. His friend vanished one night into thin air. No body, no sign of a struggle, no way off the island except by boat, and the two boats were still there. Freshly turned earth in the garden, though."

"What does that prove?"

Absolutely nothing, you twit. "It was the middle of winter—nowhere near planting season," I said. "But the constable dug for hours and never found a thing."

I stood up and put my hand on Thomas's bony shoulder. "If I were you, my friend, I'd think twice about this little expedition of yours."

The next morning, I was not surprised to hear that Thomas Weaver had caught the first train back to London. I walked over to Milford Haven to gather the supplies I would need to pass myself off as a wildlife biologist. I knew that island so well I could walk it blindfolded. Visits to several shops provided the equipment I needed: a good pair of binoculars, notebooks and sketching pencils, rubber gloves, and dissecting tools.

Two days later, the new Thomas Weaver was ready to go over to Skokholm. I had arranged with Clyde Prosser, Vandermeer's part-time hired hand, to ride over with him when Clyde delivered Vandermeer's mail on Saturday.

As he started the engine of his small boat, Clyde looked at me with his eyes narrowed down to slits in the bright sunshine. His hair was straight and black. "The Reverend don't allow any visitors on Skokkum, Robert. I'm surprised he's lettin' you come over."

"I've made arrangements with him to study the wild rabbits."

"You've been workin' out of Marloes for a year now as a fisherman. Since when are you into rabbuts?"

"I'm not. I just want to spend some time there."

Clyde was quiet for a minute or two, and I could see that he was mulling something over. "If Vandermeer is lettin' you study the rabbuts," he said, "can I still shoot them? That's the only meat my family gets—the wild rabbuts I shoot. They're mostly all sick on the mainland now."

"There are thousands of rabbits on Skokholm. Your shooting two or three a week won't make any difference. I'll only be studying small groups of rabbits, in certain areas."

Clyde nodded his head.

"One more thing. I've taken to using my middle name."

Clyde lifted his eyebrows, and it was obvious that he thought I'd gone round the bend. "What is it?"

"Thomas, so just call me Tom, all right?"

He shrugged his shoulders and said nothing, but he seemed well and truly baffled by my name change.

I leaned against the railing and watched as the blurry mass on our right began to take shape as the island of my childhood. The rose-colored cliffs seemed even taller now, years later, and the ocean was a more intense green than I remembered. The pale blue sky, stippled white with bird wings, stretched cloudless to the horizon.

As we approached South Haven, I saw my nemesis, Mattheu Vandermeer, standing on the steps of the landing. I had never seen a man with such long hair. It grew past his shoulders, sun-bleached and tangled, and now, in the fierce wind of the island, it blew across part of his face.

He caught the rope that I threw to him and secured the boat. I stepped up onto the pier and stuck out my hand. "I'm Thomas," I said, leaving off my borrowed last name because Clyde was right behind me.

"Good to meet you," said Vandermeer in a voice that was smooth and refined. His handshake was brief, his hand cool. He nodded at Clyde, who hurried off to hunt rabbits for his stewpot. Vandermeer then turned to climb the steep path up to the meadow, as I followed, happy as a sandboy as I began to live my dream, if only for a short while.

As I followed the path through the meadow of bluebells, I noticed how little the island had changed since I left fourteen years earlier, before the war. As we climbed higher, I could see that the farmhouse and the other buildings still gleamed white as chalk against the sky. The gulls circled and called raucously, and the whole island, as before, seemed to be honeycombed with burrows, with a constant scurrying in and out by the rabbits. There would be no shortage of field study subjects.

As we approached the buildings, my face grew warm, and I knew I was flushed with excitement, as well as from the wind. I couldn't wait to see Morwenn's face when she recognized me. I would have to be careful when Vandermeer introduced me to her, so she wouldn't give me away. Although she hadn't seen me since I was nine, I knew she would recognize me right away. After all, she'd raised me from the time I was three months old.

Vandermeer led me to a small hut. "You'll be staying in here," he said, as he opened the door to reveal a small, austere room that I knew well. It had been used as a guesthouse when my grandfather and I lived on the island. I'd helped to paint the wooden floor red, after the walls were carefully whitewashed. Simple wooden furniture stood just as it had when we left the island: a single bed, a nightstand, and a small desk. From the west window, I could see the ridge, inhabited, as usual, by gulls and oystercatchers.

"There's a loo in the building just behind you and hot water in the Wheelhouse boiler for washing up," Vandermeer said.

I frowned and tried to look puzzled. "Now, which one is the Wheelhouse?" I had to bite the inside of my lip to keep from laughing. The Wheelhouse, named that because of the ship's steering wheel that hung over the fireplace, had been my favorite place on the island because its nooks and crannies held bits of sailing gear, including the compass and sextant from the wrecked schooner, the *Rebecca Hawkins*. At the other end of the long room was the small kitchen that was Morwenn's domain.

"I'll show you the Wheelhouse, then give you a tour of the island. There are certain areas where you must not go because of the nesting birds." Vandermeer led me out the door of the hut, pointing out the long narrow building to our left. "My housekeeper lives there," he said, and my heart sped up, as I wondered what Morwenn would look like now. Between that building and the Wheelhouse was a courtyard where I had spent many hours playing as a child. It had not changed much. The harsh wind on Skokholm does not allow the flourishing of trees, so nothing had grown up to alter the look of the space.

As I entered the kitchen behind Mattheu Vandermeer, ducking because of the low doorway, Morwenn turned round from the stove, and I was surprised at how much smaller she seemed. Morwenn stared at me, and when her hazel eyes widened, I stepped forward and said, "Hullo, I'm Tom Weaver." I held out my hand.

"How d'you do," she said, with a bewildered look on her face, still staring at me and wiping her hands on her apron.

"This is the young man I told you about—the one who's come to study the rabbits."

Morwenn's eyebrows lifted and as she took my hand, I squeezed hers and winked. She kept staring at me, saying nothing.

"We have breakfast at seven," said Vandermeer, "then dinner at half-past twelve, tea at four, and supper at seven. Morwenn is an excellent cook." As Vandermeer turned to leave the kitchen, I gave Morwenn a quick kiss on the cheek. She drew in her breath, and I knew she had recognized me.

Vandermeer led me out into the bright sunlight of the courtyard, filled with birdcalls and my earliest memories. Surely I had re-entered paradise. We walked past the end of Morwenn's cottage, then turned north toward a wide vista of grassy plains, rocky cliffs, and birds, with the ocean in the distance. Vandermeer pointed to a three-foot stone wall. "The storm petrels are so small, they nest in the spaces between the stones."

"I've heard them called 'Mother Carey's chickens.' When do they arrive?"

"They're the last ones to come back in the spring. Should be arriving next month."

Although I knew the answer, I asked him why they were called storm petrels.

"By fluttering their wings, they can walk on the surface of the water, like St. Peter. It's said they will follow a boat before a storm, hence their nickname, 'stormies.' " This quiet man had a wealth of information, which he seemed anxious to share. "Since I arrived on the island, every day I record the numbers of each of forty different species of birds. I also document sightings of whales, porpoises, dolphins, and seals."

"Would you like me to help you with the bird census?" I said. "I'm quite good at distinguishing species."

"I record the birds at six every evening. If you'd like to join me, I would welcome your input." Vandermeer stopped and pointed at a long dry-stone wall, about three feet high. "This is called Halfway Wall. It runs north and south, as you can see, and bisects the island. It was built several centuries ago when farmers divided up the island into separate fields."

"So, the island's been farmed, and I assume it's been fished and harvested of rabbits. Has it always been privately owned?"

"I don't know much about the island's history," Vandermeer said. "I bought it in 1946 from an Englishman."

How well I knew that. We walked along a fenced area that Vandermeer seemed especially proud of. "This is an exclosure to show what the island vegetation can do when it's not grazed by rabbits," he said. "See how the heather has flourished?"

"Would it be all right," I said, "to fence off a small area as an observatory, over near Tabernacle Rock?" I wanted to bite my tongue as soon as the words slipped out of my mouth. Vandermeer had not mentioned the rock formation by name, and we had not yet passed it.

Vandermeer turned round to look at me. "How do you know the name of that?"

"I saw it on a map of the island," I managed to say. "I remembered it because it was such an unusual name." I heard a faint ringing in my ears.

"I would like to see that map. I didn't know there were any with such detail. Who drew it?"

"I don't know who the mapmaker was, and I'm not

sure I've brought it with me to the island, but I'll check." I would have to be more careful in the future.

That evening, at supper, Morwenn and I had trouble being together, with Vandermeer there, and not being able to talk freely. I had managed to say a few words to her in the kitchen before supper, but we'd not had time for a decent conversation. I knew Morwenn would be dying of curiosity. Why in the world was I using someone else's name, and what was I doing back on Skokholm?

I helped Morwenn with the dishes, and as soon as we'd finished, she returned to her cottage, and I met her there a few minutes later. Although Morwenn assured me the Reverend Vandermeer would not return to the Wheelhouse again that evening, I felt more comfortable telling my story in the privacy of Morwenn's home.

She met me at the door, and her hazel eyes were shining. "You were just a little boy when you left. I can't get over how different you look."

I hugged her. "I'm twenty-four years old, Morwenn—only a year younger than you were when we left the island." She's close on forty now, I thought. It sounds so old, but she really doesn't look that different. "You've cut your hair," I said.

She ran her hands through the dark hair that had only a few gray strands. "Do you like it?"

"Quite nice," I said. "What are you doing back on the island? Why didn't you stay in Marloes with Catrin?"

"Sit down," Morwenn said to me, pointing toward her flowered sofa. She sank into a deep upholstered armchair near the fireplace, tucking her bare feet underneath the full skirt of her housedress. She told me how she'd moved back to the island and how Vandermeer had offered her a job as his housekeeper. After all the years, Morwenn's voice still showed her surprise at this good fortune.

"Now, Robert dear, tell me about your life since I last saw you and why you're using a different name." She seemed in a hurry to skip through the details of her life, so she could hear about mine.

"Well, you know that I was shipped off to a boarding school in America, the Millbrook Academy in Connecticut. It wasn't too bad there, really."

"You were so discouraged at one point, though. I remember a letter where you complained that all the other boys were taller than you, and you felt like a loser because you'd gotten clumsy at sports."

"Really? I'd forgotten about that. I guess I didn't get my growth until much later."

"I didn't hear anything from you after 1944."

"I'm sorry, Morwenn. It was so hard to think about Skokholm and not be here."

"When the war ended, you would still have been in school, " Morwenn said. "Did you come back to England, then?"

"No, Grandfather wanted me to stay on at Millbrook until graduation. I didn't come back to England until '46."

"Didn't you ever think of coming back here, just to visit?"

"Of course I did, Morwenn. But by that time, Grandfather had already sold the island, and I couldn't bear the thought of someone else living here. It was easier to stay away."

"How is your grandfather?"

"Well, you know that his back was injured, as well as his leg. He was in a wheelchair for two years, but he can get round fairly well now, with a cane. He's been fitted with an artificial leg." I listened to the crackling of the fire. "For a while, he seemed to have lost his will to live, and he started drinking. When Mattheu Vandermeer offered him a large sum of money for the island, he took it right away. He told me later that he would never be able to live here again, since he was crippled." I stood up and walked to the window. The moon was a sliver of silver. "He never considered the fact that I might like to live here."

"Is that what you want?" Morwenn asked.

I could hear the note of disbelief in her voice. "I don't know," I said. "I truly don't." I stared out the window at red-legged oystercatchers on the dark rock of the outcropping, at the dark blue of the sky behind them. "Is there any place in the world as beautiful as this, Morwenn?"

"You sound like your grandfather when you say that."

"He couldn't have loved Skokholm; he sold it without thinking twice."

"When he first came here, I think he loved Skokholm as much as you seem to now."

"I find that hard to believe."

"It's true," Morwenn said. "He only left because of the war."

I crossed the room and sat down again on the sofa, picking up an embroidered pillow. I ran my fingers lightly over the design—an abstract flower worked in shades of orange and yellow—as I tried to gauge how honest

Morwenn would be. “I need to ask you something,” I said, “about my parents.” I saw her reaction—the raised eyebrows, the grim line of her mouth. Was she trying to “protect” me from the truth? “Did my grandfather choose to live on the island because of what happened with my parents?”

Morwenn shrugged and shook her head. She didn’t seem eager to talk about it. “He only mentioned it once, and then the subject was closed. He made that very clear.” She gazed off into the distance. “I was only sixteen, but he felt he had to give me some explanation as to why he was raising his grandson. He said simply that his son’s wife had gone mad and killed him and then had killed herself. I knew better than to ask him for details.”

“I imagine the press in London made a big thing of it,” I said. “It must have been hard for a man in his position to go through all that.”

Morwenn nodded. “I was young and inexperienced, and I didn’t know him very well. But I could see that he was upset. It took a while for him to adjust to his new lifestyle.”

“By the time I was old enough to notice,” I said, “he seemed to have made peace with his world. I thought he was happy with the simple life of the island.” I stood up and walked to the window again. The moon was higher now. “My grandfather has changed, Morwenn. He’s bitter and quiet, and he doesn’t care about much except putting more money in his banking account. He’s concerned, of course, that I’ve not already put up my plate as a doctor or lawyer. I also think he’s disappointed that I didn’t follow him into the newspaper business.” I crossed his arms and leaned against the wall. "Some parts of it I wouldn't mind, like being a press man or an editor. I hate the business aspects of it, and that's what he would expect me to take over."

* * *

As a counterfeit biologist, I first made an overall sketch of the island, which was not difficult because I'd drawn dozens of maps of it when I was eight years old. I outlined three potential locations for my field study, representing the major rabbit colonies: one just west of the Cutting, a passageway through a rock ridge at a right angle to the lighthouse path; another one slightly further west toward the lighthouse, just in front of a rock formation called the Pedestal and south of the lighthouse path; and the third just in front of Wall Rock, south of the lighthouse path and very near the lighthouse itself.

I often sat cross-legged, on a smooth part of the path, with my notebook balanced on my legs while I wrote notes on the rabbits' behavior or sketched them outside their burrows. On especially windy days, I sought shelter on the east side of the rocks near the path, sitting with my back against the boulders, looking up every now and then from my note-taking to stare at the jagged peaks of Spy Rock.

As the days passed, I filled my notebooks with observations about colonies A and B and C. I even named some of the rabbits in each colony. Distinctive features such as Alberta's unique way of hopping, Barclay's torn ear, and Bonnie's patch of white fur, helped me tell them apart.

I learned what rank each rabbit held. Ainsworth,

Barclay, and Chadwick reigned as "kings" in their respective colonies. Other males seemed to be allowed to live in the colony as long as they were not a threat, although at some point, male children of the king and queen were likely to get booted out. The parents were much more tolerant of their female offspring.

Because rabbit observation was an undemanding task, I had a lot of time to daydream. I often wondered, with only a small pang of guilt, what Thomas Weaver was doing. And then I would allow Morwenn's question—about why I'd come back to the island—to slide through my mind, but I never let it stay long enough to come up with an answer.

JOURNEY TO SKOKHOLM

Two weeks after finding the letter from Robert, I took the tube from Golder's Green, with my suitcase propped between my ankles and my duffel bag on my lap. At Paddington, I got off the tube and walked out into the warm April sunshine to wait at the intersection, with a sense that some unseen force was participating in my destiny. The traffic light changed, and I crossed the street to the train station, where the ornate metal arches stretched high into the air, and pigeons circled close to the ceiling and toddled on the cement floor, scavenging for bits of dropped food. The train from London to Milford Haven was due to leave Paddington at a quarter past one, so I had about a half-hour to wait. The aroma of mushroom pasties tempted me, but I thought of how little money I had in my pocket wallet. I sat down on a bench, crossed my legs, and smoothed out a wrinkle in my nylons. The new shoes, black leather sling-backs with round toes and high heels, were amazingly comfortable for the first time out.

If I had to skimp on food to buy clothing, so be it. I

had bought a new outfit for the trip to Milford Haven, a royal blue and black wool-tweed suit with a single-breasted jacket. It had shiny black buttons that ran from the waistline of the fitted bodice to under the narrow collar. Normally, I didn't wear black, but this royal blue tweed had been irresistible. There were deep cuffs on the long sleeves, and I had a royal blue felt beret and black cotton gloves.

Several men had given me admiring glances, and I was glad I had spent the extra money; I would rather have one nice outfit than a whole closetful of cheap ones. Even though my income was limited, I refused to wear jumble sale clothing. In the camps, I had been forced to wear the uniform jacket of a dead Russian soldier, with bloodstains that could not be washed out because I had nothing else to put on.

I stood in front of the board, watching as each new departure time was posted. The Milford Haven train would depart from platform five. I carried my bags outside to the platform and stepped up into the third car. The only passengers apart from me were an elderly couple with a young boy, and I smiled at them as I stowed my luggage. Once in my seat several rows in front of them, I allowed myself to relax and look out the window at the soot-darkened buildings along the track. As the train left London behind, I watched the sky, which was mostly grey, with short bursts of sunshine, as if it were fabric that had been ripped. Hundreds of sheep with new lambs grazed the fields, while young boys played soccer everywhere—in the grass, in the streets, in the backyards. I found myself dozing off at intervals, my head falling forward or to the side, even though I wanted to stay awake.

At Cardiff, I had to change trains, and I walked into the station, looking for the board that would tell me where to find the one for Milford Haven. I stopped a middle-aged woman, who told me the board was upstairs. The train I wanted would depart from platform three, and I hurried with my luggage and climbed aboard to find the car close on full. I sat down next to a young man who was so pre-occupied with his artist's notebook that he did not look up.

I leaned back and closed my eyes, touching the small ring of braided silver—a birthday gift from Aaron last year—that I wore on my right hand under my glove. The young man beside me looked so much like my brother Patryk, it made me want to cry. I hadn't thought about him in such a long time. To me, he was a hero, like Daniel and David—so courageous for a boy of nineteen. I couldn't think about Patryk now. What had kept Daniel safe from the lions in their den? I remembered the story, but not the details.

I looked out the window of the train, trying to concentrate on the small signs that were now in Welsh, names of towns like Hendy-gwyn and Caerfyrddin and Glanyfferi. As the train carried me closer to the coast of Wales—a place where Emil Janisch might have been living for years—the familiar fear took hold of me. I thought of Janisch on the platform next to the doctors, meeting the trains—cattle cars jammed with bewildered men and women and crying children.

One cold night in February, not long after my father's death, Nazi storm troopers had burst through the front door of the Toebbens uniform factory. About seventy-five of us, teenaged girls and young women, were dragged from our sewing machines and marched down Stawki Street. I didn't scream or cry out. I walked or ran, going along with the frenzied crowd, trying to keep from being knocked down and trampled or being slammed with the butt of one of the Nazis' rifles. Soon we reached the *Umschlagplatz.* Everyone knew this was the assembly point for transports to the death camps. There were others, old men and children and middle-aged women clinging to their terrified husbands. I searched the crowd for my mother's face. Had she been taken or was she still at home? If she was still at home, what would she think when I didn't return at the end of my shift?

As we were pushed into cattle cars that reeked of urine and sweat and human terror, I thought of nothing but how to survive the ride to wherever we were being taken. The cattle car was so tightly packed, it would be impossible to sit down. There was no food or water; we'd not had time to gather any personal possessions, unlike many of the riders in the other cars, who'd brought suitcases, extra clothing, pots and pans. I stood next to Lila and Rahel, my friends from the factory. Lila, barely five feet tall, with a long heavy braid down her back, was incoherent with terror. The pupils of her brown eyes were so dilated that she seemed to have only a faint brown circle outlining empty disks of black. Rahel, her older sister, stroked Lila's damp forehead and whispered, "hush now, hush." I felt as if I had been lifted above the whole scene. I was not quite numb—I still saw peoples' faces and heard the moans and screams and smelled the sweat and felt the other bodies crushed against me, but none of this triggered emotion. As sweat rolled down Rahel's forehead, I wiped it with the sleeve of my blouse. Lila and Rahel talked in frightened voices about what might lie ahead. I closed my eyes, and in my mind, I took myself back to Warsaw, to Grandma Lidia's elegant parlor with the camelback sofa upholstered in brown velvet, with the embroidered crazy quilt made from scraps of our family's worn-out dress clothing. I remembered holding Aunt Bella's new baby, Sarah, while I played word games with Aunt Bella and Mama.

As the train traveled farther from the Warsaw Ghetto and my mother, I began to absorb some of the terror of my companions. I felt the last remnant of our family being torn apart, with Papa and Patryk already dead, Mama alone now in the Ghetto, and Rebekah . . . God knows where. I wanted, more than anything else in the world, to see my sister again.

A woman screamed, then started sobbing. I opened my eyes and wondered if it was night or day. There had been no stops to empty the reeking, over-flowing bucket that served as a chamber pot, so we stood in our own waste and vomit. I couldn't breathe. There was not only the stench of excrement but also the acrid smell of sweat, of terror, of air breathed in a small closed space by too many human beings without water. The car was packed so tightly that we had to take turns sitting down against the sides, sliding down, weak-kneed, for a few moments of rest, a moment of sleep if one was lucky.

Sitting against the wall of that cattle car, I didn't know what lay ahead for us, but I knew that I wanted this ride that seemed like an eternity—this venture into hell—to be finished. Seeking oblivion, I drifted back to Warsaw again, to a time before the Nazis had come, to the eve of the Sabbath and the fragrance of my mother's *challah*, Rebekah's warm hand in mine as Papa blessed the wine.

I woke up suddenly, disoriented by the lack of motion, but the smell told me where I was. I got to my feet, aware of the fear in the voices of those near me, as they tried to explain to each other why the train had stopped. The doors of the railroad car crashed open, and it was still dark. I could see only a patch of the sky, which was beginning to lighten, as I stood against the far wall of the cattle car. I heard women screaming. The mass of bodies in front of me moved forward, slowly, and I heard harsh commands in German, shouting, too much noise and confusion, and the deep barking of what I knew were guard dogs, German shepherds trained to kill. Guards pulled us out, and those who did not move fast enough were kicked or hit with the butts of rifles.

The glare of the lights on the platform hurt my eyes, but I could see SS men in dark uniforms and snarling dogs on leashes. I knew the German shepherds could smell the filth and sweat that surrounded us, and I was afraid the dogs, incited by the smell of fear, would tear loose from their guards.

From the cattle car, those of us from the uniform factory were herded into a large building where we were forced to put our clothing and shoes into piles. I peeled off my clothes with clumsy, ice-cold fingers. Rahel and I had to help Lila undress. "This is not Treblinka," someone whispered. "Maybe there's a chance for us." In naked, shivering lines we moved forward to the chairs where our hair was to be cut. I sat numbly as strands of my light brown hair fell into a mass on the floor. I clenched my eyes shut to keep from crying out as the clippers bit into my scalp, drawing blood. I listened to the clippers droning, like a swarm of mad bees and the screams of women and the bark of orders in German. Lila kept screaming, "they're going to gas us."

We were put into lines again. The rest of our body hair was shaved—legs, underarms, and pubic hair—and we were pushed into tubs of a foul-smelling liquid that burned our skin like fire. Even through the shock and humiliation of these procedures, I kept my reason. "Lila," I said, "they wouldn't be doing all this if they were going to kill us." My theory was confirmed when we were handed wool uniforms and crude wooden blocks meant to be shoes.

We were assigned to barracks, crowded redbrick buildings identical except for the numbers on the outside. My block elder told us we would be working in one of the factories at Auschwitz. She told us how lucky we were not to have been sent to Treblinka. "You'd already be smoke coming out of the chimney." I looked at Rahel and Lila. What did the woman mean? Then she told us how lucky we were not to have been assigned to outside work details. I did not feel lucky. Newly bald and covered with cuts from the electric razor, I was dressed in a mangy wool uniform stained with someone else's blood and had a straw mattress crawling with lice. I moved in the slow motion of disbelief and knew only one thing for certain—

that I had stepped into a nightmare.

* * *

I awoke on the comfortable British train in a cold sweat. Fear would make me vulnerable, and I couldn't afford that luxury. I checked my watch—it was a quarter past six and still light outside. I would think of nothing except what I could see from the window. Colors flashed past—a green rowboat planted with purple bulbs, a red-painted whiskey barrel with yellow tulips. Across the water, in the distance, was a castle. On the right, a deserted beach.

When the train stopped at Milford Haven, I had a moment of doubt. I let the other passengers get off the train, while I remained in my seat. Finally, I picked up my bags and stepped down off the train. Where was the station? Having departed from the elegant Paddington, I had expected more than these two small buildings next to the tracks. I left my bags outside and entered the larger building. I asked the clerk at the desk if I could use his telephone.

In a few minutes, the taxi arrived, and the driver put my bags into the boot. He drove fast, but he seemed to know the road well, maneuvering quick turns as the road snaked between tall hedges that blocked the view. I leaned back against the brown vinyl upholstery of the taxi, trusting the driver to get me safely to the inn in one piece. I would spend the night in Marloes, a small village close to Martinshaven—the harbor where I had agreed to meet Robert at noon on Sunday. He couldn't take me over to Skokholm until then because of the tides. He'd come up with a brilliant idea, a way to get me on the island, and it had all been carefully orchestrated. Morwenn Madoc, Vandermeer's housekeeper and Robert's former nanny, had agreed to fake a back injury so that her young "cousin" from London would have to come and help out. I hoped that my London accent would be sufficiently convincing.

The taxi stopped in front of a small inn with its name, "The Dolphin House," hand-painted in green rounded letters on a wooden sign. The driver carried my bags inside, hoping for a nice tip, I'm sure, so I gave him a one-pound note even though the ride was short, and the fare only six pounds. Because it was early in the season, I was the only guest. My room, on the second floor, was tiny but immaculate, with a sink in the room and a toilet and shower down the hall.

As I looked out my window at the clock tower across the street, I knew I had to use the coming night to prepare for the days on the island. I had done this before, turned myself into stone to survive an unpredictable future. This time, I'd be better prepared. I was not a child, and the journey was my choice. As I took off my suit and changed into a white shirt and straight-cut wool trousers, I realized that I had only one night to regain control of my demons—they could return so fast to tear down my carefully-preserved sanity. On the train, memories of Auschwitz and Emil Janisch had threatened to engulf me like the ocean, to pull me under to a place from which there was no return.

I left my room and went down the narrow, carpeted stairs and past the unoccupied reception desk in the front hall. Once outside, I followed the sidewalk to the street, where cottages of stucco stood in obedient pastel queues, like the façade of a normal life the Germans were so fond of creating. I wandered down the main street of Marloes, remembering how in Auschwitz, some of the prison blocks looked from the outside like two-story redbrick cottages, in neat rows along lanes planted with trees. Even the crematoria were "disguised" by fruit trees planted in front, an attempt to hide what was happening. How could we not know, when hundreds of people marched down beside the railroad tracks in one direction and never came back, when the sky filled every day with grey smoke and the stink of burning flesh?

I stood for a while in front of a blue cottage that had no number, only the name "Louisa." Here the houses have names instead of numbers, yet I lived for so long in a place where I had no name. I moved on, stepping over uneven parts of the sidewalk, pleased that Marloes seemed to have nothing more than houses, a post office, and a pub. Only then did I realize how the noise and congestion of London had overwhelmed me. Here, the only building of any size was the church known as St. Peter's, surrounded by ancient graves with grey stone markers.

I stopped to rest on a bench beside the churchyard. What had Aaron thought when I didn't show up for work? It had been hard to leave him without saying goodbye, but I knew what he would have said about my plans. I'm sure he would have tried to stop me.

One day, I had shared with Aaron my fantasies about revenge. "I know you want to find Adolf Eichmann," I had said to him, "and we all do, of course. But isn't there anyone else you would like to find, someone who had a more direct impact on your life?"

"No one in particular stands out in my mind; they were all the same."

"What about someone like Ziereis, the commandant at Mauthausen?" I said. "I've heard he took a special pleasure in carrying out executions himself. Wouldn't you like to get your hands on him?"

Aaron stared at me with that soul-piercing look of his, until I had to look away. "Katya," he said in a soft voice, "my quarrel is with all the camps, all the guards and officers." He hesitated. "You know, the question you asked says a lot about you. Who is it that you hate so much?"

"There was an SS officer at Auschwitz—Emil Janisch," I said. "If I knew where he was, I would walk to the edge of the earth to get to him. Several people have told me they would kill him with their bare hands if they could find him."

"What would you do if you found him?"

I had dropped my head to rest my lips against my fingertips. "I have often pictured his death, which must be slow enough for him to realize who is about to kill him . . . and why." I shook my head and smiled. "A fantasy, of course."

"No, Katya," he said, "it is dangerous to have this kind of thought, even if it is only fantasy. Look what happened when the Nazis tried to turn their fantasies of a perfect world into reality."

Aaron was always the voice of my conscience. "Don't worry," I told him. "I'm not likely to find Janisch, unless I walk into hell. I believe he was killed at Auschwitz."

Aaron had been surprised. "Did you witness his

death?"

I shook my head. "No, but the idea of assassination was not far-fetched. Everyone in the camp had either seen or experienced his special brand of cruelty."

I searched for some way to express the hatred that could not be put into words. Janisch was known in the camp for his vicious attacks. Not only did the prisoners at Auschwitz have to endure endless roll calls in the heat or biting cold, while the guard in the tower counted and recounted the living and the dead, but they had to survive Janisch's brutality. He would strut in his uniform, in the gleaming black boots, the cap with the Death's Head insignia, in front of row after row of emaciated, bald women in shapeless uniforms with crude wooden blocks for shoes. Swaggering, reveling in the power of his office, he would say to us, "Now we will do exercises. *Ja*, is good for the body, good for the spirit. Everyone will do knee bends. One, two, down, up, *ja*, that's it, ten and eleven and. . . we'll only do one hundred today. More tomorrow." Long before the hundredth knee bend, my legs would tremble with fatigue. My muscles never had a chance to recover from each day's round of labor, so I was always stiff and exhausted.

"Now, push-ups," Janisch had ordered on one occasion. "Everyone on the ground. One and two and three and four . . . what is wrong with you . . . you filthy swine! If some of you need to rest, then you will all rest. Lie down and rest." As some turned their heads to breathe, he said, "No, don't look up—only down."

The grounds outside the block were rutted and uneven, and the rain had left puddles of water in some places, soft oozing mud in others. The patch of earth beneath my face was relatively firm, being one of the higher spots, but the girl beside me was not so fortunate, having nowhere to put her face except in a puddle of water. I heard the sharp inhalation of the girl's breath before she submerged her face. I heard her gasp for air a minute later, and then I heard the footsteps close to my head, and the sickening crunch of bones under Janisch's heavy boot.

I lay there, face down in the dirt, fighting the urge to vomit, but not daring to move a muscle. The awful silence was broken every few minutes by that sound as jarring as a curse, the subtle implosion of bones in the skull. When we were finally allowed to get up, I whispered to Rebekah, "Don't look." Five of our block mates were dead.

* * *

"With that many people hating you," I had said to Aaron, "you would have to be afraid of attempts on your life."

"You think he was really assassinated?" Aaron asked.

"I have no proof, and there was no retribution like when Heydrich was killed. This is what I do know. One night, we heard rifle shots. That, in itself, wasn't unusual—it happened so frequently, we barely thought anything of it." I waved my hand to dismiss this statement. "But the next day, there were rumors flying through the camp that Emil Janisch had been assassinated, and everyone was afraid, because we thought innocent people would be executed if the assassin could not be found."

"Was anyone executed?"

"No," I said, leaning toward Aaron, "no one ever saw

a body, but then we never saw him again either." I closed my eyes. "It was as if he had never existed, like so many of our families who lived only in our memories. But Janisch's memory was larger than all of the lost and dead together."

* * *

Aware of the stiffness in my hips from sitting so long, I stood up from the bench outside St. Peter's Churchyard and rubbed my arms in the chill of the approaching evening. I wondered if Emil Janisch had changed more than his name, trading the arrogant Nazi role for that of a humble clergyman. I would miss Aaron's support and guidance on this mission, but he had made his choices, and I had made mine.

I drank three glasses of red wine with supper, then went back to my tiny cubbyhole of a room on the second floor, where I lay on my bed and watched shadows on the ceiling made by a streetlight outside. When I closed my eyes, the room spun round, and color burst behind my eyelids like a kaleidoscope. I let myself enjoy the ride for several minutes, and then my eyes snapped open. What the hell am I doing? I asked myself. The other part of me, the one that refused to be peaceful and still, laughed in the darkness and declined comment.

The next morning, just before eleven o'clock, I hauled my bags downstairs to the front desk. "I need to settle up for my room and last night's meal," I said to the innkeeper, a large man who looked like he might fall asleep at any moment. As he carefully added up the charges on a small pad of paper, his wife said to me, "Are you going over to the island, then?"

"Yes, I'm to be collected at noon."

The innkeeper removed his glasses. "We could give you a lift to the harbor."

"That's very kind of you," I said, "but the walk will do me good. I'm afraid I had a bit too much of that lovely wine last night, and my head's full of cotton wool."

I picked up my bags and smiled at both of them. It was foggy and cool, and I began to walk with a sense of urgency, even though I had been told that it would take much less than an hour to reach the harbor. Soon, however, my head began to pound, throbbing just above my eyes, and I slowed my pace. I regretted drinking so much wine, and I also knew that when I was on the island, I must not drink at all. It was crucial not to let down my guard even for a moment.

Vague tingling sensations rose from the base of my spine, but I turned my attention to my surroundings, to the vast arc of sky above me, which was gunmetal grey and streaked with low dark clouds. The street was deserted. Green hedges blooming with white, pink and yellow flowers blocked my view of the ocean, but I could smell it. There was a salty fragrance of fish, a dampness in the air that warned of rain, as mist blurred the edges of buildings, dampened tall blades of grass along the lane. Sheep and cows grazed a patchwork of luxuriant fields, visible through low spots in the hedges. When the road curved, I could finally see the harbor and the rocky beach in front of it, and I walked down to the wide expanse of smooth rocks in front of the green water of the bay.

I set down my bags and pushed the hair out of my face. A narrow rock ledge ran down to a metal pier that slanted sharply downwards. Beside the pier was a white motorboat with a small cabin from which a young man emerged, wearing a short-sleeved green and blue plaid shirt and beige trousers. When he jumped onto the pier and waved to me, I noticed that he wasn't wearing shoes. I waved back and started toward the stone steps. Not a bad looking chap—lean and well built. He seemed comfortable in his own body. I walked down the steps toward the pier, as Robert Kensley came up to meet me.

"Hullo," he said, smiling, as we came face to face. He had dark eyebrows the color of his hair, and the wind had reddened his cheeks.

I set down one bag and offered my hand. "Robert, it's good to finally meet you." His handshake was firm, the hand warm.

"I thought you would be older," he said with a laugh. "I'm not sure why."

"Sorry to disappoint you."

"Oh, it's not a problem. You know how you just get a picture of a person in your mind?" He jumped into the boat, and I handed him my bags, which he stowed under the bench that ran along the perimeter of the boat. As I stepped down into the boat, Robert said to me, "I'd like to take off right away. I'm not too keen on those clouds." He pulled on a beige turtleneck jumper, ran a hand carelessly over his wind-tousled hair, then pulled on a pair of water-stained canvas deck shoes.

I didn't know what to make of him. Although he was probably rising twenty-three or twenty-four, Robert had the boyish exuberance of a teenager, with a wide grin and what seemed like boundless energy. In the cabin, he started the engine and steered the boat in a wide circle round the bay, the boat slapping the waves like a rubber sneaker. He turned toward me, raising his voice over the noise of the engine, "At least we're not fighting too much wind today."

Fog enveloped the boat between the islands that Robert pointed out as Skomer and Middleholm, giant mounds of green that rose from the ocean. I watched a flock of gulls trail behind us as Skomer disappeared into the mist.

I sat on the bench near my bags, then bent down to unzip the duffel. After I pulled out a light jacket, I slipped my hand back in the bag, underneath a wool sweater, to touch the cool metal of my Walther pistol, smuggled into England from Israel in the false bottom of my steamer trunk. After the war, I'd made a promise to myself—I would never be a victim again. In the Israeli army, I learned to shoot, and when I imagined Emil Janisch's face on the target, my aim improved dramatically.

I zipped the bag and shoved it back under the bench. Holding tightly to the metal railing, to keep from being bounced off my seat by the rambunctious waves, I could just make out a long blurred shape to the right. "Is that Skokholm?" I said, going into the cabin to stand next to Robert at the wheel.

"Yes, it is. We're almost there; it's only four miles from the mainland . . . Hey, you're not going to go crackers when you see him, are you?" Robert asked. "You know, I'm really sticking my neck out to get you on the island in the first place, since I'm playing Vandermeer around myself."

I studied Robert Kensley's profile, the tip of his angular nose reddened slightly by the wind. There were auburn highlights in his glossy hair. "Yes," I said, "just what is your little game?"

Robert flashed a smile at me. "I couldn't show up on the island and say 'hello, I'm Robert Kensley, and I'd like to take a look round for old times' sake.' Vandermeer sees almost no one." Robert spoke quickly, and his voice was animated. "When I heard that a government biologist had permission to study the wild rabbits on the island . . . " He hesitated. "I talked him out of going over there, and then I took his place."

"Pretty bold move, wasn't it?"

"Desperate men do desperate things. Did someone famous say that?" He laughed. "If not, you can quote me."

"Why were you so anxious to come back?"

He was silent for a few moments. "Nostalgia, I guess." He cut the engine speed slightly. "I grew up on Skokholm."

I watched his hands, the long fingers curled lightly round the wheel, and I tried to imagine living on an island. How different we are, our backgrounds so far apart. "Robert, we don't have much time. I need to ask you some questions about Mattheu Vandermeer."

"Go ahead."

"His lifestyle and habits. What does he live on, for instance? What does he do about food?"

"He lives off the land and the sea, to a certain extent. A local chap, Clyde Prosser, brings over staples like flour and sugar when Morwenn needs them, along with their post, although I've been doing more of the errands like that since I arrived. In return, Vandermeer lets Clyde hunt rabbits on the island."

"Does he have income from any other sources?"

"He writes books about the local wildlife. I don't know of anything else." Robert pushed a strand of dark hair out of his eyes. "So, what kind of things will you be looking for?"

"Incriminating documents. Slip-ups in conversation. Physical appearance, especially details from the SS file description."

"In your letter, you wrote that you had seen Emil Janisch in person. Aren't you afraid he'll recognize you?"

"At the time, I was a skeleton with no hair in a striped uniform. He would never have taken a second look at me, if he ever saw me to begin with. He did not think of his prisoners as human beings."

Robert frowned and was silent for a moment, gazing off into the distance. Then he turned toward me and smiled. "I'll help you in any way I can," he said. "Is there anything specific you can think of?"

I was distracted by the island, which had just begun to come in focus, with its towering cliffs and the bright green vegetation. There was a motionless shape against the rocks—was it Vandermeer? It was hard to concentrate on Robert's question. "When I need to search the house," I said, "beyond what I can do during ordinary housekeeping, if you could arrange to help him with whatever he's doing that day. You know, keep him occupied in some project."

"That should be easy to manage. Oh, by the way, you'll have to remember to call me Tom instead of Robert."

"All right, Tom, my name is Katherine Dennis," I said,

exaggerating my English accent. “Rather a respectable British name, don’t you think?”

“Absolutely.” Robert gestured toward the island. “Look there. You can just make out the puffins in the bay.”

Small dots of black and white bobbed up and down like a flotilla of tiny ships. As the boat came near them, I saw their comical orange beaks and the glossy black of their bodies. Some of them dove under the waves or launched themselves into the air to fly alongside the boat with the gulls.

“They look like toy ducks in a bath, don’t they?” Robert said.

I tried to concentrate on puffins and toy ducks, so I wouldn’t think about the man in the white shirt standing against the rocks above the harbor. I shivered involuntarily.

“Do you need another wind cheater?” Robert asked.

“No, I’m fine,” I said, but my heart fluttered and seemed to miss a few beats. Jagged cliffs loomed high above the water, and the cries of gulls overhead echoed my inner turmoil.

THE JOURNAL

My grandfather has refused to put up bail money for Katya, and I can understand his point. He doesn't know her, so why should he trust her to not go skiving off? Aaron Levy has no money for her bail, either, although he has managed to scrape together funds for Katya's barrister. If I had anything at all of value, I would sell it. If Skokholm belonged to me, I would sell it to the first person who bid for it, just to buy Katya's freedom. There is a question of ownership since Vandermeer's death, but if it reverts to the previous owner that would be my grandfather, and here we are, come full circle.

When I think of Katya in that jail cell, I feel so helpless. If I could take her place, I would do it. It was my wretched curiosity that started the whole chain of events in motion and my negligence that allowed things to end the way they did. If only I'd not gone to the mainland that afternoon. If only the storm hadn't kept me there overnight. If only . . . A person could go mad with these thoughts.

The hardest thing I ever had to do in my life was to take Katya over to the mainland after Vandermeer's death. It wasn't that she resisted in any way—in fact, it was her cooperation that broke my heart. We had agreed to meet at her room, so I could carry her luggage. When she opened the door, I'd caught my breath because I'd never seen her in anything but trousers and long-sleeved white shirts. She'd managed to put on a short-sleeved white blouse and a grey pleated skirt, and her short hair had dried in waves around her face.

"These buttons were a challenge with my left hand," she said to me, and she took out a small leather wallet from her bedside table and put her money into the pocket of her skirt.

I held out the Iron Cross to her. "I couldn't find the journal."

She looked puzzled. "Vandermeer wouldn't have had time to move it," she said. She refused to look at the Iron Cross, but she ran her thumb over its edges, under the velvet wrapping.

I picked up her bags, and she followed me. On the way to South Haven, we crossed the rabbit-grazed turf made hazardous by thousands of burrows. The sun was hidden behind dark clouds, appearing for a moment as a small bright disk, then slipping back.

Katya held her injured arm against her torso and walked with her feet splayed for balance, because the stone ramp down to the harbor was slick. Puffins bobbed up and down in the turbulent waves below us, and I wondered if we'd be able to take off, since it was close to high tide. I tried not to think about the waves rising at

Crab Bay, and yet, in a part of my mind, I couldn't help wishing the waves would take him, pull him under to the bottom of the bay, where he would never be found. Here at South Haven, the white foam crashed up to the top steps of the landing, all the way to the spot by the low white wall where he had stood, on that first day, to greet Katya. The waves washed over the spot where he had stood and then slipped back into the sea, again and again, as if to erase all memories of him.

I watched her step carefully to the edge of the platform with the Iron Cross, now uncovered, in her left hand, and I wondered if the slight shivering of her body was from the cold or from the thought of the Iron Cross at the neck of Janisch's uniform. She stretched her arm back and threw the Iron Cross as hard as she could. It flew like a small dark bird, then dropped into the ocean. The sun broke through the clouds with a pale, diluted light, but the sky was still grey. I tried to imagine what she was thinking.

I reached out my hand to steady her as she climbed into the boat. She sat down on the bench near the railing, watching me, and said, "I'm sorry to have gotten you involved."

I was the one who should have apologized. I checked the gauges in the cabin of the motorboat and started to turn on the engine, but then I stopped and looked over at her. She was shivering violently. I pulled off my jumper and draped it round her shoulders.

"I'm not entirely blameless," I said. "It was my curiosity that started this whole thing."

"True, but you've no guilt in his death. You weren't

even on the island at the time, and I'm sure you can find plenty of people on the mainland who will testify to that." She touched her neck gingerly as if it hurt her to speak.

Just before I started the engine, I said to her, "Do you think this will come to trial?"

She nodded. "It will, most certainly. I'm a stranger to these people, and they thought Vandermeer was a quiet clergyman who studied birds." She turned round to watch the island disappear as I steered us toward the mainland, where we would face the consequences of our actions. "And if they find out who I am," she said, and didn't finish her sentence. Although I couldn't see her—she was behind me—I knew she would be holding her left forearm against her body, as she often did, to hide the blue numbers tattooed into her skin.

* * *

We need to find Vandermeer's journal. Katya was translating passages from it in our last days together. While the material did not prove he was Emil Janisch, it suggested that he was not using his real name, mentioned the words murder or murders, and indicated loyalty to Hitler. Unfortunately, when I went to look for it in Vandermeer's house, just before I took Katya over to the mainland to turn herself in, the journal was not where Katya had told me to look. Morwenn was in his bedroom, going through papers at his desk, and I had a strong feeling she had taken it, though she denied it later.

Two days after Vandermeer's death, I went back to see her. I cut the engine just outside of South Haven and looked at the cliffs of the island—jagged red sandstone—with a sense of wonder. With Vandermeer gone, it might be possible to live on the island indefinitely, except that Morwenn blamed me, at least in part, for what happened. I climbed the stone steps, past the old limekiln, up the path through the meadow of bluebells toward the white buildings that stood so clean and pure against the sky.

In the courtyard between the Wheelhouse and her cottage, I found Morwenn on a bench with an open book in her lap and a steaming mug of tea beside her. A white bedspread and some tea towels flapped in the wind on a washing line. For a moment, I was a boy of nine, and everything was right in my world. As I sat down next to her, I recognized the call of a sedge warbler, as it trilled and chirped, unseen, from dense vegetation near the wall.

I wasn't sure what to say, because her last words to me had been bitter. She finally looked up from her book, unable to ignore me any longer. I took her hand and stroked the back of it gently with my thumb. "How are you?"

She didn't answer for a moment and still wouldn't look at me. "The only man I ever loved, Robert." She flicked away a tear from her right cheek. She stood up suddenly, and the book fell from her lap into the bare dirt of the courtyard.

I knew she wasn't ready for the truth about him. "Katya has to stay in Marloes. She can't go back to London."

Morwenn turned back toward me, crossed her arms as if to protect herself from even speaking about Katya. "Are they going to take her up?"

A moment of panic made my mouth go dry. "I don't

know."

She sat down again beside me, picked up her mug of tea, and ran her fingertips along its rim. She stared straight ahead of her, as if she were in a trance.

"I'm truly sorry I didn't talk to you after I found the Iron Cross, but I knew you wouldn't want to hear anything against Mattheu."

"I still don't, Robert."

I found myself pulling on my earlobe, a habit I had tried to break. "I know, and I wouldn't bring it up unless it was important. Katya's future is at stake."

"Why should I care?" Morwenn said, as she turned toward me. "She ruined mine."

"What if we could prove that Mattheu Vandermeer was really Emil Janisch and did all those things that Katya said? Could you understand, then, why she came here?"

"She killed the wrong man. An innocent, good man." Morwenn stared off into the distance as she said this, as if I weren't there, and she gripped the mug so tightly, I wondered if it might break. "What I hate most is that I let you talk me into lying so she could come."

"She had to find out who he was, Morwenn."

"She was wrong."

"How do we know that? Wouldn't you like to find out the truth?"

Morwenn remained silent for a moment. "I'm trying to cope with things the way they are. He's dead—I'll never see him again. I hate that you've brought up these other possibilities."

"You know that Katya was translating Mattheu's journal before he died."

"Yes."

"But it disappeared, and I know it wasn't with the things that the investigators took with them." I leaned towards her and took her hand again. "There are passages in that journal that would help Katya."

She got up from the bench, and I followed as she stalked into the Wheelhouse. At the sink, she filled the mug with water.

"Morwenn, please."

With her back to me, she untied her apron, folded it, and placed it on the kitchen counter, then turned and walked past me as if I were invisible.

THE BIRD WATCHER

The first time I saw Vandermeer, that day when Robert brought me over from the mainland, I was puzzled by the fact that he didn't look like Robert's sketch. He stood against the dark rocks just above the harbor, and his hair was down to his shoulders and bleached by the sun. He was more slender than Janisch had been, and there was something else about his face that I couldn't quite put my finger on, beyond the mustache and full beard that Janisch wouldn't have had. With his hands in the pockets of his khaki trousers, he walked down the steps, and although I avoided his eyes as I collected my bags, I felt him watching me. As the boat touched the landing platform, Vandermeer said, "Hello, Thomas." Still not looking at him, I pretended to search under the bench for something, and I realized that I had never heard Janisch speak English. Vandermeer's voice was smooth and cool, but heavy with Teutonic overtones. I straightened up and turned toward Mattheu Vandermeer, who took one of my bags and then the other, setting them down on the rock stairs while he gave his hand to help me out of the boat. When he touched me, a current like electricity shot up from the base of my spine. The roar of the waves crashing against the rocks and the intensity of the sunlight made me dizzy for a moment, and I closed my eyes. This was not the time to pass out. Vandermeer said, "Are you all right?" At the sound of his voice, my eyes shot open, and I found myself looking into his deep-set blue eyes, in the tanned face with creases lining the wide forehead. With the light brown hair growing down to his shoulders, he looked like a painting of Jesus of Nazareth that I once saw in a London museum, and I wondered what Robert was up to, since his sketch of Vandermeer had shown a beardless man with short dark hair. This man looked very little like Emil Janisch, whose face had been pasty, with the receding chin and the short dark hair slicked back, almost shaved above the ears. This man's grip was firm, the hand cool and strong, and for a moment, I allowed myself to hope that he was not Emil Janisch. I had sworn to Aaron that I would know Janisch's eyes, but now I wasn't certain of anything.

"Yes, I'm fine," I said.

Robert climbed out of the boat behind us and took one of my bags. "Reverend Vandermeer, this is Katherine Dennis."

Mattheu Vandermeer nodded to me. "Welcome," he said, as he turned and began to climb the steps. A man of few words. We followed, while huge white gulls watched us from the top of the rocks beside the path, as it rose steeply and curved in front of a small stone building.

"An old limekiln," Robert said. Between the stones

grew clumps of fragrant white flowers, which Robert said were sea campion.

Just past the limekiln grew masses of bluebells, swaths of violet across the green of the island. Fleecy white clouds dotted the pale sky, and a gentle breeze tossed my hair. I didn't want to think about the possibility that the ordinary-looking man ahead of us could be a monster called Emil Janisch.

When we reached a broad meadow, the path curved to the left, still climbing upwards. A rabbit scurried through the bluebells just ahead of me, then I noticed they were everywhere—light brown shapes in constant motion, except for the ones who froze, motionless, as I passed. Bluebells ran down to the sea campion above the rock cliffs of the harbor, which Robert had called South Haven.

As we turned to the right, I saw several white buildings in the center of the island. Robert pointed them out: "The farmhouse, where Reverend Vandermeer lives; the smaller place to the right where I am staying, and that's Morwenn's place in the center, where you'll be staying, and of course, on the far right, the Wheelhouse which has the dining room and the kitchen. The farmhouse, by the way, was built in the seventeenth century."

I listened to Robert's chatter with most of my attention focused on the silent figure of Vandermeer. How much would I see of him? How often would he leave his house so I could search it? Damn. What if this was just a wild goose chase, like Aaron said?

We passed an overgrown rock wall that ran

perpendicular to the path. "That was built hundreds of years ago," Robert said. "Notice the herringbone pattern of the rocks. These walls used to divide the island into fields when it was being farmed."

I smiled half-heartedly and thought that Robert would make an excellent tour guide. Vandermeer, as we walked, had said nothing and did not even turn round. I studied the back of his head, his walk, his build. Janisch had been at least twenty pounds heavier and had walked with a certain stiffness, as if he were wearing a back brace. The man ahead of me on the path moved with an easy grace. His voice could be that of Janisch but all I ever heard from Janisch were his sharp commands in German, so the tone was different.

Around the clustered buildings, the terrain was wide and flat, the grass heavily grazed by rabbits and honeycombed by their burrows. Vandermeer stopped in front of the farmhouse and turned around. As he handed my bag to Robert, Vandermeer said to him, "Why don't you take Miss Dennis to see her cousin and then you can show her around the Wheelhouse." Vandermeer gave me a slight nod before turning to walk toward the farmhouse. Then he turned back abruptly. "You've come too late to fix tea," he said, "but I'd like supper at seven." I nodded, hoping that Morwenn could talk me through this challenge to my culinary skills. I had never bothered to cook much, since I'd lived on my own for seven years.

I followed Robert toward the long narrow building between the farmhouse and the Wheelhouse, and he stopped on the porch in front of the closest door. I wanted to confront him about Vandermeer's appearance, but it was not the right time. As if reading my mind, Robert said, as he opened the door, "Well, what do you think? Is he Janisch?"

My own doubts and fears had made me edgy, and I bit back the angry response. "I don't know yet, Thomas," I said, with the irritable control one would use to placate a demanding child. "I don't want to talk about it right now." I walked into the small room, with its two windows, the narrow bed covered with a green wool blanket, the tiny wooden nightstand, the small desk and one chair.

"You'll have the best view from this room," he said, ignoring the tension in my voice. "Eastern window—hope you're an early riser. Why don't we go and say hello to Morwenn."

I took a deep breath, suddenly anxious about meeting the woman who had every reason to resent me.

Robert started out of the room, but I said, "Hold on a second," and he turned back. "How does she feel about doing this?"

"Well, she'd rather not, of course. She's always been very active, and pretending to have a back injury involves a lot of sitting still, which she hates." He paused. "But she's doing it as a favor to me."

"Can we trust her not to say anything to Vandermeer?" I glanced through the window at the rock outcropping, which was covered with seagulls and red-legged oystercatchers.

"She couldn't say anything to Vandermeer about you without implicating me also. The last thing she wants is to get me booted off the island."

"I hope you're right," I said.

I followed Robert to the other end of the long building, where he knocked on a blue-painted door.

"Come in." The voice was undeniably Welsh. We entered a small living room, where a woman of about forty sat on a wood-framed sofa with her bare feet propped up on a stool, crocheting a blanket with baby-blue yarn. She wore a dark green housedress, from which the bottom button dangled by a thread. Morwenn tossed the handwork aside. "I'm tired of this mug's game already, Robert," she said. "I'll be goin' round the bend soon. You know I don't know how to just sit."

Robert walked over and kissed the top of her head. She reached up to pat his face. He said, "It's Thomas, remember?"

"Thomas, my arse. I've known you as Robert since you were in nappies, and I'll call you what I like in my own house."

Robert took my hand and pulled me forward. "Morwenn, this is Katherine Dennis."

Morwenn rolled her eyes to the ceiling and said sharply, "Not your real name, is it, ducky?" Through the rounded Gaelic lilt of Morwenn's Welsh accent, the undertones of sarcasm were unmistakable. Morwenn stared at me. She had the olive-toned skin that seldom burned in the sun, but there were the beginnings of crow's feet round her eyes.

Robert said to me, "Morwenn is the only mother I've ever known."

That's right, Robert. You know how to play the old girl, don't you? And she thinks you make the sun shine. I held out my hand to Morwenn and said, "I know this must be hard for you, and I'm very grateful."

Morwenn put her feet carefully on the floor and stood up. She was two inches taller than I was. "I'm not used to being cooped up here, but I've had to play the invalid for several days already. There's only so much sketching or crocheting I can do before I get sick of it."

I gave her my best smile. "I wonder if you could give me a few pointers about cooking for Reverend Vandermeer." I watched her face, but there was no smile in return.

"I don't use cookery books, so I can't just hand you a stack of recipes. Most of what he likes is simple food: creamed potatoes and runner beans. And I'll tell you how to do the plum cake and Cornish pasties."

I knew I was completely out of my element, and I also didn't want to be tied up in the kitchen all day. "Do you have any suggestions for tonight?" I said. "I'm at a loss." I glanced at Robert, who had made himself comfortable in one of the armchairs.

"There's a bit of leftover stew you can heat up. I made a double portion right before my tragic 'injury.' "

"Morwenn, I am eternally grateful. Cooking is not one of my strong points."

"Hopefully, you'll not be here very long. I don't like playing games with Mattheu, and I'm only doing this because Robert asked me to." She looked at me and then smiled at Robert. "I've never been able to say 'no' to this boy." She sat back down, picked up the handwork, and started crocheting, the hook flashing between the yarn and the body of the blanket. I realized that Morwenn's loyalty to Vandermeer was surpassed only by her desire to keep "her boy" on the island as long as possible.

IN KATYA'S DEFENSE

When I visited Katya in Carmarthen, I normally took the afternoon train from Milford Haven or Haverfordwest and went to see her in the evening. Carmarthen was not the closest town to the island of Skokholm. By all rights, the trial should have taken place at Haverfordwest, but the courthouse there had been destroyed in a fire six months previously and had not yet been rebuilt, so the Guildhall in Carmarthen had taken on the overflow of cases. Carmarthen, laid out on the north bank of the River Tywi, was originally a Roman fortress, dating back almost two thousand years. In the history of mythology, it claimed importance as the birthplace of Merlin the Enchanter.

Now, in 1953, there was little to suggest that Carmarthen had ever been a site of any great glory. It had evolved into an important market town, famous for its woolen industry and its ports, but there was not much of interest in its architecture except for the handsome Guildhall. This was the two-story brownstone Georgian, in the heart of the city, where the trial would take place.

On my way to an appointment with Mark Wickham, Katya's barrister, I paused for a moment to admire the Guildhall's graceful front façade, with its Ionic columns, Palladian windows, and mullioned door.

I'd agreed to meet Mark at 10 o'clock that morning, so I'd stayed over instead of returning to the island. His office was on a side street, just off the square in front of the Guildhall. I arrived at five minutes before ten.

He met me at the door and invited me inside, apologizing for the clutter. Mark was a few years older than I was—in his early thirties, maybe. His hair, dark and slightly damp, looked like he'd just gotten out of the shower. His secretary was ill with pneumonia, he told me, and he admitted that he was not a tidy person by nature. The room was lined, ceiling to floor, on all walls, with bookshelves, which were crammed with books of all sizes. Stacks of books spilled over onto the floor, each one with slips of white paper marking references. "You know," he said, "I have a great deal of trouble staying inside on a day like this. Would you like to take a walk?"

Although I'm not normally prone to claustrophobia, being any place besides that drab little office sounded appealing. He grabbed his hat and we started walking, instinctively, toward the river.

"We'll be lucky if Kevin Sperry doesn't call you as a witness for the Crown," Mark said. "If you take the stand, they'll ask you why it was so important to return to Skokholm."

Morwenn had asked me the same thing, that first night back on the island. "So, Robert, why have you come back?" To see you, of course, I'd said. She told me I'd always been a good liar, but she smiled as she said it. I laughed, but I could give her no other answer. My feelings for the island bordered on reverence. I was so obsessed with its raw beauty; it might have been an exotic lover. How could this be expressed, except by opening my mouth and spouting insane poetry? I was not willing to do that in a court of law.

"I remembered Skokholm," I told Mark Wickham, "as the only place where I had been happy. I just wanted to spend some time there." I chewed on my thumbnail. "I can give nothing but a dusty answer to that question."

"What was your relationship to Mattheu Vandermeer?"

"We got along well, I fancy, because of our shared interest in birds. He seemed to respect my knowledge about the island wildlife, even though he was puzzled about how I could be so familiar with it."

"Kevin Sperry will ask you how you got Thomas Weaver to change his mind about going to the island."

"That won't come off very well, will it?"

"It would be helpful, of course, to have a copy of Katya's letter about the investigation of Vandermeer."

"I thought it best to burn that, under the circumstances."

"So there's only your word."

I bit the inside of my lip. "Which isn't worth much, is it?"

"You went to the island posing as Thomas Weaver. You arranged for Katya to come and be Morwenn's 'cousin.' That's already two strikes against you."

"I could testify that Katya gave me the letter for

Aaron."

"Aaron could testify about that, and we wouldn't have to face the issue of your credibility."

"You've defended two women accused of murdering their abusive husbands. How will Katya's defense be different?"

"We'll have to prove that her life was in danger, at the moment she killed Vandermeer, without any personal history of his violence against her. This may involve bringing out his Nazi past—his capacity for murder—but that's exactly what the Crown wants us to do."

I stopped on the banks of the River Tywi, stood with my hands behind my back. "It's a fine line, isn't it?"

He didn't answer but sighed heavily. "I hate to see that girl go to prison for the rest of her life."

The thought of this terrified me. "There's got to be something I can do."

"You mentioned a journal," Mark said.

"I'm sure Morwenn took it. I've tried to convince her to give it to me, but she's dug her toes in."

"Do you think the Crown might try to prove that Katya killed an innocent man? That he wasn't Emil Janisch after all?"

"They could win with that ploy only if we don't use the Nazi angle. And I'm afraid we'll have to. Mattheu Vandermeer the bird-watcher is just not a credible assailant."

OBSESSION

My first night on Skokholm Island was painfully long, and I couldn't get to sleep until almost dawn. As I lay for endless hours on the hard mattress of that bed, I couldn't get warm, in spite of the six wool blankets over me. Finally I got up, stood in wool socks on the red-painted floor, and realized that I was warmer out of bed than in it. Somehow, the mattress had absorbed the cold dampness of the sea air. I crawled in between the blankets, leaving a layer of them over the mattress, and found the secret to staying warm. But my mind could not rest—I kept dragging the Christ-like image of Matthew Vandermeer over the arrogant face of Emil Janisch in my memory. I stripped away the mustache and beard from Vandermeer's face, trying to picture the receding chin and pronounced cleft between Janisch's nose and upper lip. Still, the two images did not fully match. On the island, playing with memories of his face was a lethal game.

The sun rose early at the western edge of Wales, and although the colors of the dawn were gentle, the wind was not. It roared outside my room, rattled the door and windows, battered green plants outside, and ruffled the feathers of gulls on the rocks.

I began my first day as a domestic helper in a fog of exhaustion and irritability that left me off-balance. My first job was to fix breakfast. Morwenn had dictated the menu the day before: scrambled eggs, tomatoes, toast, and bangers. My hands shook as I cracked eggs into a blue ceramic bowl, and the contents of one egg landed on the counter in a shining mass, which then dripped onto the floor. "Blast," I said to myself, as I scooped up the oozing yolk with a dishrag and tried to wipe the clear slime of egg white from the dark tiles. I looked up when I heard footsteps on the stone floor of the dining room. Through the arched doorway I saw Matthew Vandermeer, dressed for work in a denim shirt and well-worn khakis. I looked at my watch; it was precisely seven o'clock. I poured his coffee into a ceramic cup and carried it into the dining room, where he sat in his chair at the far end of the fifteen-foot dining table, leafing through a bird magazine. When I set down the coffee on the table in front of him, he said good morning to me, but he seemed distracted. He had difficulty making eye contact for more than a brief moment.

I returned to the kitchen and scrambled the eggs, while the bangers sputtered in their own grease in another pan. Breakfast I could handle—it was supper I was concerned about. I put toast and sausages on a plate for Morwenn, then carried Vandermeer's plate to him.

Absorbed in his magazine, he didn't look up. Probably not used to the company of strangers, especially young women. Or was this my own paranoia? I saved a generous portion of everything for Robert and covered it with another plate. I tried to eat, but could only manage three bites of scrambled egg and a slice of tomato.

On my way out the door to deliver Morwenn's breakfast, I met Robert in the courtyard, his damp hair curling round his forehead, making him seem even younger than he was. He smiled as he said to me, "Did you sleep well?"

"Yes, thank you." Within Vandermeer's hearing, I preferred to keep my relationship with Robert on a formal note, instead of admitting that I had slept badly. "I've got to get this to Morwenn before it gets cold. Your plate's on top of the cooker."

As she ate her breakfast—examining each piece of toast and each banger, for what?—Morwenn reviewed with me what needed to be done each Monday: scrub the kitchen floor, tidy up the Reverend Vandermeer's house, and do the washing. I decided to start with Vandermeer's house, hoping for a chance to search it. Scrubbing the floor and washing clothes sounded like something Cinderella should be doing, but I would have to play the game.

I filled two buckets with hot water from the boiler and carried them to the sink. As I did the washing up, I daydreamed about what I might find. If I were fortunate, there might be something really damning, and I could write to Aaron and ask for his help in getting indictments, an extradition—Janisch would have to be extradited to

Poland. I stopped myself in this train of thought. What if Vandermeer was exactly who and what he claimed to be, and Robert was truly a flake?

I threw rags, soap, and a scrub brush into one bucket, then filled a second with clean water. I walked toward the farmhouse with the clamor of gulls in the sky far above me, but kept my eyes on the uneven terrain beneath my feet. It was impossible to walk more than five feet anywhere on the island without stepping into a rabbit burrow.

The front door was painted black, and the latch clicked loudly when I pressed the handle. As I pushed open the heavy door, I had the sensation I should duck my head because the doorway was only two inches taller than I was. I stepped into the entryway and closed the door gently. Behind me, to the right, was a small alcove in the corner, with a wooden stand holding two black umbrellas and a gnarled walking stick. How strange. With the strong constant winds, how could they use umbrellas? The floor of the entryway seemed to be made of stones, painted red, and I knew it would be difficult to clean, because of the layers of dust gathered in the valleys between them.

Straight ahead was another door, which I assumed led to a spare bedroom. The entry hall, to the left, was lined with shallow bookshelves on either side, and the door at its end was painted red like the floor. I glanced at the books on the shelves—mostly bird guides and books about local flora and fauna—just what one would expect in the library of a nature enthusiast. I also noticed a layer of dust on the books—from the wind, I wondered, or from lack of use?

With my thumb, I pressed the lever of the door handle. The clamor of its metal latch was even louder than the first. As I pushed open the door, I jumped involuntarily when I saw Mattheu Vandermeer in an armchair beside the fireplace. He was writing in a black leather notebook, and he held a cigarette in his left hand. "Yes?" he said.

So much for detective work. I forced myself to smile. "I was going to tidy up in here. Should I come back later?"

With unhurried, precise movements of his elegant hands, he capped the fountain pen and closed the journal. "No need," he said, as he stood up. "I'll move into the other room." He placed the cigarette carefully in the notched side of a glass ashtray, which he placed on top of his journal with the fountain pen. He looked at me for a moment, with a slight smile, as he crossed the room and disappeared into his bedroom, closing the door behind him.

I stared at the bedroom door. I would kill to get hold of that journal. He's got in his hands what I need to see, I thought, as I began to straighten the couch cushions on the wooden sofas. Where might he keep it? At least I know what it looks like. Maybe he'll finish and go out while I'm here. Then I'll know it's somewhere in this room. It's probably nothing—notes on birds he's seen recently or a list of supplies he needs to finish some project.

As I swept up the fireplace ashes into a dustpan, I wondered if there were people who could truly read another person's thoughts. I wished I had that power, to be able to enter the mind of Mattheu Vandermeer. If I found some clue to his identity, I could go back to Aaron, to ask for his help one more time. And yet, the thought of entering Janisch's mind made my hands tremble.

I let my thoughts drift to my most common daydream—a face-to-face confrontation with Emil Janisch, who would be unmasked and compelled to speak the truth. If I found guilt in his emotional repertoire, that would be satisfying, but I would still seek prosecution. One person can't feel enough remorse to pay for the deaths of thousands.

I looked over the room. The floor, of course, needed to be scrubbed, but there were also dusty windowsills and smeared panes of glass, as well as sofa cushions to clean and re-arrange. I picked up one of the embroidered pillows. It had a black and white puffin on a green background, surely Morwenn's handiwork. The room had the feeling of a woman's loving touch—the pillows, the gingham curtains on the window. I wondered how close Morwenn had gotten to the Reverend Vandermeer, who seemed so unapproachable. It would make my mission more dangerous than I had thought.

That evening, after a disastrous meal of roast beef and Yorkshire pudding, I stood in front of the kitchen sink and watched gulls circle in the sky, their cries muted by the glass of the window. Even though it was late in the day, the sun was still visible at the western end of the island; Robert had told me it didn't set until close on ten p.m.

In the kitchen warmed by heat from the oven, I let my hands relax, comfortable inside rubber gloves, in the hot dishwater, and I made no effort to scrub burned Yorkshire pudding from the pan. Too tired to be a cook, a maid, I thought, as I bent my knees slightly and braced them against the front of the sink to arch my back. Every muscle in my body ached from a day of scrubbing and sweeping. The sleepless night had fogged my brain, and there would be so little benefit from this fatigue. I had burned the roast, but the potatoes were undercooked. I will not do this again, I thought, this wasted day with nothing to show for it.

I heard footsteps behind me and knew without turning round that it was Robert, because of the lemony scent of his after-shave lotion. I flicked water from my gloves and turned to face him, wondering why I was up to my elbows in greasy hot water on this God-forsaken island.

"Hi . . . is there anything I can do to help?"

His face was flushed, probably from some exertion more pleasant than doing dishes, and I resented his freedom. He had so much energy, like a puppy, and it annoyed me because I was so tired. I wanted to say, tell me why you wrote that damn letter, but I held my tongue. "No, your timing is just great," I said. "I'm almost done." And even though I tried to keep the anger and frustration out of my voice, Robert frowned slightly. I stripped off the rubber gloves, damp inside from invisible punctures.

"I was wondering if you'd like to go for a walk," he said. "The sunset will be beautiful tonight, with all these clouds, but you can't really see it from here."

I shook my head as I threw my gloves into the sink. "We need to talk."

Robert backed up instinctively. "Why? What's wrong?"

I looked over his shoulder at the door to the courtyard.

"Does he ever come back here in the evening?"

Robert shoved his hands into the pockets of his khaki trousers. "I don't think so, I mean, it's highly unlikely. You see, his evening routine is practically written in stone, as is his afternoon routine and his morning routine." As he moved to stand beside me, leaning against the kitchen counter, Robert checked his watch. "Right now, I should think, he will be engaged in silent contemplation of the New Testament. At eight thirty, he will review the daily bird census in that huge notebook of his. At nine o'clock, he will blow out the propane lamp in his living room and retire for the night."

I mimicked Robert's English accent. "You should think? You should think he would be engaged in silent contemplation of how insane this whole idea of yours was to begin with." I heard my own voice rising, against my will.

Robert grinned at me and touched my cheek gently. "You get these little spots of color in your cheeks when you're angry. It's rather charming."

I slapped his hand away and crossed my arms in front of me as I leaned against the sink. My deepest desire at the moment was to strangle him. "Robert, is there any possibility that your love of this island, and your desire to spend more time here, has caused you to build this 'Nazi' aspect in your mind? Have you possibly lost your mind? Could that be why you didn't just ask Vandermeer yourself about the Iron Cross, which, by the way, I have yet to see?" While I slammed these words at him, I watched a look of surprise cloud his face.

But then he smiled, a wide grin that lit up his brown

eyes. “Well,” he said, “aren’t you a bit wound up.”

My voice was calm and controlled. “Wound up,” I said. “Do I seem wound up to you, Robert?”

“Do you think he’d really tell me the truth about that Iron Cross?”

“All right,” I said. “You’ve made your point.”

“I’m not as balmy as you seem to think I am.” He pushed a strand of hair out of his eye. “We’re missing that sunset.”

I wouldn’t let him off the hook so easily. With my arms still crossed, I scooted along the edge of the kitchen counter, away from him. “Have you spent so much time with Mattheu Vandermeer, that you know his every move, his every thought?”

In an attempt at redemption, he offered, with a shrug, “Vandermeer has a schedule, all neatly hand-written, which maps his day from sunrise to sunset. I found it when I was snooping through his bureau, right before I discovered the Iron Cross. He’s the dullest man I’ve ever met.”

“Dull,” I said, “is an understatement. But, what the hell were you doing, looking into his bureau? Playing the spy? With the difference between what I see and your pencil sketch, I’m beginning to doubt his being Janisch.”

“What do you mean? I thought your group wanted leads like this one. Okay, some artistic license with the pencil sketch . . . but his isolation, and the Iron Cross—isn’t that important?”

“How would I know?” I said, as I fingered the small pearl on a fine gold chain around my neck. “All I know is that his house is clean, and his meals have been cooked, and I haven't slept, and my whole body aches, with nothing to show for it. Oh, except for your charming smile and wild stories."

Robert thought for a moment. "Okay, I've got an idea."

"It had better be good." In spite of myself, I felt a smile forming at the corners of my mouth.

"It is," Robert said, too quickly. "It is."

"All right then, let's hear your wonderful idea."

"I know I can buy you an hour, right now. I can tell Vandermeer I'm concerned about the rabbits on the far side of the island—the ones beyond my colonies. I've seen some that are acting strangely—something like that. I'll keep him occupied looking for the 'sick' rabbits." Robert sighed. "That will give you some light, and time to at least find the Iron Cross, which is in the bottom right-hand drawer. I'll come back before him, on some pretense, to let you know he's on his way."

I stretched my back, rubbing the small of it that ached so badly. "Okay," I said. "I think that's a good start. I really need to find something, Robert. This can't be just an outing for a bored little rich kid who wants to play at catching bad guys."

I regretted the words as soon as I said them. Robert's face hardened, and I knew I'd gone too far. "It is a good plan," I said, " I just need something to go on. All I see is this man in prayer and meditation, and it's not doing my soul much good."

* * *

I entered Mattheu Vandermeer's house through the front door and the inner door with their clacking latches and pushed open the door to his bedroom, which was oddly shaped. The room was twice as long as it was wide, and a narrow bed under a small southern window took up half the longest wall. An enormous mahogany desk with an inlaid pattern of lighter wood inset several inches from its edges dominated the other half of the room, with another small window to the east. I sat down in the straight-backed wooden chair, at the desk that had yielded the Iron Cross, which I needed to see and to touch. I needed to know that it was real, regardless of Robert's sketch or anything else. As long as the Iron Cross was there, I could hope. I didn't want to use the propane lamp, although the light outside had begun to dim.

I found the velvet-wrapped bundle in the drawer, just where Robert had told me to look, and I held it in my hands, feeling the shape of the medal. I unfolded the velvet carefully, noting the direction and depths of the folds, to be able to put it back exactly as I had found it. The Iron Cross, dark metal rimmed by white, was all too familiar to me.

I had first seen the Nazi uniform when I was twelve years old. The Iron Cross made me think of death, even now. When I could bring myself to touch it, I held it in my hand with the cross lying over the tops of three fingers, light in my hand as I weighed it. I tried to be objective about this bit of metal. If thrown into a fire, it would melt into a worthless lump. I wrapped the Iron Cross, replaced it in the drawer, and checked my watch. Forty-five minutes left. If I had a desk like this, I told myself, I would keep my journal in the top right-hand drawer. I opened it and found three pieces of yellowed writing paper with Vandermeer's daily schedule underneath, on a fresh white page, neatly written in blue ink, every hour of the day dedicated to some worthy activity, just as Robert had described it. Proof of a compulsive personality, nothing else.

In the drawer below were two small rings with keys in various shapes and sizes and a folded map of Great Britain. Again, I pulled open the bottom drawer, where the Iron Cross lay hidden in its cloak of velvet. There were two brown ledgers and a small book with a white leather cover, with two words—probably Dutch, I didn't recognize them—embossed in ornate gold letters above a gold cross. I thumbed through the gilt-edged pages—a prayer book?—and put it aside. The ledgers revealed that Vandermeer had recorded his household expenses down to the penny for his entire stay on the island. Was this his attempt to live simply, to emulate Thoreau at Walden Pond? Or was it just an elaborate farce, a game of survival?

The next drawer had blank white stationery, two Parker fountain pens, a half bottle of blue ink, and a book of stamps. As I closed the drawer I wondered if Janisch would risk disclosing his location and if so, with whom would he correspond? The next drawer held nothing but receipts and tax bills. I decided to come back to it later, when I could look at each item more closely.

As I opened the bottom drawer, I felt pressure inside my head and wondered if the tight muscles in my neck would lead to a headache later. I slipped one envelope from the middle of the stack and studied the handwriting—a precise, rounded script that slanted to the left. Maybe it was a fellow bird fancier comparing notes on the migration of kittiwakes or cormorants. The

Reverend Mattheu Vandermeer, General Delivery, Marloes. It was the return address that surprised me: J. Dengler, Villa General Belgrano, Argentina. I knew this was a Nazi gathering place. I counted the stacks of envelopes and did the math in my head—eight stacks, roughly twelve letters per stack—close on one hundred letters. How much could one say about cormorants or kittiwakes, I wondered as I checked my watch again. I would have another half hour, if Robert kept his promise. Could I trust him with my life? Did he realize what could happen if Emil Janisch found me there?

I opened the envelope on top. It contained a two-page letter, written in German, dated the 29th of April, 1952, but I understood and spoke German better than I could read it. I closed the drawer and sat back in the chair, with the letter in my hands. I stared at the rough texture of the white paint on the wall. If I took one letter from the bottom, would he notice? Only if he counted his letters every day, which wouldn't surprise me.

I saw the light flash as Robert had promised. Damn, why was he so early? I stuffed the letter into its envelope, then tossed it back in the drawer. I dashed out of Vandermeer's bedroom and out the front door of the farmhouse, then dropped, out of breath, onto the low bench against the stone wall. Robert's voice seemed to come out of the dark sky, and it startled me. "I was wondering if you'd like to go for that walk now."

His face was shadowed by the twilight, and I stayed on the bench for a moment, before I finally got up and followed him along the far side of the Wheelhouse, where I knew that Vandermeer couldn't hear us. "Did you overestimate things again, like the amount of light before sunset? Or did you underestimate Mattheu Vandermeer's willingness to break his precious, carved-in-stone routine?"

"We weren't that early coming back," Robert said, and there was an edge to his voice that I hadn't heard before. "Surely you had time to find the Iron Cross."

I kept my mouth shut, wanting to scream at him, wondering if he realized the dangers of this game and how important—how crucial—small things could be. The sun gleamed in the west, and I wanted to look at it, but I kept my eyes focused on the narrow path as we walked.

He waited for what he obviously considered a prudent amount of time before he whispered to me, "So, did you find it—the Iron Cross, I mean. Am I right?"

I hated the eager look on his face and his absolute confidence that he would be vindicated. Not so easily, I thought, and I stopped walking and crossed my arms as he turned back toward me. "There's just one thing I need to clear up with you before I go any further with this, or with you."

"What?"

I smiled, hearing the uncertainty in his voice, and I began to walk again. "That sketch your grandfather sent to Aaron showed a clean-shaven man with extremely short hair, much darker than Vandermeer's. It did remind me a lot of a monster named Emil Janisch. So, I arrive on the island, to be greeted by a gentle bird-watcher who looks a hell of a lot more like Jesus than a Nazi, and you're asking me why I'm not thrilled to find an Iron Cross, which could be here for any of a hundred different reasons. Excuse me, Robert Kensley, but just what do you think you're doing?"

Now Robert stopped and touched my arm. "Look," he said, "I've already admitted that I took some artistic license with the sketch. I knew a Nazi would never have long hair or a beard. Also, it's unlikely Janisch's hair would have been lightened by the sun at that time, so I drew his hair darker and shorter, and I took off the beard." He shrugged his shoulders.

I looked toward the sunset. "I'm surprised you didn't draw him in a Nazi uniform."

"Now there's an idea."

"It's all a joke to you, isn't it?"

"No," he said softly, "it's not a joke, Katya. Not before and not now. Maybe I didn't really understand before."

I was surprised by the sincerity in his voice; maybe I had misjudged him. "Okay, you may be right. I'm exhausted, but I did see the Iron Cross. Maybe I'm on the right track after all." I didn't tell him about the letters; I had him at a distance, where I intended to keep him. "But I need a block of time."

"I'll keep him away tomorrow for three hours. I promise. We'll be working to finish the shed we started last week." He lifted his eyebrows. "See what you can come up with."

I shivered, and Robert took off his jacket and put it round my shoulders. "You know, Robert, I found your sketch only because we were packing up files to be put in storage. They were being sent to Israel for safekeeping." Reminded of the loss of my job, I felt vulnerable. "Aaron believes that someday the files will be needed again, but I don't have his faith. I believe it's come to the wire—it's now or never." I looked at Robert. "I was the only one there who actually knew Janisch. The sketch meant nothing to the rest of them."

"I thought your organization followed up on leads like that."

"It would, normally, but when your letter arrived, we were shutting down. Aaron had finally given up, frustrated by the small number of indictments and convictions we were getting for all our work."

"So," Robert said, "am I correct in assuming that you're doing this on your own?"

"Yes." I avoided his eyes by pretending to examine a rabbit carcass on the path, pushing it gently with the toe of my shoe.

"Why?"

I knew that Robert was studying my face, but I refused to look at him. I needed to know what kind of person could kill so carelessly, and what made him enjoy it so much. Would Robert understand this? "I have to find out if this man is Emil Janisch," I finally said to him.

He took a deep breath. "Does Aaron Levy know where you've gone?"

I shook my head. "He'll figure it out. We had quite a row about Janisch before I left." I watched Robert's face, serious now, as he gazed off into the distance.

"Tell me how the Documentation Center functions," he said. "What do you do? Where does the money come from?"

Not wanting to have this conversation any closer to Vandermeer's house, I stopped just after we made our way across the marsh. I explained to Robert about the files made up for each known Nazi officer, with details supplied by the testimony of survivors. "We also keep files on the locations of potential witnesses," I said, "so we can find them if a Nazi comes to trial." The ocean roared behind us.

"So you'll have to start a file for me?" he asked.

"Have you witnessed any crimes? You could only testify about finding the Iron Cross."

"I was just kidding," he said. "Can't you take a joke?"

"Some things I don't joke about."

He shook his head. "I'm sorry, I don't mean to offend you. And I really do want to learn more about what you're doing."

I pushed hair out of my face. "For a while, we put ads in Yiddish newspapers, asking people to come forward with information, but then the word spread, and people knew who we were and what we were doing, and they would come to us on their own. Our offices were right there in the middle of the Jewish community, in Golder's Green."

"What about the money?"

"The operation was funded by private donations. For a variety of reasons, certain governments have chosen not to pursue suspected war criminals. People like Aaron and myself have devoted their lives to keeping track of former Nazis. Aaron and I make a good team; we've worked together for three years."

I thought of the long days and countless evenings spent with Aaron, doing this work, finding in it reason to live again, and I realized I missed Aaron very much. "I do most of the interviewing and then the transcribing. Then Aaron goes over the details. He spends days, weeks, referencing and cross-referencing. He goes through every document, sifting it for the smallest details. Reading and comparing the personal accounts of survivors, Aaron will eventually discover a pattern, and with that small pattern he will soon be able to compile enough information to bring action against a former Nazi. Just watching him has taught me how to interview more carefully—what questions are most likely to bear fruit later under Aaron's close inspection."

"Why is he quitting?"

"I'm not sure 'quitting' is the right word—maybe 'retiring.' " I searched for a way to explain to Robert, and to myself. "He's tired; he's spent so much time on what is becoming a hopeless cause. Even when Nazis are brought to trial and convicted, someone will come along and release them. Out of ninety-six hundred Nazis sent to prison, there were only three hundred left in June of 1950. God knows how many have been released since then."

"How can that be? How can that many people who are guilty, convicted by a court, go free?"

"Now you see why funding is drying up. People don't want to waste their money, if it ends up being for nothing." I said quietly, "I'm not sure how it will be now, without the work. Having a purpose, I believe, is what saved us."

"I'm not sure you've answered my question," Robert said. " Why are you doing this, on your own, without Aaron Levy?"

I ran the toe of my shoe round the opening of a rabbit

burrow. "I told you—I want to find out if this man is Janisch, and if so, does he have a conscience?"

He took hold of my arm. "Is this a vendetta?"

I stared at this young man I barely knew, whose face was now shadowed by the falling darkness. He was kind, he was a good listener, but he had not yet earned my trust. "He's the big fish we need to catch right now," I said.

Robert walked me back to my room, and when we said goodnight at the door, the sky's dark blue was the same color as the ocean. I entered the dark space and felt along the end of the bed for my torch, which I propped on the bedside table while I lit a taper. The lamp hissed and glowed with green light.

Restless, unable to consider sleep, I thought about another walk, but with the heavy cloud cover, there was no moon. I did not want to chance stepping in a rabbit hole and ricking an ankle. I didn't want to use up the batteries in my torch, so I pulled my journal from under the mattress and sat down at the small desk. I had debated whether or not to bring the journal to the island. It would be dangerous if Janisch got hold of it, but in the end, I decided to take the risk. He had no reason to suspect me of being anything other than Morwenn's cousin, and besides, I always kept the journal hidden. The one thing I would not give up was the emotional release of writing down my thoughts, feelings, and memories. By the soft light of the propane lamp, I began my first entry on the island:

2 May, 1953: I have been on the island of Skokholm for slightly above 24 hours, and I am filled with doubts about what I hope to accomplish. Back in London, when I thought about coming here, I was so sure of my plan. I would make the journey, meet the man who called himself Mattheu Vandermeer, and I would know right away if he was Janisch. I didn't count on him looking so different from Robert Kensley's sketch. I must say, it's thrown me off balance. The man lives in seclusion here, and he is either a quiet man of God or a killer playing at charades. When I look at him, I am baffled by the change in his appearance, even beyond the longer hair and the beard, the weight loss, and the tan.

I keep asking myself over and over why I've come, if the chances are good, as Aaron says, that he'll never come to trial. Why have I put myself at risk? I feel such a responsibility to do the right thing, and I'm not sure what that is, except that I know I must identify Janisch. I'm not sure I can see beyond that.

ROBERT

In spite of her nonchalance about the whole matter, I could see that Katya was beginning to grow restless. I tried to visit her at least twice a week, coming over to the mainland on Vandermeer's boat, then taking the train from Milford Haven or Haverfordwest to Carmarthen, which was not very far. She seemed glad to see me each time, but we would often end up arguing. I knew it was how she got rid of tension, and I tried not to take it too personally when she made comments that were hurtful.

One evening, I realized that it might help her to write down her feelings in a journal, and I convinced the matron to let Katya keep a notebook and fountain pen in her cell. She told me that she would not share what she wrote, but I had not expected her to do so. From that time on, though, she seemed more relaxed, and she told me that she spent hours during the day writing, and she would soon need a second notebook. I was eager to keep her supplied with writing materials—it was something concrete that I could do for her. Aaron Levy encouraged me in this—he said Katya had kept a journal as long as he had known her and that it might be especially therapeutic for her now.

Soon after Katya's arrest, I found Aaron in a pub one evening after I'd visited her. He'd stayed on in Carmarthen because his work in London was finished. He smiled and motioned for me to sit down, although I knew he didn't like me much. Aaron was always the gentleman, though, and would never be impolite. I'm not sure he ever went out without a three-piece suit, bowler hat, and umbrella.

"You're not going back to London?" I said.

"Not yet. I've some loose ends to tie up here."

"That barrister you hired for Katya—that Wickham fellow. I talked to him yesterday. He's a good chap."

Aaron rubbed his forehead. In spite of his polished appearance, he looked tired. "He's got a massive job ahead of him. I just hope he can handle it."

"I suppose you'll testify," I said.

"Undoubtedly."

"Look, Aaron, I know you think I'm mixed with too much water."

He said nothing. Being polite didn't require him to lie.

"I want to help Katya," I said. "Any way that I can."

He sighed and shook his head, and then he stood up. "You've done enough, Robert. Why don't you just stay out of it?"

With some people, you just can't win. It wasn't my fault that a storm kept me trapped on the mainland, the night that Janisch died. Katya had sent me over—she'd asked me to take a letter to be mailed to Aaron—and she'd said it was urgent, so I ignored the brooding clouds and took the boat over to the mainland, against my better judgment. I had no idea what she was planning that evening—did she know I would be unable to return until morning? How different things would have been if she'd confronted Janisch in my presence.

IN THE LION'S DEN

Robert had promised to keep Vandermeer away for three hours, so I sat at his desk again for a proper search. I glanced at my feather duster on top of the desk—my excuse for being in his house—and reached for the large notebook on top of the desk. When I brought his coffee to the house every evening after supper, I had seen Vandermeer working on this record of his island's wildlife. It was eighteen inches square, with sheets of graph paper divided into quarter-inch squares. The first page was a neatly-printed title page, with "SKOKHOLM ISLAND WILDLIFE: 1953" centered in large block letters. Two inches below, centered also, was "Recorded by Reverend Mattheu Vandermeer." The title of "Reverend" seemed detached and stilted, as if he needed to remind himself of this part of his charade.

The birds and animals on and surrounding the island were listed, not surprisingly, in alphabetical order, from "Blackbird" to "Wood Warbler," each species assigned one horizontal row of squares, so the number spotted by

Vandermeer could be recorded each day. The birds were catalogued meticulously, down to the last sparrow, but the entry for rabbits was a row of question marks. Why does he bother to put them down at all, when they can't be counted? I closed the notebook and replaced it, turning my attention to the desk. I ran the fingertips of both hands along the smooth surface of the desk, opening my mind to impressions. There were no images, no sudden flashes of brilliance or insight, so I leaned down to open the bottom drawer, which had nothing but letters. I took one from the bottom of the first stack and made sure the stack remained in alignment. Resisting the urge to glance at the letter, I slipped it into the pocket of my skirt. I knew, somehow, that the letter would be helpful, and this lifted my spirits. I closed the drawer and pulled open the top right-hand one, taking Vandermeer's schedule from beneath the writing paper. Again, I read the entries for each hour. What kind of person would put his life into such small constricting boxes of time? I replaced the schedule and closed the drawer.

From the drawer below, I pulled out the map and unfolded it carefully on the top of the desk. An ordinary map of the British Isles—no marks or notations of any kind. I refolded it and put it back in the drawer, which seemed empty with only the map and two sets of keys. For the first time since I'd entered the room, I heard the ocean from the east window, which I'd opened so I could hear signals from Robert or any sounds of Vandermeer's return.

I leaned down to open the bottom drawer, placing the two ledgers and the small book on the desk, then picked up four issues of *Bird Watch* magazine from the stack. I flipped through the first one, listening to the soft noise of the pages flicking past my left thumb—birds and more birds appearing for an instant, disappearing with the others. Nothing. Fourteen more magazines—I didn't know why I was compelled to count them. All empty, nothing but black and white photographs of birds on the inside, and one huge bright bird on each cover.

One issue remained in the bottom of the drawer. I pulled it out and tossed it on my lap, arching my head back to stretch the tight muscles in my shoulders. As I picked up the magazine and started to flip through the pages, a bankbook of navy-blue leather dropped into my lap. It had twenty neat entries, dated from June of 1943 to February of 1952. Not a very active customer—twenty entries in nine years. Which bank? I flipped past the check record to the remaining blank checks. In the lower left-hand corner was the imprint: Bank Leu; Bahnhofstrasse 32; Zurich, Switzerland. Why does he need a Swiss bank account? My heart sped up, as I returned to the check register. Some of the entries were in German, but the sixth one, in the column for the payee, caught my eye—William Kensley. The amount recorded in the next-to-last column was 75,000. The purchase of Skokholm Island: 5 April, 1946. The balance of the account was recorded, in blue ink, as 100,000. I touched my lips. One hundred thousand Swiss francs. Tucked into the check register was a business card. "Dr. Jakob Finster, 35 Upper Woburn Place, London, W2." A German name. I copied it, with the address, onto a piece of scrap paper I had tucked into my skirt pocket.

I replaced the bankbook inside the magazine and tossed it into the bottom of the drawer, just in front of the Iron Cross. So much Jewish gold, confiscated from bank accounts and pried from the fingers of the living and the mouths of the dead, had gone into Nazi pockets. Through the open window, I heard Robert. "Look over there, to the west. Is that a peregrine?" His voice was abnormally loud, and I knew he was stalling Vandermeer and trying to warn me at the same time of their early return. As quickly as I could, I replaced the other magazines, the two ledgers, and the prayer book.

I would not have time to leave the house without being seen, so I grabbed the feather duster and slipped into the living room. I swept the duster across the spines of books on the shelf next to the bedroom. Vandermeer wore a khaki jacket, and the wind had tangled his hair. I tried to keep my voice light and my tone casual as I said, "Have you noticed, Reverend Vandermeer, these books are starting to show some damage from the salt air?" I pulled one from the shelf and ran my fingers along the edges of the cover.

"Really?" he said, and he walked across to where I stood. "Let me see." He took the book from my hand. Was it an accident that his cool fingertips grazed the inside of my wrist? He would not look at me, but kept his attention focused on the book in his hands. He flipped through the pages. "The dampness in the air seems to be making the pages stick together. I'm not sure what we could do about it."

"If you have any volumes," I said, "that are especially valuable, you might want to consider putting them into some sort of air-tight storage."

Vandermeer stared at me with his usual expression of blank despair, and I relaxed enough to wonder if he had ever been happy at any time in his life. The slight smile he gave me seemed to be an effort. He walked past me into his bedroom and closed the door, while I prayed that I had left everything in its place.

I hummed a song I'd learned in London, as I dusted the room. He opened the bedroom door in less than a minute. I hadn't expected him to come back out; I'd only planned to wait a decent interval before leaving. He took a step towards me, his face still bright red from the sun and wind, his long hair sun-bleached, so different from the pasty skin and clipped dark hair of Emil Janisch. But the eyes that stared back at me could be his eyes. He gestured with a slender hand at the bookshelf, and said in his heavily-accented English, "No need to dust those books. Morwenn did it just two weeks ago." Clearly, he wanted me out of his house, but was it just a desire for privacy or was it paranoia?

"As you wish," I said, and I turned and walked toward the red door with his eyes on my back like arrows of fire. In the entryway, I dropped the feather duster into the stand in the alcove that held the umbrellas and the walking stick and tried not to panic when the latch stuck on the front door. I had to press twice before it lifted and allowed me to escape.

Out of Vandermeer's house and his view, I stood for a moment and took a deep breath, putting my hand into the pocket to touch the letter. I sprinted round the corner to Robert's hut and knocked on the door as hard as I could, trying to ignore the pain in my knuckles. "Robert!" I said, not wanting to shout. "Hurry up."

The door opened, and Robert stood in the doorway, his face as red as Vandermeer's, and he smiled at me. "Hey, come on in. Sit down." He sat, cross-legged, on his bed, and there were no chairs, so I remained standing. "It's not exactly posh here. Sit down," he said, patting the gray wool blanket. He looked up at me. "Go on, sit, you look like a frightened rabbit."

I realized my heart was beating as rapidly as a rabbit's, and that it wasn't entirely from the jogging. I sat down across from Robert. "I thought you were going to keep him away for three hours."

"I tried, honestly I did. But he insisted on coming back early."

I felt awkward perched on the edge of Robert's bed, and the wool blanket was scratchy and rough through the thin fabric of my skirt. "Why? What did he say?"

"That he was tired." Robert massaged the back of his neck. "Katya, he's been asking questions about you."

"What kind of questions?"

"What I thought of you. Had I spent much time with you? As if he wanted to know what our relationship is."

"What were his exact words?" I didn't trust Robert's evaluation of Vandermeer's remarks—I wanted details of what Vandermeer had said. Was he suspicious of me?

"Well, he started off with, 'What do you think of Morwenn's cousin?' . . . 'Katherine?' I asked innocently. 'Oh, I think she's quite nice.' Then he asked me if you were involved with anyone, and I said I didn't know."

I heard the question in Robert's voice. "No," I said,

"I'm not involved with anyone."

"What if he's falling in love with you? I've seen the way he stares. I can't say that I blame him. You are quite beautiful, you know."

I rolled my eyes to the ceiling. "I am no oil painting, and if he's in love with me, I might as well pack it up and go home tomorrow. He's definitely not the man I'm after. Emil Janisch had no heart; how could he fall in love with me or anyone else?" I paused, amazed at his childish lack of sophistication. "It's called 'lust,' Robert. Whoever the man is, he's probably been celibate for many years." I was repulsed by the thought of Janisch being attracted to me.

"How do we know he's been celibate?" Robert said. "What if he has a secret lover on the mainland?"

I lifted my shoulders and rolled my head from side to side, while I considered Robert's ridiculous notion. "What about Morwenn?"

"Morwenn? She's practically my mother." His face flushed deep red, even beyond the sunburn.

In spite of my attempt to remain serious, I laughed. "That doesn't make her a nun, you know. And she's only thirty-eight now." He was such an innocent, so trusting, and so dangerous because of it. I would have to be careful.

"Morwenn and Reverend Vandermeer? I wonder. " He paused but dismissed the subject with a wave of his hand. "What did you find in Vandermeer's desk?"

"Letters. Close on a hundred, from someone named Dengler in Argentina." I pulled the envelope from my pocket. "Now, it's possible they're just corresponding about birds here and in South America, but look at this return address."

"J. Dengler," Robert read, "Villa General Belgrano, Argentina. What does this mean?"

The screeching of gulls outside became louder for a moment, and I leaned back against the wall and stretched out my legs. "A lot of Nazis live there."

"Interesting," Robert said, "but it still doesn't prove anything, just because he has a pen-friend there."

"And an Iron Cross," I said. "And the letter is written in German." I pulled out the two pages of featherweight stationery.

"Let me see that." He was silent for a moment. "Oh, this should be interesting. In the last paragraph, see the word 'liebling'? That means 'darling.' I've an idea this is not a fellow naturalist writing about cormorant migrations."

* * *

After supper, we did the washing-up together, with Robert drying the plates and silverware after I scalded them in the soapy water of the dishpan. "I also found a business card this afternoon," I said to him, "with the name 'Dr. Jakob Finster.' "

"In the desk?"

I nodded. "Tucked inside a bankbook which was hidden in a *Bird Watch* magazine. The entries are in German, and the balance of the account is large—100,000 Swiss francs."

"Swiss?" Robert said. "Oh, that's interesting. Quite a generous nest egg for a retired clergyman, wouldn't you say?"

"The thought had crossed my mind." I swished my

hands in rubber gloves through the hot water of the dishpan. "One of the entries was to William Kensley in May of 1946."

"The sale of this island," Robert said, and I heard the bitterness in his voice. He continued to dry the plate he was holding. "What did he pay for it?"

"Seventy-five thousand francs."

"I always wondered about that." He set down the plate on the kitchen table and went over, with the dishtowel in his hand, to stare out of the steamy window over the sink. "I hated Mattheu Vandermeer from the first moment I heard of him, because I blamed him for the loss of my home."

I had never seen Robert so serious, his usual mask of good humor replaced by a look of sadness, and I realized that his love of Skokholm was as strong as any attachment he had to the people in his life. In those rare moments when he revealed himself to me, I felt a tenderness toward him that was normally covered over by irritation with his cheerfulness, with what had always seemed like false gaiety. "So," I said, "we seem to have a common enemy." I, too, looked out the window at the ever-present gulls, aware that our reasons for hating this man were worlds apart.

He turned to me. "Why is the doctor's business card so important?"

"It may mean nothing, but I'll make some inquiries in London. If Finster is a plastic surgeon, he may have records we could subpoena. A real bonanza would be photographs—before and after."

"What for?"

I poured the dishwater down the drain. "Janisch may have had his nose altered. Those photographs would be especially important if he's had his blood type tattoo removed. He has to be identified in court either by eye-witnesses or by the information in his SS file." I peeled off my rubber gloves. "Make sure you always check the mail first; I don't want him alerted by an envelope with a suspicious-looking return address."

"All right." Robert hung the dishtowel to dry on the back of the kitchen chair. "By the way, you missed a fabulous sunset last night."

I took a deep breath, trying to identify the scent of Robert's after-shave. Something musky, with a hint of citrus. "You know," I said, "the sun might actually set again this evening. We could have another go at it." I dried my hands on the tea towel and untied my apron, hanging it on a hook beside the cabinet.

He smiled at me, and I followed him out of the Wheelhouse kitchen, closing the door behind us. We walked toward the sun and the western end of the island where the lighthouse stood, brilliant white. I wanted to enjoy the beauty of the evening, without slipping into regrets about the past or worries about the future, and he seemed to sense my need for reflection. We listened in silence to the scattered cries of seagulls. Like a jewel, the sun dangled from clouds that were rose and apricot.

"When we had to come away from the island, it was like my soul was ripped out. Nothing has been the same since." He stopped and leaned against a huge moss-covered boulder, part of a rock outcropping.

"Nothing is ever the same as when we were children,"

I said, and I inhaled deeply to keep myself in the moment, enjoying even the dank aroma of seaweed, while the wind blew strands of hair against my cheek.

Robert ran his fingers over the green moss of the boulder. "My roots are here, Katya. I'm not sure I can be happy anywhere else. This place is so extraordinary when the sun is bright, and the sky is that cornflower blue, because all the colors are so vivid—the bluebells and the red sea campion and the purple sandstone. If an artist tried to paint these colors, they would seem exaggerated." He looked off into the distance. "And then there are days when mist surrounds the whole island and floats just over its surface—it's too beautiful for words."

Unable to share his sentimentality, I didn't know what to say. "I'd no idea you felt so strongly about this place." I looked at the rock-strewn path through the outcropping, at the fragments of tracks he had shown me where the tram once ran from the lighthouse down to South Haven. "You're lucky to have a place where you can feel happy," I said.

There was nowhere on earth I could escape my past. I picked a bell-shaped white flower from the sea campion and held it to my nose, while I listened to the waves on the rocks of Crab Bay. The scent of honey, a beautiful sunset, a handsome young man. In different circumstances, it might have been enough. Gulls circled above us, wailing—they always seemed to be saying, "no, no, no." There would be little joy for me if there were the slightest chance Emil Janisch was alive and free, especially if he was alive and free on this island.

* * *

The next evening, it was still light outside at eight o'clock when I took Mattheu Vandermeer his coffee. Before I knocked on the inner door to the living room, I stood in the entryway listening to him play Beethoven's "Choral." I recognized the intense beauty of the adagio, where violins carry much of the melody. Enjoying the variations in intensity and tone, the resonant skill of his art, I listened for as long as I dared without chilling the coffee. On other nights, when I entered the room, he always stopped playing. But now, as I handed him the coffee cup, he surprised me by looking into my eyes, and his usual "thank you, Katherine" seemed warmer.

"The 'Choral' is one of my favorite pieces," I said, and I knew my face had flushed. "Were you playing the adagio just now?"

He put down the cup. "Would you like to hear the rest?"

I nodded, and a chill ran through my body, as if a snake had slithered over my bare foot. My heart pounded as he motioned for me to sit down. He stood before me, slender and elegant in dark trousers and a white shirt, open at the neck, holding the violin across his left forearm and the bow in his right hand. He had the look, for a moment, of a self-conscious schoolboy, and he gave me the closest thing to a smile he could manage—a deepening of the creases that ran from under each eye downward, curving round his mouth and ending in the dark beard. Mattheu Vandermeer lowered his face to the violin and played for almost fifteen minutes, the entire adagio performed without a discernible error, his bow moving on the strings like a dancer, the fingers of his left hand long and pale, balancing upon the frets.

I was almost seduced by the skill of his playing, by the tender notes coming from his violin, but then I closed my eyes and saw Emil Janisch's face and the nightmare scenes began to play out, in slow motion. The anger twisted in the center of my chest like a knife blade.

When he finished playing, he lowered the violin and looked at me. I stood up and froze my face into the smile that would allow me to say, "You play beautifully, but your coffee has grown cold."

"I really shouldn't drink coffee in the evening." He smiled again, and I sensed that he was about to take a step toward me.

"I have to go," I said, pulling the hood of my jacket up over my hair, as I avoided his eyes by looking at the clock on the mantel. I walked between the bookcases in the entry hall, and as I stepped outside, the damp cold took my breath away. I hoped that, when the time came, it would not be necessary to seduce him. Surely, he would be able to sense my hatred—my desire to tear his flesh or stop his breathing.

* * *

When I was alone in my room on the island, I tilted my wooden chair against the doorknob, so the legs would scrape on the floor and wake me if the door were opened from the outside. At night, the loaded Walther pistol lay on the side table within reach of my right hand. If I was investigating Janisch, he could also be suspicious of me. All it would take is one slip by Robert or Morwenn; even a well-intentioned comment could be my death warrant. I knew Janisch would not hesitate to kill me. He had invested too much in this ruse to be found out, to be unmasked by a Polish Jew, and a woman as well.

THE ABSENCE OF LIGHT

I went to visit Katya on Tuesday evening. The matron, Miss Palmer, was a tired-looking woman of about forty whose pale coloring was overwhelmed by the dark blue of her uniform. I always greeted her by name and chatted her up a bit, and she seemed to like me. When I signed in each time, her smile seemed genuine, not the mechanical cheerfulness of some government employees.

As we walked from the reception area to the cellblock where they kept Katya, Miss Palmer explained that Katya was their only prisoner at the moment. "She never gives us any trouble. We let her stay out in the exercise yard for two hours when the weather's nice, just check on her frequently. The only thing you worry about, with these quiet ones, is that they'll hurt themselves somehow. We had a woman two years ago who tried to slit her wrists with a sharpened toothbrush handle. Don't worry—we found her in time. I shouldn't be telling you this. We keep a close eye on your lady, even when she's not aware of it."

We walked past cell after empty cell. "It was lovely you brought that notebook," she said. "Katya is always writing in it when I go past her cell. Sometimes, she just sits and stares into the empty cell across the hall. She doesn't even speak to me then—it's almost like she's in a trance."

"Maybe she's dredging up things from her past," I said.

Miss Palmer lowered her voice. "Those numbers tattooed on her arm—was she really in a concentration camp?"

"Auschwitz."

She shook her head, and I wondered how she could be so sympathetic to one of her prisoners. I asked her how long she'd been matron there, and she told me almost six months. She seemed ill-suited for the job. I had always thought a prison matron should be more substantial, physically, and more hard-hearted. Maybe she'd had a mother or a sister who'd been abused, and she was sympathetic toward women who killed men in self-defense, but I didn't want to delve into Miss Palmer's personal life.

When we reached Katya's cell, she was writing in her notebook. As she unlocked the cell, Miss Palmer gave me a small triumphant look, as if to say "you see what I mean about the journal." Katya looked up and smiled as she put the cap on her fountain pen. "Look," she said, wiggling the fingers of her right hand. "No cast."

"Smashing," I said. "How does your wrist feel?"

She flexed and extended it to show me. "Not bad. A little stiff, but Dr. Crowther says to keep moving it. I'll have writer's cramp for sure by the end of the day. It's such a joy to be able to write with my proper hand."

Her initial elation seemed to subside, like air being let out of a balloon. "How's Morwenn?"

I leaned against the bars of Katya's cell. Should I outline Morwenn's devastation—the crying jags, the broken crockery, the episodes of vomiting, the refusal to eat, the days when she never got out of bed?

What I said to Katya was that Morwenn didn't talk much any more. "She used to chatter about anything and everything. I believe she's having a hard time making a decision—she wants to stay on the island, but she's also thinking about moving back to Marloes, to live with Catrin."

Why was it so hard to tell Katya the truth about Morwenn? I guess I was trying to protect her. There was no way I could tell Katya what was really going on with Morwenn without it sounding like an accusation.

MARKERS FOR THE DEAD

When Robert took the constable of Marloes over to the island to pick up Vandermeer's body, I stayed behind. I sat in a chair facing the constable's cluttered desk and tried to ignore the throbbing pain of my arm in its new plaster cast. The door opened behind me, and when I heard Aaron Levy's voice, I stood up, afraid of his reaction. I was also relieved that he had come. He looked at the cast on my arm and started to touch my neck but then drew back and shook his head. "Why didn't you talk to me?" he said.

"I tried, Aaron. You wouldn't listen." Reaching behind me to grasp the armrest, I lowered myself carefully into the chair.

Aaron stood for a moment with his hands in the pockets of his trousers, looking down at the floor. "You should have told me what you were planning." He glanced at me, then pulled up another chair and sat down.

"You'd only have tried to stop me." I pushed my hair back with my left hand.

"Of course I would, Katya. I worry about you as if you were my own daughter. I would have tried to stop her, too."

I looked over Aaron's shoulder, at the clock over the desk. If asked, I would have said I was an honest person, in spite of those deep wounds that I concealed even from Aaron. Sometimes, I hurt him with blunt words that just slipped out of my mouth. I knew my words would sting, and I didn't really mean them, but he never insulted me in return. Sometimes, I apologized and cried and told him I didn't know what was wrong with me.

"I hope I haven't disgraced you," I said to him now.

"Is that what you think? Oh, no, no." He got up from his chair and took a step toward me, bending down to touch my shoulders. His beloved face was close to mine as he looked into my eyes, and the shadows under his eyes seemed darker than usual. "No, Katya, my concern is for your safety. Look what could have happened to you on the island. He nearly killed you." Aaron straightened up.

I touched my neck where it was swollen and tender. "He could have done, yes, but he was not allowed to have another victim. I'm safe now, Aaron."

"I hate to think how it might have turned out." His brown eyes searched my face as if trying to memorize it. "Katya . . ."

I stood up from the chair, and his arms round me made me feel like I'd come home.

"Thank God you're alive," he whispered. He stood, holding me gently, with his eyes closed. "You could go to prison," he said softly.

"Look around you. I am in prison." I smiled and pulled back from him.

"You know what I mean—for a long time. And we probably won't be able to afford bail for you."

"Aaron, it's all right. It will give me time to sort things out."

Silence hung between us for a few moments. "How does it feel?" he said. "Is the world different, now that he's gone?"

I was suddenly so tired I couldn't stand up, and I sank into the chair and leaned my head back against the wall. Aaron bent down again and kissed my forehead. "I will do everything in my power to help. You know I would walk to the ends of the earth for you."

When the constable returned, he told me I could go, but I would have to stay in Marloes or Milford Haven and would have to give him my address. Under no circumstances was I to return to London. Aaron asked him if I was being charged with anything, and he said no, but I had to be available for questioning.

I booked a room at the Dolphin House, where I'd stayed before my trip to the island, and Mr. Welby gave me the weekly rate. The sixty pounds that I'd taken to the island would soon be gone, and I would need to have money wired from my account in London. Aaron had promised to help arrange that for me.

I didn't have much appetite, although I hadn't eaten since the night before. My throat still hurt when I swallowed, so I ordered a bowl of soup. It was more than I could eat, thick and full of vegetables, and served with a generous slice of Mrs. Welby's homemade bread. The room was deserted, except for an old man at the bar who spent an hour nursing a pint of dark ale.

Aaron had asked me to have supper with him, but I told him I wouldn't be very good company, and he respected my need for solitude. I couldn't help thinking of the first time I met him—had that only been four years ago? It seemed like I had known Aaron all my life.

I was sitting on my own at a sidewalk café in Jerusalem, trying to see how long I could make one glass of red wine last, when I noticed a man two tables away. He was staring at me, and I stared back at him with what I hoped would be a hostile expression. He didn't look away. Tired of this game, I turned my head and pretended to watch people across the street, but from the corner of my eye, I saw him move toward me.

"Excuse me, please." He spoke in Hebrew, but the Polish accent was unmistakable. "You look like someone I . . ." He couldn't finish. This time I stared at his face out of curiosity. I thought for a moment that he did look familiar, like some faces do. My uncle Moshe had had the same small, rather deep-set eyes and a high forehead creased by lines. But I wasn't looking for companionship that night; I was involved in a fascinating relationship with my glass of Cabernet Sauvignon.

"May I sit down?" he asked. "My name is Aaron Levy."

What the hell, he's probably harmless. I'd noted the gray hair, the shadows under his eyes, the black yarmulke. I nodded to him, then gestured with a wave of my hand toward the chair across from me.

I told him my name, which seemed to be the permission he needed to sit in the chair I had waved him towards.

"How long have you been in Israel?" he asked me.

"Six months."

As he studied my face, I felt my cheeks flush, and I wasn't sure why. "What do you do here?" he asked.

"I'm a nurse."

He smiled, and I felt he was staring past me, but I held my ground and waited for the next question. How little information can I give without unforgivable rudeness? If he chooses to occupy my space, the least he can do is carry his own weight in the conversation.

"And what about you, Mr. Levy?" I'm sure my voice did not conceal my hostility, which grew by the moment.

He seemed to come out of his reverie. "I've been here six months also," he said. "When I first saw you, I couldn't help staring. And now I see your eyes are like my daughter's, clear green, like that stone. What is it? Peridot, I think."

His gaze was so intense, I had to look away. I glanced at my watch. Half-past nine. I hated this empty small talk, this casual banter about nothing.

"Where do you come from?" he asked. The usual questions—I'd come to expect them—asking really, are you a member, are you one of us?

"Warsaw." The last of my wine tasted bitter.

"You are also Polish?"

"Yes." To avoid his eyes, I ran a finger along the rim of my wineglass. "So," I said, "what is it you do in Israel?"

"I collect testimony from Holocaust survivors."

So that's what he wanted. I looked down at the sleeve of my white shirt—at the long sleeves I always wore—

knowing that he had not seen the numbers on my forearm, but had guessed. I leaned back in my chair. "So," I said, hearing the coolness in my voice, "what's the point of writing all that down?"

"We use the testimony to get indictments against Nazi war criminals."

An idealist, I thought. Out of touch with the reality of the world. I wondered how long he would stay if I insulted him. "Where is your daughter, and how old is she?" A sarcastic smile as I added, "Do older men approach her in cafes?"

From the pocket of his shirt, Aaron Levy took a silver lighter and a pack of cigarettes and tapped one out. "My daughter would have been nineteen this month." I regretted my careless question. His daughter was two months older than Rebekah, who would have turned nineteen in June. I motioned to the waiter. "I'll have another glass of wine." I was not as heartless as I was trying to pretend I was.

"And I'd like some coffee, please," Aaron said. He flipped open the lighter and held the blue-orange flame to his cigarette. "And you?" he asked. "Do you have family?"

All I could do was hate him for reminding me and stare down into my empty wineglass. Tipping it up, I let the last drop slide into my mouth, as the waiter arrived with another glass of wine, which I gulped like water to ease the familiar tightness in my throat. I refused to let this stranger named Aaron see my pain, so I swallowed wine to block out the thoughts and memories that could hurt me. Finally, I set down the glass and took a deep breath, shrugging my shoulders, as Aaron gestured at himself and at me, with the hand that held his cigarette and said, “We could drown in our past, couldn’t we?”

At the next table, a man and woman laughed together. They were holding hands across the table, their eyes locked in the fascination of early love. A warm April wind blew up one corner of the red cotton tablecloth. As I rubbed my forearm, as if it were an itch that could never be relieved, Aaron reached out and touched my sleeve over the numbers, as if to bless them. “You were also in the camps,” he said in a quiet voice.

“Yes.” I stared down at my hands, at the moisture I could feel on my palms, and took deep breaths to quell the nausea. Now he will share his story—everyone has a story, and I don’t need any more pain. As he spoke, I pretended not to listen by staring at the waiter, following his quick movements with my eyes.

“From the Plaschau labor camp near Krakow,” Aaron said, “I was sent to Mauthausen in Austria, on a temporary work detail at the munitions factory.” His voice was flat, as if he had repeated this tale a thousand times and was tired of it. “I did a lot of different things in the camp, but later, I wondered if we had made the bullets that were used on others, in other camps. When the work was done, they were through with us, and they planned to kill us. I knelt at the edge of a pit, with twenty other men, waiting to be shot in the head. They shot five men ahead of me.” He paused and looked away from me, focusing on something in the distance. “You know what that feels like, to have death so close you find yourself splattered with someone else’s blood.”

I stood up, almost knocking over my chair, and turned away from him—this man who wanted to bring back what I had learned to push away. "I'm sorry," I heard him say, and I turned back and saw the look on his face and sagged back into my chair. "Sometimes," he said, as he gently touched my arm again, "it is a good thing to talk about it, with someone who knows."

"And sometimes it isn't." I pulled my hand back, as if his touch was fire, the same that had burned the tattoo into my skin. Then I watched as Aaron removed the silver cuff link from his left shirtsleeve and pushed it up. The numbers on his forearm—64662—looked like the ones on my arm. Small blue numbers. I said to him, as if thinking out loud, "It's strange, I used to love the color blue. Now I don't recognize it as a color, only as a feeling that I want to push away." I saw Aaron's mouth curve slightly into a tentative smile.

But then I felt the iron bars wrap themselves round my heart again, and I heard myself say in a strained voice, "Don't think you feel what I feel or even know what I feel, because we existed in different places and we had different experiences. You cannot know my pain." I said this to him even though I knew that our experiences were more alike than different. "You can't walk around in my head because I don't indulge in that sort of thing. We are not the same!" I wanted to keep this man at a distance. It was as if giving any part of myself to him would somehow diminish me, and there was so little left of myself to give.

He stared at me for a moment, then continued as if I had not attacked him. "An SS officer from Plaschau recognized me and pulled me out of the line. He told the other officers I was too good at painting trucks to be shot. I was sent back to Poland, to Majdanek, where I worked in the kitchen until the liberation."

"What about the tattoo? You had to have been in Auschwitz."

"For a short time—only a week—and then they sent me to Majdanek."

Before I could stop myself, I said, "How did you feel when you lived and all the others with you were shot?"

Aaron looked down at his hands. "What do you expect—that I hate myself every day, that I believe I should be dead also?" He took a sip of his coffee. "No, I believed even then I was saved for a purpose."

"That's how we rationalize it, don't we?" I couldn't believe the barbs that were coming out of my mouth. I called for another glass of wine, knowing I would have a hangover in the morning, but at that point, I didn't care.

Aaron looked at me. "Just after the war ended, I thought I was cursed—the only survivor of my whole family. I was lost. I thought there was no point to being alive. But everything I do now is for them. Every night I am certain I have spent that day earning this life I was given." He paused and rubbed his forehead, as if he had a headache. "How do you cope?"

I lifted my glass and admired the ruby-colored liquid. It was like a jewel—my magic potion—and I curved my lips into the obligatory half-smile reserved for strangers.

"It's no good," Aaron Levy said. He touched the stem of my wineglass as he stood up. "Haven't you noticed the memories are always there, waiting for you when you wake?"

Without regretting my behavior towards him, I watched him walk away. The wine had done its job, and I savored the familiar warmth circling round my brain, the taste of red wine on my lips and their slight tingling.

Aaron had been more persuasive at our second meeting—I couldn't numb myself with alcohol because I was on duty. A fortnight after meeting Aaron in the café, I'd found him in the dayroom of the psychiatric ward at Mt. Hadassah, where I worked as a nurse. He was seated in a chair across from one of my patients, Mrs. Isaacson, a tiny grey-haired woman being treated for depression.

"You have to get permission from her doctor!" I'd yelled at him. Again, I flinched at my harsh tone, at the unexpected anger this man evoked in me. He seemed surprised to see me there. "I work here, remember? Does Dr. Kelemen know you're interviewing her?"

"Of course," he said. "Do you think that I would just walk in here?"

"I'm sorry for interrupting." I was well and truly embarrassed by my verbal attack.

Aaron smiled and shook his head. "It's all right. Forgive me for being short with you. I should have cleared this with the nurses, also."

Mrs. Isaacson stared at me with vacant brown eyes, her grey hair straggling round her face. I looked at Aaron and softened my voice as I said to him, "You should go ahead with your interview."

"I would like to speak with you when I'm done here," he said. "Please, it's important."

Caught off-guard by his request, I looked at my watch

and said, "Meet me in the cafeteria downstairs at half past noon. I have only forty-five minutes for lunch."

An hour later, I hurried downstairs and found Aaron waiting for me. "I'm sorry to be late. There was an emergency on my ward."

"Is everything all right?"

"No one's dead, if that's what you mean. I can't really say more than that." We shoved our trays down the line in silence. I reached out for food, not really caring what I ate—one of our patients had just tried to hang herself with the sheet from her bed. She'd been discovered, luckily, just as she was stepping off the chair, so the only visible sign was an abrasion on her neck. The emotional trauma—the despair that would drive someone to end her life that way—was invisible.

As I took my silverware, rolled in a paper napkin, I thought about the eighteen-year-old who'd tried to slash her wrists the previous week with a fork from her place setting at dinner. So caught up in the lives of these women, I almost forgot that Aaron was there until it was time to sit down. We chose a small table near the window.

"I'm glad our paths crossed again," he said.

"Why?"

He looked at me, then shook his head almost imperceptibly. "You seem so hostile. Are you like this with everyone, or is it just me?"

I put down the sandwich and reached for my coffee. There was nothing I could say to this, and I was aware that my silence might well be interpreted as more hostility.

Aaron said, "I was actually surprised that you agreed

to meet me for lunch."

"I surprised myself." I smiled and looked into my cup, knowing that Aaron was studying my face and aware of some new, unidentified feeling at the edge of my mind.

Aaron put down his fork. "I need your help. I told you before about the work I do, but I've finished here in Israel. I'm setting up a documentation center in London next month." He lit a cigarette. "My colleagues here love the work—they believe in it—but they all have families, and they don't want to re-locate. Their dreams are to raise their children in Israel, which I understand. I'm trying to find people who would be willing to move to London. The pay is not outstanding, but the rewards on another level are tremendous. You're a nurse. You must have some degree of compassion for people, and you're also a survivor." Aaron hesitated. "Would you consider coming with me?"

"London?" I couldn't believe what he was saying. "After all I had to go through to get to Israel? I've put down roots here." It wasn't completely true, but I needed to fight him. I thought of my tiny apartment on the outskirts of Jerusalem, the lonely evenings in the dingy living room where I existed, not really knowing or wanting to know how to live with other people.

He leaned forward as he said to me, "It's the chance of a lifetime."

"Really. How do you figure that?"

"Maybe you can do something about your demons instead of being haunted by them."

I wanted no part of a crusade. "How about if I just live my life in peace?"

"Is that what you're doing? If you've found peace of mind, I'd like to know your secret."

I hated being wrong, and this arrogant man seemed to have all the answers. Hoping to accelerate and end the conversation by playing along, I said to him, "If I were to go to London, what would I be doing there?"

He sat back in his chair and smiled. "Interviewing other survivors, making a record of everything—names, places, events. It's important that we reach these people before their memories fade."

I crossed my arms. "I've spent the last six years trying to forget what happened. Why would I want to go slogging about in other peoples' misfortune?"

"Do you enjoy your work here at the hospital?"

"Sometimes." I thought about London and the crowds of people. The first few days there, I had thought the sheer energy of the place would kill me—the constant noise of buses and automobiles and the breath-taking force of subway trains blasting into stations. Doors slammed constantly in the flat where I lived—above, below, and on either side—shaking me down to my bones. London was a great noisy beast, restless and violent. When I had lived there after the war, while training at St. Bartholomew's to be a nurse, I couldn't wait to immigrate to Israel, which represented solidarity and the chance to distance myself from all things European. I knew I would never be completely satisfied wherever I was, but the thought of a new start was appealing. It was a first step. I opened my mouth to speak, but stopped myself.

"What?" Aaron said.

I looked out at the caramel-colored landscape. "I don't

understand why you are so eager to dredge up the past. What will you gain? Those memories lead only to our darkest places—black holes where our hearts used to be. Nothing good can come of it."

"How will you live your life?" he said to me. "Will it count for anything, in the end, that you have been on this earth?" He pushed his plate aside. "Last week, I met a young man from Lodz, named Dodek Klimas, who was imprisoned in Plaschau when I was, although I did not know him at the time. His father was at Plaschau with him and died of typhus. His mother and younger sister were left behind in Lodz when the men were sent to the labor camp.

"After the liberation, he returned to Lodz to find out what happened to the rest of his family. Dodek met a former neighbor in Lodz, who had been present during the first transports from Lodz to Chelmno. The neighbor told Dodek that he had seen Dodek's mother and sister as the trucks were being loaded. The sister, only eleven, was torn from her mother's arms because she had no work certificate. The mother, desperate, ran up to a Nazi officer, dropped to her knees and begged him to spare her daughter's life. The officer, according to Dodek's neighbor, pulled the woman up by her long blonde hair and shot her point-blank." Aaron leaned back in his chair. "Do you know why this story is so important?"

I helped myself to a cigarette from Aaron's silver case. I didn't smoke very often, but there were times when I needed something to steady my hands. Aaron lit it for me, and I inhaled deeply, blowing the smoke up toward the ceiling before I answered. "I've told you—I see no good reason. This story is the same as thousands of others."

"The world needs to hear the truth," he said. "When a Nazi comes to trial, the survivors' testimony against him is like a marker for the deaths of so many. Otherwise, the victims are nameless and too easily forgotten. But I am sure you have your own stories to tell."

"No." If he expected me to open up and tell him everything, he was sadly mistaken.

"Why do you work here, Katya?" He waved his hand to include all of the hospital. "Here are horror stories, different, but still a hospital full of emotional torment and pain. Is this so different from interviewing survivors?"

"Yes," I said. "This is so very different." I stubbed out my cigarette. "Here there are people in pain, but they have lives to which they can return. They have names, and they have families who love them. They are people, not rats useful only for target practice." I crumpled my paper napkin and threw it on the tray. "So, tell me, Mr. Levy. Are you looking for revenge?"

"Only justice," he said, as he wrote something on a piece of paper. "Since we have been victims ourselves, how can we be anything less than just?" As he stood up, he said to me, "Here is my phone number. Why don't you consider my offer for a few days?"

I picked up the slip of paper and watched the slump of his shoulders as he walked toward the door. He turned round for a moment, searching my face with his eyes. I nodded and held up my hand as if to wave but drew it back abruptly.

For the first time in years, I did not feel anger or fear. Somehow, I was emptied, all the barely-contained panic gone, and what was left in its place was something I had forgotten—the quiet feeling of having something to give meaning to my life.

After finishing my shift at the hospital, I grabbed a quick supper in the hospital cafeteria and returned to the darkness of my apartment, intending to fall asleep on the sofa. When I closed my eyes, white light burned in my brain—the smoke of the crematorium at Auschwitz. To stop those thoughts, I got up to pace the floor of my small familiar living room—the length six steps, the width only five.

I had not said the word "Auschwitz" that day, but Aaron Levy had dislodged buried memories. I thought of the dream where I am dancing in a long dress of turquoise silk. We are all free, our families and our former lives restored. Nothing has changed. It is all the same, in the dream, as before. We eat and drink and listen to beautiful music. I laugh with my fellow prisoners who are now my childhood friends.

The music stops. Five Nazis in grey uniforms and glossy boots march into the room. We hear the click of their boots on the dance floor, but we can no longer see them, because the lights have gone out. I am back in the terrible darkness of the camp. What a cruel joke to spoil the celebration. I want to attack these nameless men, but I need to see their faces. I turn on the lights.

One SS officer sits motionless in a chair in the center of the room—the others have vanished. We stand in a circle of women round one man. No one speaks. There are enough of us to kill him. And yet, we hesitate. No one wants to make the first move. In the end, by silent consent, we spare him—this little man who has no power over us. We lock him from our minds and go on with our dancing. It is the dancing that helps us forget the past. I hadn't told Aaron about this dream.

"How will you live your life, Katya?" His recent question—the question of the day—would not let me sink into the oblivion of sleep, until I clutched his telephone number in my hands, holding it between my palms like a prayer.

DARK OF THE MOON

On the train from Milford Haven, sometimes I close my eyes and remember how Katya looked on the island. When I thought she wouldn't notice, I would catalogue the elements of her beauty. The wheat-colored hair against alabaster skin. The angle of her jaw, her cheekbones, the turquoise of her eyes in a certain light. The grace of her fingers picking spring onions from the garden or smoothing round loaves of bread before they went into the oven. She made me want to write poetry. Then she would see me watching her. She would stiffen and become self-conscious. I loved most the colors of her hair in sunlight. And the porcelain of her neck above the white shirt, with only the top button left undone, and the slender wrists and the warmth of her hand if I managed to brush it with my fingers while we translated the letters.

I wanted to touch her, to hold her, to make love to her, but it never happened. She said she always had to be on guard—to watch her back. She tried to tell me how dangerous this Janisch fellow could be, but I guess I was in denial then. If I believed that Vandermeer was Janisch, I would have to admit that someone I cared about was in danger. Looking back, I see that it was still a game to me, although I swore it was not.

There was one evening when she let me hold her for just a little while. I'd asked her to take a walk with me, just after dark. We headed toward the lighthouse, side by side, placing our feet carefully to avoid the rocks and half-buried pieces of track from the old tramway. She said to me, "I'm a bit jumpy tonight. I'm not sure I'll sleep."

"Let's go down to the Quarry, then," I said, "and watch for shearwaters. They may fly in tonight because it's so cloudy." The darkness was broken at ten-second intervals by the beam of the lighthouse, and we made our way past it and climbed down, with the help of my torch, to a small rock ledge. The ocean breeze was strong and smelled like fish.

We sat next to each other on the cold surface of the rock, and Katya seemed to relax a bit. "It's beautiful here," she said. "I can see why you love it. Under different circumstances, I think I might enjoy it, too."

I heard the shearwaters calling in the distance. "Listen," I said, as I grabbed her arm. The three-note calls grew stronger. Chee-caw-go, chee-caw-go. Soon the air round us was filled with a dense web of black wings. With a flash of white, they turned as a unit, flying east with perfect choreography.

"That's lovely," she said. "How do they fly like that in the dark?"

"I don't know. Maybe they bounce their cries off land masses, to help them find the island first and then their burrows."

"So they navigate," she said, "by the echo of their cries."

"Or maybe by the stars."

Katya stood up and rubbed her arms. I put my arm round her shoulders, and I could feel her shivering. "You're freezing," I said. "We'll go back."

She scrambled up from the ledge, grabbing at bits of vegetation to steady herself, and I followed close behind in case she should slip. When we reached the lighthouse, we stopped beside the wall of its courtyard to catch our breath. In the flash of the lighthouse beam, I caught a glimpse of Mattheu Vandermeer, about fifty feet ahead of us on the path. I knew from Katya's sharp inhalation that she had seen him, too. "What the hell is he doing out here?" I said, keeping my voice low because he would surely be able to hear us.

"I don't know, but I don't want to see him right now."

"We can wait here in the courtyard. Give him a chance to finish whatever he's doing." We climbed over the low part of the wall and sat with our backs against the cool stucco. Katya was still shivering, whether from nerves or from the cold, I don't know, but it seemed natural for me to move closer and put my arms round her. She put her head on my shoulder, and a little shudder ran through her before she finally relaxed. We sat in silence, listening to the rhythm of the ocean, and I wondered what he could have done to her to instill such fear.

TRUTH AND LIES

One day, since Vandermeer was out on the bay setting crab pots, I had the chance to take his library apart. If he returned early, as before, I would grab my feather duster again and hope for the best. I moved the books out, two at a time, in order to dust behind them. On the second shelf from the top, behind two huge volumes of *Brown's Commentary on the Bible*, there was a slim, black leather journal.

This journal was smaller than the one in which I'd seen Vandermeer writing when I first arrived on the island. I held it in my hands, ran my fingertips over the smooth leather. The book had a leather clasp that slid out easily, and the pages were gilt-edged. It was written in German, in the elegant script I recognized as Vandermeer's, and all the book's pages were filled. Although there were no dates, the leather of the journal had the smooth well-worn texture of age, and I guessed it might have been completed several years ago. I wanted to sit down, but it was safer to stand up beside the shelf, so I could replace the journal in a few seconds if I had to. In the front, I found Bible verses in English.

> "The Son of Man shall send forth his angels, and they shall gather out of his kingdom all things that offend, and them which do iniquity;
> And shall cast them into a furnace of fire: there shall be wailing and gnashing of teeth.
> Then shall the righteous shine forth as the sun in the kingdom of their Father. Who hath ears to hear, let him hear."

> "Attend unto my cry; for I am brought very low: deliver me from my persecutors; for they are stronger than I.
> Bring my soul out of prison that I may praise thy name: the righteous shall compass me about; for thou shalt deal bountifully with me."

> "Out of the depths have I cried unto thee, O Lord.
> Lord, hear my voice: let thine ears be attentive to the voice of my supplications.
> If thou, Lord, shouldst mark iniquities, O Lord, who shall stand?
> But there is forgiveness with thee, that thou mayest be feared."

> "The Lord is gracious, and full of compassion; slow to anger, and of great mercy."

Why these verses? Vandermeer's fear of judgment, his hope for forgiveness? It would take too long to translate even one page. Certain that the small book held the key to Vandermeer's identity, I replaced it with great reluctance.

The next day, Robert brought me a letter from London, from the office of the doctor whose card I'd found earlier. I had made an inquiry into the nature of his medical practice. His secretary was kind enough to let me know that Dr. Jakob Finster was a surgeon who specialized in facial reconstruction. I waved the letter at Robert. "I was right."

"So Finster is likely to have done the surgery."

"Yes, but he could well have removed the blood type tattoo at the same time. Since Janisch looks so different, he can't be identified by witnesses."

"So," Robert asked, "what's the next move?"

I ran my fingers along the edge of the table. "I need to spend some time with that journal I found yesterday. He has to have written something that will betray him—why else would it be hidden like that? Everything else we've found has been circumstantial." I looked up at Robert. "Do you think you could get him off the island tomorrow? A trip to the mainland, or something?"

He slapped the table and stood up. "Katya, I think you're in luck. He just told me he'd be going over to Grassholm tomorrow to check on the gannet colonies."

"Lovely," she said. "Maybe God is on our side after all."

* * *

The next morning, Robert had watched from Purple Cove until he saw Vandermeer's boat headed toward Grassholm, a small rounded island in the distance. He sprinted on the path from Twinlet Bay, past the North Pond, across Halfway Wall, then across the heath to the farmhouse. He found me in Vandermeer's living room, already flipping through the journal, with the dictionary in my lap. With the books cradled in my arms, I stood up, walked to the bookshelf, and pointed out to Robert the two large volumes of *Brown's Commentary*. "This is where he keeps it, behind these two. For some reason, he doesn't feel comfortable leaving it in his room. I intend to find out why."

"Can you do this outside?" Robert asked. "If you sit on the bench against the wall, you're somewhat sheltered from the wind and you have a clear view of me signaling from South Haven. You can also hear the sound of his engine when he gets close enough."

I went outside with him and sat down on the bench against the dry stone wall that ran from the farmhouse alongside Robert's hut. The tip of the Wheelhouse was to my left, with Skomer off in the distance. The harbor, South Haven, lay straight ahead, out of my range of vision because it was so far below.

With Mattheu Vandermeer's journal in my hands, I felt triumphant and certain that my efforts would bear fruit. I watched for a moment as Robert made his way across the open space leading to South Haven. One or two gulls flew across, but all the gulls were silent for now, and I heard only the songs of two birds and the buzzing of flies. The sky was a clear blue, with high clouds to the left and a bank of low-lying clouds across the horizon. I wished that Vandermeer would get marooned on Grassholm and not be able to return for the night, but it was too much to hope for, since there was only a gentle breeze that could not keep him from landing. I opened the journal, forgetting to breathe.

Morwenn had come out to enjoy the sunshine in Vandermeer's absence, and she sat down on a bench near me. "Why would a Dutchman write his journal in German?" I asked her, not expecting an answer. She didn't talk to me much these days. Morwenn only shook her head and walked away from me toward the Wheelhouse.

Glancing down toward South Haven, I saw Robert perched on a ridge overlooking the harbor. I opened the dictionary and began the tedious work of translation. A half-hour yielded only the knowledge that Mattheu Vandermeer was a compulsive list-maker. He had made endless notes to himself about things he needed to do in the future, such as mapping the location of bluebells and white bluebells on the island, and clearing the rain gutters of debris. A lesser black-backed gull, which I had learned to distinguish from the herring gulls because of its darker wings and yellow legs, perched on a small mound of earth about twenty feet away and scolded me loudly for being there.

I stood up for a moment to keep my legs from cramping. The sun, above the gleaming white farmhouse roof, cast a short shadow of the chimney. Flies buzzed and circled and gulls just over the garden wall squawked and flapped their wings. The high clouds to the left had vanished.

Maybe I should go back and search the house again; this journal may be worthless. From deep inside, something urged me to continue, the silent voice that usually led me in the right direction. I'll do five more pages. I leafed through the journal, scanning for key words or even a gut feeling about their contents and then turned over one more page to begin a word-for-word translation. My heart skipped a beat, then fluttered, as the first sentence revealed its meaning: "I am tired of living in this desolate place, without friends, without my name."

"Without my name," I said aloud to the gull that waddled past. The next word, "Gewissen," German for conscience, made me realize that I'd struck the mother lode. "My conscience . . . has demanded that I seek peace." Good luck, I thought. How does a man sleep at night after murdering so many?

Robert was still in the same spot, but a sense of urgency made my heart speed up. My mouth was dry, but I didn't dare stop to get water. "I have examined . . . my life . . . carefully . . . and I conclude . . . that I am not a murderer." I wanted to throw the journal on the ground, as if his words were blasphemy and would poison me just by reading them, but I was still curious to know how the bastard rationalized all those deaths.

I had begun the next sentence when I heard Robert calling out to me. He was running toward me, about fifty feet away. "You weren't watching. He's back." The sound of Vandermeer's engine had not reached me.

As I caught a glimpse of Vandermeer's sun-bleached hair from a distance, I stood up and tried to decide whether to duck into my room with the dictionary and journal or to take the journal back to the farmhouse. In either case, I would have to return one of the books to its proper place at some point. I decided to walk calmly to the farmhouse, with the slim journal hidden at my side.

After replacing the journal as quickly as I could

behind the *Brown's Commentary*, I put the dictionary between books on the entry shelves, knowing that I could retrieve it later without much trouble. I walked out of the farmhouse with my cleaning bucket, aware that Vandermeer could see me but deliberately not looking in his direction. When I heard Robert's voice, I was grateful for his effort to buy me more time by engaging Vandermeer in a conversation. Leaving the cleaning supplies on the porch in front of my room, I went inside and shut the door.

Janisch. I sat on my bed and stared at the wall, while in my mind, a scene played itself out. The man known as Mattheu Vandermeer sits at the desk built by William Kensley. All the other furniture in the room he has built himself, out of pine boards brought over from the village of Marloes: the small dresser, the simple slatted bed frame, and the nightstand. Now, he sits on the hard, straight-backed chair and stares at the white wall above the desk. Vandermeer runs work-roughened hands along the smooth design of the desk, which is bare except for two sheets of writing paper and a fountain pen.

He leans down to open the bottom drawer on the right side and takes out a small piece of folded black velvet. He sits back in his chair and unfolds the cloth to reveal the dark metal cross, set off against the velvet by its light outer rim. Running his finger along the symmetrical outlines of the cross, as he has done each day on the island, Emil Janisch hears the songs of glory, sung in strong young German voices by the light of a thousand torches—the heady wine of power that he cannot forget.

I pulled myself back from that image. Further proof

was needed, of course, but the chances were good that the journal contained more incriminating entries. I wondered if I had enough courage to steal it during the night. .

According to Robert, if he could be trusted, Vandermeer retired early, so he would most likely be asleep if I waited until half past ten. I would need to go through two doors without them clanking loudly, since both doors were close to Vandermeer's bedroom. Would I have a chance to oil the hinges? I could lay throw rugs in a path through the entry to minimize the sound of my footsteps on the floor. The most serious problem remained: how to lift the door latches without making a sound. If it were done ever so slowly . . . The thought of being discovered by Vandermeer filled me with a raw fear that made it hard to breathe. What excuse for being in his house would be plausible in the middle of the night?

* * *

I stood at the kitchen table, dicing potatoes and carrots for the evening meal. Every now and then, I glanced out the large window to my left, over the sink, to watch the gulls or to go over in my mind, one more time, my plan for the night. I would walk barefoot across the low-grazed turf to the farmhouse, while Robert checked for Vandermeer's bedroom light from the south side of the farmhouse. After his signal, I would open the front door as slowly as possible, although this first latch would not be as critical as the inner door.

Once inside the front door, it would be three steps to the hallway on the left. Four steps through the hallway would bring me to the inner door, so close to Vandermeer's bedroom. After opening this door with great care, I planned for two steps to the bookshelf—remove both volumes of *Brown's Commentary*, place each one on the floor and lay the other books sideways to keep them from falling.

I focused my attention on the carrots, which tended to roll as I diced them, but out of the corner of my eye, I saw someone in the kitchen doorway. Thinking it was Robert, I started to say, "Are you ready for tonight?" but checked myself just in time. Mattheu Vandermeer stood there, his face tanned above a white long-sleeved shirt, and in his hand was my German-English dictionary.

Oh, God. He had never come to the kitchen at this hour. My first impulse was to put down the knife, so I could wipe my hands on my apron, but my fingers refused to let go, and I felt them tighten on the handle. My mind raced, weighing the possibilities, the options, the lies. He looked at me and said, "Is this yours?"

I couldn't even think of a good lie. "Yes, where did you find it?"

"On my bookshelf."

"Really?" I said. "I must have left it lying around some place. Thomas probably thought it was from your reference collection." I dropped the knife and gestured towards the dictionary. "I'm trying to learn some German, you see, for a trip later this year."

"Where are you going?"

"To Berlin." I gripped the table's edge with my left hand to keep my fingers from trembling, aware that I was swaying slightly. God, why did I say Berlin? I widened my stance for better balance and crossed my arms.

He studied my face, but he didn't smile. "Have you seen the shearwaters come in at night?" He leaned against the wall, and I looked into the terrible eyes of Emil Janisch as he said to me, "The shearwaters fly only at the dark of the moon. Otherwise, the greater black-backed gulls can see to attack them; they split the shearwaters right in half. I'm sure you've seen the carcasses all over the island."

He turned as if to leave, then turned back, with the smile that was not really a smile. "But that's the way of nature, isn't it? Predator and prey." Just then, his smile vanished, replaced by the chilling look I knew so well from my memories and nightmares. I stared after him, thinking of the sharpness of the knife on the table between us. How much did he know about me? I was unwilling to leave without solid proof of his identity, even though I knew it would be wise to get away as soon as possible. I stood in the Wheelhouse kitchen, staring at the doorway through which he had disappeared. To calm myself, I scooped up handfuls of the chopped vegetables and threw them into the soup kettle. With the knife, I cut careful slivers of celery, then tossed them in with the carrots and potatoes. I covered the vegetables with spring water and put the pot on the stove to simmer.

At the kitchen table, I looked at the palms of my hands, straightening out the fingers until the muscles and tendons stretched, then clenched my fists, thinking of Janisch, weighing the options. He could run at any moment, disappear in the middle of the night to sail for South America or Spain. I watched the doorway and listened for his returning footsteps, but he was more likely to run than to kill me. I must now secure two pieces of evidence; my intuition about the man could hardly be presented in court. One more go at the journal—it would have to be soon, but not tonight—then I must check him for the scars and the blood-type tattoo. It would be too dangerous now to seduce him, so I would drug his coffee with the medication from the Israeli pharmacist, and with any luck, Janisch wouldn't remember a thing.

MASQUERADE

I had been back on Skokholm four and a half weeks when I found the diseased rabbits. I'd never paid much attention to myxomatosis before—I'd seen a few carcasses on the mainland—but there was no mistaking the grotesquely swollen heads. Two young males staggered in pathetic circles near the main entrance burrow of the colony in front of Pedestal Rock. I hadn't counted on becoming part of an intensive field study of the "myxy," as the farmers called it. Nevertheless, I put on rubber gloves and caught the dark brown rabbit, which was not difficult because the poor creature could barely see through its swollen eyelids.

As I examined the rabbit, I tried to think what to do. I remembered something about the myxy, on Skokholm, when I was about six years old. My grandfather had wanted to get rid of the wild rabbits that were ruining his gardens, so he asked Sir Alden Smith—a funny little man with bad teeth—to inject some of the island rabbits with myxomatosis, knowing that the disease would spread rapidly.

Only a few of the rabbits besides those originally injected actually died, and in less than three months, the population was thriving. I'd been glad at the time, because I thought it was cruel to make the rabbits sick.

I released the brown rabbit, thinking there must be some reason for the island rabbits' immunity. A dark speck moved on my rubber glove—a rabbit flea, which the island rabbits never carried.

My grandfather had once proposed the theory that since the rabbit flea required the blood of a pregnant doe in order to reproduce, rabbit fleas could not survive on Skokholm because of the short breeding season. Skokholm's does had significantly fewer gestations than their mainland counterparts. A natural check, I thought, on the population that had no land predators and would otherwise outgrow its resources.

I captured the second rabbit and combed through its fur with my gloved fingers. It was a light brown one with patches of white fur, and the fleas were easy to spot because of the contrast. If fleas were the vectors for "myxy," this might explain the immunity. What puzzled me was why the island rabbits were now suddenly showing up with fleas.

I walked back toward the farmhouse, then turned west on the path to North Pond. I knew Vandermeer would be there, since he had mentioned wanting to observe the mallards and the Canadian geese. My head ached, and the back of my neck was tight.

The gulls circled overhead with their incessant cawing. Vandermeer sat motionless on the ground, his back against the hide. He was writing in his bird notebook. "Reverend Vandermeer, I have some bad news. I've found two rabbits infected with myxomatosis."

"Are you sure?" I could have sworn I saw the trace of a smile.

"There's not much doubt, sir. Their heads are swollen to the point where they're nearly blind."

"Any signs of illness in the others?"

"Not that I can see."

"Well, you'll need to get rid of the infected ones. Take them to an open area where there are no burrows and burn them."

"I should like to put them out of their misery first, sir. Do you have a gun?"

Mattheu Vandermeer gave me a strange look. "There is a rifle on that high ledge in the Wheelhouse."

Katya, who had been in Morwenn's cottage when she heard the shots, met me on the path. She looked at the burlap sack and Vandermeer's rifle. I held up the sack. "Two rabbits infected with the 'myxy.' If it spreads, all the rabbits could be dead in ten days, and I'll have no reason to be here."

* * *

Three days later, Vandermeer sent word that he wanted to see me. When I knocked on the door of the farmhouse, there was no response. I knocked again, harder this time, until my knuckles began to sting. In a few minutes, Vandermeer appeared at the door, his hair lit up by sunlight from the east window. His eyes narrowed when he saw me.

"Katherine said that you wanted to talk with me."

Vandermeer stared at me with those ice-blue eyes. Finally, he motioned for me to come in. He was wearing rumpled trousers and a long-sleeved white shirt, and he seated himself in a straight-backed chair near the fireplace.

He nodded once, as if he were royalty, indicating that I might be seated. Vandermeer's intense stare unnerved me, along with the sudden formality, and I sat on the edge of the sofa. My mouth was dry.

Vandermeer stood up and walked to the window. When he looked back at me, a muscle twitched in his jaw. He crossed the room and took a Bible from the mantel, pulling a white envelope out of it. "This came a week ago, from the British Wildlife Society in London. They apologize for the fact that Thomas Weaver did not show up on the appointed day to begin the field study. They write that he has changed his mind about the study, and they greatly appreciate my cooperation in having made arrangements for him to come over."

"May I see that?" I said, buying time. Vandermeer tossed the letter to me and sat down in his chair. There was no return address on the envelope; no wonder it had slipped past me. I gave him a faint smile and shrugged. "You've caught me, and obviously, I owe you an explanation." I hesitated, looking out the window into the garden, gathering my thoughts. "My earliest memories are from right out there," I said, pointing to the garden. "Morwenn tells me that she used to take my pram out there and sit with me for hours. She swears that even as an infant of ten months, I was fascinated by the birds that flew over us." I looked at Vandermeer, trying to judge his reaction, but his face had no expression. "I had to come back here, you see. I'm William Kensley's grandson. My name is Robert."

He stared at me as he ran his long fingers over the cover of the Bible. "So that's all it was? You just wanted to visit the island?"

"I've been known to do some pretty balmy things." I wondered if Vandermeer suspected he was being investigated.

"And Katherine Dennis is truly Morwenn's cousin?"

I hesitated for a fraction of a second. "Of course. Who else would she be?"

Vandermeer shook his head, his thin lips curved into a faint smile. "I know it's early in the day," he said, "but would you join me in a glass of sherry?"

Vandermeer's chummy remark set off alarm bells in my head. Trying to make my tone sound casual, I said, "Sure, why not?"

Standing up slowly, Vandermeer picked up the decanter that stood beside the clock on the mantel. He poured the amber-colored liquid into two glasses from a tray on the side table and handed one to me. He held his own glass up in a toast. "I commend you for your honesty," he said, "as well as your cleverness."

If you only knew, you would not salute my honesty

Vandermeer sat down again near the fireplace with a faint smile. "I have a confession to make. Those two infected rabbits were from the mainland. I knew the infection wouldn't spread, but I was testing you."

"Did I pass?"

"Only too well. You knew so much about the disease,

you either had to be a genuine wildlife biologist or you'd been to the island before. I began to suspect the latter, when I remembered your remark the first day about Tabernacle Rock."

I took a sip of my sherry, which was lukewarm and sweet, and reminded me vaguely of licorice.

Vandermeer set down his glass, his face serious, his pale eyes boring into mine. "I thought you might be investigating me—some relative seeking revenge."

My heart skipped a beat, and my shoulder muscles tensed. I spoke slowly and carefully, "What do you mean, sir?"

Vandermeer continued. "With too much time to think about things, I suppose I've gotten paranoid." He rose from his chair again and walked into his bedroom.

Staring at Vandermeer's back, I put my glass on the coffee table, estimating the distance from my chair to the door. When Vandermeer returned with the black velvet bundle in his hand, I waited for him to speak. He pulled his chair closer to me and sat down, leaning forward.

"I've never told anyone this, except Morwenn," Vandermeer said, and my heart began to pound. I reached for my glass and gulped sherry.

Vandermeer took a deep breath, fingering the velvet. "I came here in '46 because I killed someone in Amsterdam. Since I was a man of God, I could no longer look out into the eyes of my congregation and preach to them when I had broken one of His most sacred commandments." He avoided my eyes, turning to stare into the fire.

I wanted to ask him the name of the person he'd killed, but I didn't have the courage to interrupt. Almost in a trance, I sat listening to Reverend Vandermeer's smooth voice, with the sherry making me feel so heavy, as if it was too much of an effort to move my arms or legs. Vandermeer's words became tangled inside my head, and I found it harder and harder to concentrate.

"During the war," Vandermeer said, "the Jews of Holland were in great danger, so my wife and I took in a Jewish family and hid them for one year. I know someone gave us away to the Nazis, because they went straight to the door of the secret place where we had hidden the Rosens. They took away the whole family—a mother, father, and two little boys."

I found myself trying to read Vandermeer's eyes—was he telling the truth or was he lying? What does truth smell like—is it more like licorice or firewood? It was hard to keep my eyelids from drifting shut.

After pausing for a sip of sherry, Vandermeer continued. "I was taken up for hiding Jews—a crime punishable by death."

Through the fog in my brain, I chased a fleeting thought—did Vandermeer emphasize the words 'a crime punishable by death'?

"My wife was eight months pregnant," he said softly, "and when they started to take me away, she began screaming. A Nazi officer shot her. I was not even allowed to hold her in my arms as she died." Vandermeer's eyes took on a distant look. Before you could say 'knife,' he turned in his chair and threw his wineglass against the stones of the fireplace.

I could almost feel his despair as he said, "I had to carry that memory—the look in my wife's eyes right after she was shot—a look of such terror, and I knew she was afraid not just for herself, but for the baby and for me. During the whole time I was in prison—they decided not to kill me but to work me to death—I held that Nazi officer's face in my mind. When I escaped from the train taking us from one prison to another, I made my way back to Amsterdam. I found that man one night, in a tavern downtown, and I followed him when he left." Vandermeer sat with his hand over his eyes, then looked at me. "I killed him," he said. "I came up behind him and I slit his throat, and as he lay in the street in a pool of his own blood, I stood over him and looked into his dead eyes and that Iron Cross on his uniform made me so angry. How could a monster like that be allowed to wear a symbol of our Lord?" Vandermeer unwrapped the velvet to reveal the Iron Cross, which he held out to me.

"I grabbed hold of this Iron Cross and ripped it from his uniform. In the shadows of that alley, I held in my hand this medal of honor, warm with blood that grew warmer in the palm of my cold hand until it burned as if with the fire of hell. I realized in one sickening instant, that I was now a murderer too, no better than the Nazi who killed so carelessly."

I was shocked that Vandermeer had revealed this to me. What reason could he possibly have, unless he were a man so burdened by his guilt, that to tell another human being would be some measure of healing? I'd not heard one false note, and I was inclined to believe the story, in spite of Katya's allegations. I managed to say, almost choking on the words, "Why did you keep the Iron Cross?"

He glanced at me for a moment but his eyes were wild, darting round the room as if he were having trouble focusing, and he was breathing heavily. "I kept it," he said, "to remind myself of my guilt." Vandermeer stared at the Iron Cross in the palm of his hand.

There was an awkward silence—I was unable to speak. I sipped my sherry and avoided looking at him. The Iron Cross, the seclusion, even the journal entry about not being a murderer—it all fit together so bloody well. I am such a fool. For a moment, I was tempted to make a full confession of my own sins, especially snooping through things that didn't belong to me, lying and more lying to get a Nazi hunter onto the island to investigate an innocent man. I wished that I had never found the Iron Cross. "I'm so very sorry that I lied to you, sir," I said to Vandermeer, knowing that I could not reveal Katya's identity, even to this man of God who would surely understand. If Katya wanted to tell him, that was her business. The truth was that I didn't want to admit to more lies.

I ran my fingers over the floral design of a pillow. "Under the circumstances, no one could blame you for killing that Nazi," I said. "You're too hard on yourself." I stood up. "I'll make arrangements to be gone from here by Friday at the latest." I took several steps backward, fighting the urge to run.

From Vandermeer's house, I walked back to my room and sat on the bed, staring at the wall and thinking about what Vandermeer had said. I should leave—that would be the decent thing to do, to stop the deception. Mattheu

Vandermeer was a man who had been grievously wronged, and I regretted my part in his investigation. I knew Morwenn wouldn't want me to go, so I decided to put off telling her, because I hated to see her cry.

I got up from the bed and walked out of the hut, heading west through the rock gates, past the fenced area called the "Exclosure" where Vandermeer studied island vegetation untouched by rabbits. I walked on the spongy path, climbed over the low wall, where the path led up in a gentle curve to the brown wooden hide at North Pond. I swung open the heavy door.

Inside, I sat on the narrow bench and opened the viewing window. In the distance lay Skomer and Middleholm and part of the mainland. Gulls floated on North Pond, pushed backwards by the strong wind, bobbing their heads down to drink and to wash off the salt brine, then flying up and landing a few feet ahead, drifting back to the same spot in a few moments. Three oystercatchers stood scattered in the wet grass between patches of water, which were now splattered by raindrops. Vandermeer's revelation had shocked me, and I went over his words in my head.

Something startled the gulls, and they took off from the pond, wheeling into the sky in all directions, their cries breaking the silence of the island. I stood up suddenly and bent my head down to clear the doorway of the hide, and as I looked up, I felt dizzy. I had to shut my eyes against the sun's glaring light. Perhaps I should consider breakfast. I've had nothing to eat this morning, and the sherry's making my head spin.

* * *

When I found Katya, waiting for scones to bake, I told her what had happened. She sat back and crossed her arms. “So he’s got your number. Did he know the name of this Nazi he’d supposedly killed?”

“No, but he’d memorized his face. Everything makes perfect sense now—the Iron Cross, the reclusive lifestyle.”

She leaned forward and touched my arm. “When you walked in here, you said his story was incredible. That’s because it’s one big lie.”

I rocked back on two legs of the wooden chair, holding onto the table’s edge. “Listen, I know you’re sure he’s Janisch, but what real evidence do you have? The bank account and the plastic surgeon’s card prove absolutely nothing. Even the German woman could be no more than a foreign pen friend.” I let the chair legs crash forward onto the floor tiles. “And you admit that you didn’t recognize him when you first saw his face.”

She pressed a fist to her mouth. “But now I know why he looks different.”

“What he told me makes sense,” I said, ignoring Katya’s remark. “Every detail rings true.”

She stared over my shoulder into the dining room. “Of course he would know the details because he was there when it happened, except that he was playing a different part. He was the Nazi officer. Robert, think about it. He’s had seven years to polish this story.”

“No, you’re wrong on this one, Katya.” I leaned forward. “You weren’t there to hear him tell it. I was there. I heard his voice, I saw his eyes and the expression on his face—I believe he’s telling the truth.”

She stood up and walked past me. She turned back toward me and leaned against the kitchen wall. “In the camps,” she said, “we learned never to trust anything that came out of a Nazi’s mouth.”

“I guess I’m gullible because I take things at face value. The man was spilling his guts to me, and I didn’t hear a single false note.”

“He played it perfectly,” she said, “just like his violin sonatas. Why would you want to believe his lies?”

I stared at her. “I don’t think you’re being objective.”

“Objective?” she said. “Perhaps that’s what someone could be whose war effort was making blackout curtains and serving on bird-banding committees in Connecticut. I spent those memorable years experiencing horrors that you cannot even imagine.”

She might as well have slapped me in the face. I stood up suddenly, the pulse beating in my ears like a drumbeat. As I walked past her out the kitchen door, I said, “I don’t know why he’d bother to tell me this, unless it were true.”

MEMORIES AND DREAMS

What I had said to Robert, as he stalked out of the Wheelhouse kitchen that morning, was that Vandermeer spun his tale because he suspected me, and he knew Robert would relay the lies as some great revelation of truth. But, of course, Robert didn't hear any of this. As soon as he told me "The Reverend Mattheu Vandermeer story," I knew I was on my own, as far as anything else I hoped to accomplish on the island. He'd accused me of losing my objectivity, but I knew it wasn't true. Why hadn't he questioned the fact that this Dutch minister wrote his journal entries in German? And, more importantly, from whom was Mattheu Vandermeer hiding? Did Robert honestly believe there was a warrant for Vandermeer's arrest in Amsterdam for killing a Nazi during the war? According to Vandermeer, he "couldn't face his congregation," so why didn't he just quit the ministry and do something else? There was no need to retreat to the edge of the earth, unless he had committed a crime. Janisch had committed so many, he couldn't even keep track of them.

Robert, of course, has since admitted his error in believing Vandermeer. He tends to trust people, even when he should not, and Janisch played the part of Mattheu Vandermeer the Dutch clergyman with incredible attention to detail, including the prayer book in Dutch and the Bible verses copied in English in the front of his journal.

Robert is certain that Morwenn is hiding Vandermeer's journal, and I tend to agree with him. He's searched the entire house, and I don't think Vandermeer would have had time to get rid of it. He's tried to explain to Morwenn how much we need the journal to help prove that Vandermeer was Janisch. She refuses to discuss it. He, in turn, refuses to search her room, saying that would violate her trust in him, which is already on shaky ground. He says he'll think of some way to convince her to give it up.

Meanwhile, I continue to write in my own journal, which Robert brought soon after my cast was removed. Now the green spiral notebook and black fountain pen are my most precious possessions, and I am fortunate to be able to keep them in my cell, even though I could slit my wrists with the nib of the fountain pen or do some damage to myself with the wire from the notebook. Perhaps they trust me more, because they know I am a survivor. If I endured what I did in the camps and the Warsaw Ghetto, why would I take my life here in this place that feels more like a safe haven than a jail?

Every day that the weather's nice, they let me stay outside for two hours. I love the fresh air and the chance to walk, and I go round and round the perimeter of the wall—seventy-one steps if I keep them a moderate length. Such small pleasures. Sunlight on closed eyelids. I hear automobiles outside, although I can't see them because the wall is too high. What I can see are cloud formations, which change shape from moment to moment if you watch them closely enough. I also see birds flying overhead, which reminds me of the island, which is sometimes a good thing and sometimes not. It depends on what I choose to remember.

Although I can't see any trees, to mark the passage of the seasons by the changes in their leaves, I can feel the air outside getting just a little colder every day. It has been four months since the coronation of Elizabeth as Queen—four months and eleven days since I killed Mattheu Vandermeer. We are close on the same age—she's a year older—but our lives have been so different, even though we had a common enemy, Hitler, in our teenage years. She is married and has two small children. From this point on, without question, our lives will diverge even more.

I write things like this in my journal—insights that I think are especially profound, at least at the moment I come up with them. I tend to write page after page, once I start. It's almost like I can't stop, but then it's not like I have much else to do. I dread the coming days, when autumn will slide into winter, and my outdoor excursions will be curtailed by snow or rain. Being outside, even for just a few minutes a day, is what helps keep me calm.

I'm starting to have dreams that repeat themselves. In one of them, I'm on an endless driven belt that runs through a tunnel so narrow, I have to turn sideways. The walls are crooked, all of them curved, and I am in danger of smashing into them. There is no way to stand up straight. The movement of the belt forces me toward the end of the tunnel, where there is nothing, and I am always haunted by the dream for several days.

I had dreams like this in Auschwitz, on the rare occasions when I slept deeply enough to do so. It's not surprising that my sleep, in those days of hell, did not refresh me. When you must spend all of your time concentrating on survival, you cannot allow the distraction of nightmares.

The first thing I learned in Auschwitz was that physical survival depended on one thing—having a cup for soup and water. Such a simple thing. A fellow Pole in the men's camp gave me a bit of string and a nail, and with a rock, I pounded the nail through the rim of the cup. I was able to wear the cup under my jacket by threading the string through the hole in the cup and then using the string for a belt to hold my pants up. My baggy trousers were made for a large Russian soldier, not a skinny Polish teenager.

Emotional survival depended upon being able to endure pain, hunger, thirst, and humiliation. Every third Sunday with nauseating punctuality, we were lined up to be shaved again, not only our heads but also our legs, underarms, and pubic areas. As another example of Nazi sadism, those who were forced to shave us were Jewish men and boys. We suffered great humiliation, because even a married Jewish woman did not expose herself to her husband. Those poor Jewish men, equally embarrassed, tried to be gentle with us, but they were forced to run the clippers with such speed that drawing blood was the rule and not the exception.

THE STORM

Morwenn left today to visit her sister in Marloes, before the weather gets too dicey between the island and the mainland. I did something well and truly horrible, but it wouldn't be the first time for me, would it? I went through Morwenn's drawers and searched every nook and cranny in her cottage, looking for that damned journal. Since I'd already taken apart Vandermeer's farmhouse, that left the Wheelhouse, which I considered an unlikely hiding place, and roughly three thousand rabbit burrows, which I had no intention of searching.

The only explanation, as far as I can see, is that she either took it with her or she's thrown it into the ocean. I hope and pray it's not the latter. Eventually, she'll come to her senses and turn in the journal as evidence. Right now, I'm sure she thinks this is her revenge against Katya.

When I saw her last week, Katya seemed to be having some anxiety about her upcoming trial, although she put on a brave front for my sake. She told me she had thought about the future and wondered if she would have one. Would there be too many years in prison to endure? Days and months and years—overwhelming concepts, she said. She supposed she would reach some sort of equilibrium—some comfort in a daily rhythm and maybe small glimpses of happiness every now and then. She's not asking for the world.

I sat in with Aaron Levy and Mark Wickham yesterday, in one of their war council sessions, where they hash out the fine points of Katya's defense. I know they both think I'm a fool, but on occasion, I have something valuable to contribute. We agreed that the best strategy for Katya was also the most dangerous—to prove Janisch's capacity for murder without strengthening her motive. In other words, we would need to establish Janisch's background as a Nazi without emphasizing his truly sadistic nature. Katya had shared a few things with me about Janisch that I found difficult to believe, but Aaron assured me his behavior was not unusual among Nazi officers.

"If he'd left the blood type tattoo," Aaron said, "we'd be in good shape. Not many people have the letters AB under their arm."

Mark rubbed the side of his face. "He was too smart for that. The autopsy report shows only a small scar there."

I added my two cents worth. "The autopsy report on Vandermeer shows a scar on the right seventh rib, as does the SS file description of Janisch, if my translation is correct."

"It's not enough to prove anything," Mark said.

Aaron looked at me. "We need the journal."

"I've tried everything I can think of."

"Keep thinking," Mark said. "Keep trying. It's our only hope."

Even after she was certain that Vandermeer was Janisch, Katya had taken his journal one last time, in the middle of the night. She'd found some particularly incriminating passages, with which she hoped to convince Aaron to help her get Janisch extradited. That was when she came to me, just after midnight, and asked me to take a letter for Aaron over to the mainland. The weather that day was not the best, but she had told me this was extremely urgent. I was fortunate, in that the storm struck when I was only a mile out of Martinshaven, although I had difficulty landing.

I remember that afternoon as one of the worst in my life. Chilled to the bone and exhausted from bringing the boat safely into the harbor at Martinshaven, I'd sat at a table in front of the fire at the Foxes Inn, my hands wrapped round a steaming mug of tea, waiting for it to cool. The rain had drenched my clothing and hair, and droplets of cold water now ran down into my shirt collar.

It was three o'clock in the afternoon, and I was the only customer in the pub. The owner, Brian, who was a friend of mine, gave me a towel for my hair, and we sat and watched out the window, as it poured with rain. "Do you know how I can get hold of Clyde?" I said, as I blotted my face and neck. "I need to have him collect Morwenn's cousin and me from Skokholm on Friday morning." A sudden crack of thunder made us jump, and we grinned at each other.

"He's living with his mum now," Brian said, "he and

his children, just down the road from here. You should go and chat him up when the rain stops."

"I will." I sipped the hot tea and closed my eyes, wondering how Katya was. Our shared adventure, it seemed, was coming to an end. Now that I had seen my beloved island in the hands of another man, I wasn't sure there was anything else in the world for me. There was nothing that I really wanted, except Katya, and what did I have to offer? Certain that the storm would prevent my return to the island that evening, I felt cheated out of precious time with her.

I heard a car pull up outside, and I looked out the window to see a man in a black overcoat step out of a taxi and open an umbrella, turning to slam the car's door before he bolted up the sidewalk. The stranger entered the pub's doorway, where he stood dripping onto the slate floor, closing down his umbrella. He wiped his hands with a white handkerchief from the pocket of his coat and nodded at Brian and me. "Good afternoon," he said.

Brian rose to his feet. "May I help you, sir?"

"Yes, I hope so." He paused. "I was told this is the closest village to Skokholm Island. Is that correct?" A Londoner, I thought, from the accent. I leaned forward to hear the conversation between this stranger and Brian, wondering why he was asking about the island and if it had anything to do with Katya. What she had done, coming to Skokholm to investigate Vandermeer, was because of the letter I wrote to my grandfather, and the last thing I wanted was for Katya to be in trouble with the authorities.

"Aye," said Brian, "this is the closest, except for Martinshaven, and there's not much there besides the harbor." We heard the roar of the engine as the taxi drove away.

I noted the elegant cut of the black overcoat, the raindrops beading on polished shoes. The stranger pulled off the overcoat, shook it out, and laid it across the back of a chair, as he said, "I'm trying to locate a young woman who might have gone over to Skokholm a couple of weeks ago. When this storm lets up, do you know where I could get transportation over to the island?"

No time wasted on formalities. The game had just become more serious, but whose side was this stranger on?

Brian looked at me, and I nodded my head and stood up. "Whom are you trying to find, sir?"

"Katya Denys. She's a colleague of mine—I'm Aaron Levy."

Of course. Katya had spoken about him, but why would he come all this way to find her? "I think I can help you, Mr. Levy. I'm Robert Kensley," I said, stepping toward him to hold out my hand.

Aaron shook my hand vigorously and said, "Robert!" His voice was full of both surprise and relief.

I motioned for Aaron to join me and sagged into my chair. "Why don't you sit down?" I noted the creases in Aaron Levy's forehead, the general air of concern, although his facial expression was pleasant enough. Brian left us alone at the table and busied himself drying glassware at the bar.

"Katya disappeared from London after she found your letter, which your grandfather had passed on to me. I can only conclude that she's followed Vandermeer's trail to the island. Am I correct?" I saw the worry in Aaron's eyes as he said, "Do you know if she's okay?"

"She's on the island now, but she'll be coming back to the mainland on Friday. I'm making arrangements for us to be collected from Skokholm on Friday morning." I studied Aaron's face, the brown eyes and olive-toned complexion, the careful mouth with small even teeth.

Aaron waved to get Brian's attention. "Might I have some tea?" Brian nodded, and Aaron said to me, "What luck to run into you here."

"She said you'd probably figure out where she'd gone." I would explain it all to Aaron, and Katya would be exonerated. Then I would face only my grandfather's anger.

After Brian set down a small teapot and a cup and spoon, Aaron said, "May I ask what she's found out?"

I was grateful to be able to explain what we'd learned and to underline my part in the mistaken investigation. "I'm afraid I made some false assumptions when I found that Iron Cross. First, I assumed it belonged to Vandermeer and that made him a Nazi. Secondly, I assumed he was hiding out because he was a Nazi—what other reason could there be?" I massaged the back of my neck with one hand. I felt like a foolish schoolboy, not an adult and certainly not Levy's equal. "I was wrong on both counts. Vandermeer took the Iron Cross from a Nazi officer that he killed in retaliation for the murder of his wife and child. It would have been enough to tip anyone over."

Aaron's spoon clattered onto the table. "He's been hiding out, at the edge of the earth, because he killed a

Nazi? I do not condone revenge killings, but he's certainly in no danger of prosecution."

I paused for a moment. "It's a moral issue for him," I said, "rather than a legal one. He killed the man in a fit of rage, and he says he couldn't face his congregation after what he'd done." I spread my hands open, palms up. "He ran as far away as he could and since then has lived this ascetic life on the island."

Aaron gazed off past me and hesitated before he said, "He's put himself in prison, the poor devil. He would never have been prosecuted for that killing."

Something dark gnawed at the pit of my stomach, as Aaron lit a cigarette. Why couldn't Vandermeer have simply given up the ministry? A twinge of doubt fluttered across my mind, as I repeated my own words. "He said he couldn't face his congregation." I wondered if losing a wife and child had truly sent Vandermeer around the bend.

I pulled myself back to the present, to Aaron Levy who sat across from me sipping tea and smoking a cigarette. "Oh." I reached into my coat pocket to find the letter, amazingly dry considering how soaked my clothing was. "This is from Katya, probably repeating what I just told you about Vandermeer. She obviously felt it was important to let you know your instincts were correct. I'm certain she planned to return to London after coming off the island Friday."

Aaron crushed out his cigarette and opened the envelope, smiling as he unfolded the single sheet of paper. "I've been worried about her; she'd never disappeared like that . . . " His voice trailed off as he read the letter. "Dear God." Aaron tossed it on the table in front of me. "He didn't kill a Nazi."

The taste of bile came up in my throat. With the letter in my hand, I whispered, "How do you know?" because I was afraid to read it.

As Aaron stood up from the table, he gave me a cold, hard look that made me feel like an adolescent who had questioned authority. I watched him walk to the window, where he stood looking out at the sheets of rain that continued to fall. I pictured myself going back to the island in the storm, fighting the waves, winning against all odds. I would save Katya, because I was the one who had put her in danger. And I also knew that to even try to get back to the island in that kind of weather would be suicidal. My heart beat like a war drum as I read Katya's letter, her cramped handwriting illegible in several places, so that I had to stare at the words before I could make them out.

I dropped the letter and put my hand over my eyes. What had I done? I looked up at Aaron, who had returned from the window and stood watching me. "She's alone on the island with him, except for Morwenn, who'll be staying put in her house." What had Katya planned to do? I wondered if she would seduce Vandermeer to get the information she needed.

Aaron leaned forward on the table. "Who's Morwenn?"

"His housekeeper . . . and my former nanny. That's how I got Katya over there. Morwenn agreed to pretend that she'd injured her back and needed help."

"So Morwenn's in on this?"

"Not really. She agreed to the deception only because I asked her to." I thought for a moment. "In a pinch, she'll side with Janisch. I believe she loves him, and she still thinks he's a Dutch minister." I leaned back in my chair, feeling drained. Something in the fireplace popped violently, like a muted rifle shot, and I jumped. "I've really been playing the goat, haven't I? He had me convinced, with that incredible story about how he came to possess the Iron Cross."

"The Nazis were master liars. He's had a long time to perfect this cover." Aaron stood up and walked again to the window. "Any idea when the rain might let up?"

I shook my head. "We'll leave as soon as it stops, I promise you. Why wouldn't Katya tell me about this last part, about the passage in the journal?"

Aaron stared at me. "Obviously she didn't trust you."

I crossed my arms and leaned back. "I'm sure that's true. I showed rotten judgement on more than one occasion, but the worst of it was when she questioned Vandermeer's Iron Cross story, and I sided with him."

"The fact that Janisch bothered to share that story," Aaron said, "tells me that he suspects something. We need to get Katya off the island. Go back, tell Janisch that your ride's not available Friday and you'll be leaving on Thursday instead."

"She has a gun," I said.

Aaron's face drained of color. "She's playing with fire." He pulled himself to his feet and walked to the window. "This bloody rain! I hope to God the storm breaks soon."

"There's no way to predict," I said. "I'll leave as soon as it's humanly possible. I feel like I've betrayed her. She tried to tell me Vandermeer was lying, but I chose to believe him instead." Surely he realized how much I cared for Katya and that I'd not deliberately put her in harm's way.

He gave me a half-smile, which was all that either of us could manage. "You couldn't have known, Robert. You were never there in the camps, living with the Nazis' deception, day after day. I would expect Emil Janisch to be an accomplished liar, as smooth as obsidian."

THE TRIAL

The fact that I was a foreigner and had killed one of their own—maybe that's what had drawn the crowd. The benches of the visitors' gallery were filled with people who looked delighted to have gotten a seat. Some, I am sure, were Welsh fishermen and their families from Marloes and Milford Haven, who had known Reverend Vandermeer only by name and reputation as the owner of Skokholm Island. I would guess that among those Welsh citizens were no more than a handful who could boast of actually having met him. According to Robert and Morwenn, his involvement with the mainlanders had been minimal. Welsh villagers, though, understood the notion of place and would fiercely defend ties to the land, so they had a sense of loyalty to the man who had owned the island. Why should they trust me, a woman about whom they knew nothing?

Those who watched me enter the dock probably noticed that I straightened my shoulders and lifted my chin, since I knew I was under scrutiny by every visitor in the gallery. Spectators may have whispered among themselves that I did not seem afraid, with some taking the opposite view. Perhaps the young woman was well and truly terrified—she could be facing the noose, after all—and she could cope only by pretending not to care. They watched the back of my head—I could feel it—my hair done up carefully in a French twist, and when I turned my head to the side, to look out the window, I heard whispers about how pale my skin was.

Although many of the spectators looked round the courtroom, wide-eyed and smiling, as if they expected to be entertained by the proceedings, they observed a respectful silence, and they bent their heads to whisper to each other as if they were in church. In some ways, the courtroom had the feeling of a church. Dark wood ran twelve feet up the wall, topped by molding, with mullioned windows above. A balcony, high on the wall to the left, was carved from a glossy, dark wood, and below the balcony was a clock with hands frozen at five minutes past one. A huge formal painting of some officer in a red and white uniform hung over the judge's chair, which had an ornate carving on the high, arched back and a red leather seat. On either side of the officer's portrait were the official seals of Great Britain and Wales. Like church pews, carved wooden benches faced each other on either side of the courtroom, with the barristers' table in the center. The prosecutor sat facing the judges' bench, with his back toward the defendant and the spectators, while Mark Wickham sat at right angles to the prosecution, going over his notes and occasionally pushing an unruly strand of dark hair back up under his grey bench wig. The court clerk, a tall woman with auburn hair in a stylish bob, stood at her table just in front of the judges' bench, shuffling loose papers and re-arranging notebooks.

The twelve jurors filed into the courtroom and took their seats in the row of benches to the left of the barristers' table: three gray-haired women, two women in their twenties, one older man with a limp, a dark-haired middle-aged man, and five younger men, ranging in age from mid-twenties to late thirties. They all wore carefully-impassive expressions, along with their Sunday-best clothing, as if to show how seriously they took their assigned task. None of them had the courage to look at me for more than a moment or two.

Just under the familiar smells of coffee and floor polish and damp wool scarves, there was a faint musty scent, as if the navy-blue carpet had been damaged by water. The air in the courtroom was chilly, so most people had not taken off their coats. I turned my attention to the window to escape the piercing stare of the guard, seated on my left, who watched me like a hawk. A ten-foot Palladian window dominated the right-hand wall of the courtroom, framing a view of the square below—a cluster of shops and houses round an open area guarded by a bronze statue of a soldier from the Boer War. I saw people coming and going—people with no more to worry about that what they would have for their tea that evening. Those ordinary people pulled overcoats more tightly about them and clutched their hats in the fierce wind, which stole a black hat from the head of a young man. A small girl in a red coat dashed after the rolling hat, retrieved it, and gave it back to the young man. Above the line of shops, the sky was gunmetal grey, completely overcast, with the kind of diluted light that I had been told was typical of February in Carmarthen.

The key to survival was to be invisible, but now I had become the unwilling center of attention. I could feel the eyes on the back of my neck, weighing my guilt or innocence, judging me for what I had done. I allowed my glance to sweep over the twelve upright citizens of the jury and laughed to myself, knowing that I was entitled to a trial by a jury of my peers. How many of these good people were survivors of concentration camps? How could they presume to judge me? When I shifted my weight, the wooden chair on which I sat seemed out of balance, as if one leg were shorter than the others. I twisted round for a moment to glance at the people in the visitors' gallery. Neither Robert nor Aaron would be there. As potential witnesses, they would be barred from the courtroom until their testimony.

I'd been in the prison in Carmarthen for nine months waiting for this trial, with only a small window near the high ceiling of my cell, from which I could see no trees, only bits of the sky and the gray streaks of cloud and sometimes the moon. For two months, it had been too wet or cold to go outside for exercise. Now, back in the same courtroom where I'd been arraigned, I watched the wind wreak havoc on the square below. I knew the winds would be harsh back on the island, and I wondered how high the waves would be.

We were asked to rise just before Judge Mulholland entered and seated himself in the massive carved chair in the center of the judges' bench. Kevin Sperry, as the Crown prosecutor, rose to make his opening statement. I could only see his back, but he was a short man and seemed to be more stout than slender. I'd seen the rounded contours of his face above the black robe, when he moved about the courtroom before the proceedings began. He painted the worst possible picture of what I had done, claiming that I had intended to kill Emil Janisch all along—citing the drugs, the gun, and my obvious motives—but that I had killed an innocent man, Mattheu Vandermeer, who didn't have a vicious bone in his body. So that's the game Sperry wants to play. He'll deny Vandermeer's true identity because it would throw sympathy toward me. He's right—we don't have much to go on. We have no Mattheu Vandermeer to put in the prisoners' dock, so that witnesses can point to him and say, "That's him. That's Emil Janisch." All we have is one lousy autopsy report, with one scar that matches another scar in the SS file. Kevin Sperry has taken a wise path.

I watched as Mark Wickham got up slowly. From his position at the barristers' table, as he faced the jury, he was in profile to the visitors' gallery and to me. He told the jury that the defense would prove, beyond a doubt, that the man killed on Skokholm Island was not Mattheu Vandermeer—that he was instead a former Nazi commandant named Emil Janisch. I heard the murmurs of excited voices behind me, and Judge Mulholland pounded the gavel for silence. My barrister then said that he would show how Emil Janisch would have killed me if I'd not shot him first. How Mark intended to do this, I wasn't sure, considering the fact that there were no witnesses, unless you counted me.

When Mark sat down, Kevin Sperry called his first witness—the person who could do the most damage to my case—Morwenn Madoc. She approached the witness box as if she were trying to make as little noise as possible with her worn leather pumps. She looked unusually pale dressed in a black suit, with matching hat and gloves. The grieving semi-widow. Did everyone know that she had lived as Vandermeer's wife for several years? I guessed that it had not been kept secret at the time. She held the Testament in her left hand and raised her right, which trembled only a little. After being sworn in, Morwenn seated herself in the box and smoothed down the fabric of her skirt.

"State your full name," said Kevin Sperry.

"Morwenn Madoc."

"And your place of residence?"

"Skokholm Island." Morwenn pressed her lips together tightly.

"How long have you lived there?"

"Twenty-five years, except for a time during the war."

"Where did you live during that time?"

"I lived with my sister Catrin in Marloes for three years. I don't like having so many people about, so I went back to Skokholm and lived on my own."

"Then what happened?"

"Reverend Vandermeer showed up one day, to look at buying the island. He was amazed to find me there, I can tell you that." Morwenn sat forward in her chair. "He didn't say much to me at all, that first time. He walked the island for about three hours, then he left without a word." She rubbed her forehead with two fingers. "He came back a few days later and told me he'd bought the island from Lord Kensley. I expected him to tell me to pack up my things and get off his property. Instead, he offered me a job as his housekeeper."

"What year was this?"

"1946"

"Did you live in his house?"

"No, I had a cottage of my own." She straightened her shoulders and lifted her chin, as if to dispel the rumors about Mattheu Vandermeer and herself.

Kevin Sperry smiled at Morwenn. "Were you happy there?"

"I was content," she said, twirling a strand of her dark hair round her finger. "I had my goats and my garden and someone to take care of."

"How long had you worked for Mattheu Vandermeer at the time of his death?"

"Six years."

Kevin Sperry leaned forward on the barristers' table. "What sort of person was the Reverend Vandermeer?"

"He was a strange man, to be sure—he kept his distance from people, but I suppose the same could be said of me." She paused. "No one came to the island except Clyde Prosser, who delivered his mail and did odd jobs for him. But Reverend Vandermeer was good to me—very kind—and he worked all the hours God sent." She gazed out the window to her left for a moment. Morwenn then looked down at her hands in her lap, and she took a deep breath. There was a faint smile on her face.

"Reverend Vandermeer was one of the most gentle men I ever knew. Sometimes there would be shearwaters that would fall to earth, exhausted from flying so far. He'd put them in a box and take care of them until they could fly again."

"What did you think about the possibility that Mattheu Vandermeer might have been a Nazi?"

"Enough to make a cat laugh."

"But Robert Kensley had found an Iron Cross."

"It wasn't exactly a trout in the milk. My brother-in-law has a German pistol from the war—that doesn't make him a Nazi."

"Was Mattheu Vandermeer in the habit of drinking alcohol?"

"A tot with his supper, every now and then."

"Was it part of his routine to be served coffee in the evening at his house?"

"Aye."

"And who served it?"

"I did, until Katya Denys came, and then it was her job." Only then did Morwenn glance at me. From the look on her face and the tone of her voice, I realized, in that moment, just how much she hated me. But Kevin Sperry didn't care who hated whom—he just wanted to show my golden opportunity to drug Vandermeer's coffee, when the issue of pentobarbitone came up. And Morwenn certainly didn't mind putting the cat among the pigeons.

Sperry then asked Morwenn about her relationship to Robert Kensley, and she explained that she was his nanny until he was nine years old. "Then the Kensleys moved back to London, just before the war."

"When was the next time you saw Robert Kensley?"

"In March of last year, he came to the island."

"Under what circumstances?"

"He just showed up one day. It took me by surprise, to be sure."

"He showed up with no warning?"

"Not exactly. The Reverend Vandermeer had told me a young man was coming out to study the wild rabbits, but then Robert showed up, calling himself Thomas Weaver."

"Robert Kensley was posing as someone else?"

"Yes."

"Did he tell you why he'd come back to the island?"

"He said it was to see me, but that was more of a joke than anything. He'd made no attempt to contact me in years."

"Then what happened?" Kevin Sperry asked.

"One day, he came to me with a letter from her." Morwenn looked at me again.

"The defendant?"

"Yes."

"And what did Robert ask of you?"

"He said that a young woman from London wanted to come out to visit him and could she pose as my cousin?"

"What was your first response?"

"I told Robert no, I wouldn't do it." She shook her head. "But Robert begged me. He said he'd go back to London if she couldn't come out, so I gave in."

"What did you see one day, when Vandermeer was off the island?"

"Katya had Vandermeer's journal."

"How did she explain that to you?"

"She admitted that she had not come to visit Robert—that she was investigating Mattheu Vandermeer because he might be a former Nazi she had encountered in Auschwitz."

"What did you see on the defendant's forearm?"

"Blue numbers, tattooed into the skin. The things they did in those camps would make anyone crazy."

Mark Wickham stood up. "Objection, M'lord. The witness is speculating."

"Sustained."

"One last question," Sperry said. "When was the last time Miss Denys had seen this man she thought Vandermeer might be?"

"1944."

"Nine years before she came to the island?"

"Yes."

Kevin Sperry sat down at the barristers' table, and Mark Wickham stood up immediately.

"So, Miss Madoc, your employer, Mattheu Vandermeer, had been very kind to you—he offered you a job when he found you living on the island, he provided you with your own cottage. You, in return, kept house and cooked for him, is that correct?"

"Yes."

"And you had some loyalty to him because of what he'd done for you?"

"Yes."

"You were angry when you found out that Robert and Katya had deceived you. Isn't that right?"

"Of course I was angry."

"Did you report to Mattheu Vandermeer what was going on?"

"No."

"Why not?"

"I wanted Robert to be able to stay a little longer."

"So you were willing to deceive Vandermeer also?"

"It wasn't my idea."

"No further questions for this witness." Her most damaging testimony was about our deception, but if she participated in that, even to a small degree, her accusations lose some ground. Every one of us had a part in the masquerade.

* * *

Richard Thompson had trained as a physician immediately after World War II and had not been in practice long enough to be tired of his work, just the five year minimum required to serve as coroner of Dyfed County. He was a large man, not so tall but broad enough in girth to be considered substantial. He wore a dark gray suit, with a white shirt and blue tie. As he took the oath, his chubby cheeks were slightly flushed, his eyes watered down and pale behind thick glasses.

Kevin Sperry approached the witness, skimming a hand over his immaculate white wig. "Dr. Thompson," he said, "could you please verify that this document is the report of the autopsy you performed on Mattheu Vandermeer." Kevin handed Dr. Thompson a slim manila folder, and Dr. Thompson flipped through the pages.

"This is my report, yes."

"Could you read out the cause of death for Mattheu Vandermeer, as written in your report of the victim's autopsy."

Dr. Thompson read from the first page: "Cause of death, Mattheu Vandermeer, as determined by autopsy performed 23 May, 1953. Gunshot wound to the chest, rupturing the thoracic aorta." A loud crack on the roof drew everyone's eyes to the ceiling for a moment. With no visible signs of damage, we shrugged it off as a bit of flying debris.

"Could you also read to us from the report concerning your discovery of pentobarbitone sodium in the victim's bloodstream? In the fourth paragraph of page three."

Dr. Thompson cleared his throat twice and coughed. "Excuse me. 'A significant amount of the drug pentobarbitone sodium was found during blood tests.' "

"Doctor, can you tell us what pentobarbitone is used for?"

"It's a barbiturate, often used before surgery to induce sedation."

"I understand this medication has a rather unpleasant taste. Could this be masked by a strongly-flavored substance like coffee?"

"I suppose so. In coffee made with chicory, for instance, you'd probably not notice the taste at all."

"Where can pentobarbitone be obtained?

"It's used in hospitals, but sometimes doctors will write prescriptions for patients with intractable pain."

"What are the side effects of the drug?"

"Large doses result in coma," said Dr. Thompson, "and eventually death. Smaller doses produce dizziness, loss of balance, euphoria, and lack of muscle coordination."

Kevin Sperry put his hands down and leaned forward

on the barristers' table. "You say that large doses could lead to coma and eventually to death. So, this is a potentially dangerous drug, is it not?"

"Yes."

"And it was found in Mattheu Vandermeer's bloodstream?"

"Yes."

"And how much was found in his bloodstream?"

"Enough to make him sleepy and affect his muscle coordination and judgment."

"No further questions, M'lord."

Judge Mulholland called for the court to adjourn for the day.

ROBERT

Now that the trial had started, I did not return to Skokholm between visits to Katya but stayed, instead, with my grandfather's brother in Carmarthen, who was delighted to have a houseguest. Katya seemed fairly calm on the evening of the first day of her trial. I would have been shitting bricks if I were in her shoes.

"According to Morwenn's testimony today," she said, "Mattheu Vandermeer was a saint, and I killed him by mistake because I'm crazy from being in the camps. That was clever of Sperry, having Morwenn be somewhat sympathetic towards me. I know what she'd really like is to see me hang."

I sat down in the only chair, since she had taken up her usual spot on the bunk. "Mark says Kevin Sperry will probably downplay the issue of Vandermeer's identity, since he knows we have so little to go on."

"If only we could find that journal," she said. "Do you think Morwenn will stay here in Carmarthen for the rest of the trial?"

What she meant was, if only you could find that journal, Robert. She wasn't able to do much looking herself. "I imagine she'll stay in Marloes with Catrin," I said. "It's a short train ride from Milford Haven over to Carmarthen. I could go back to the island and take things apart one more time."

"She's probably keeping it with her," Katya said.

"She won't be able to read a word of it, except the Bible verses you said were in the front."

"If she loved him, she'll want to keep something of his, for sentimental reasons."

"If it's on the island, I'll find it." The search for the journal was so frustrating for me, because so much depended on my finding it, and yet, I knew that Morwenn had not only taken the journal but had denied doing so. I guess she figured that I had lied to her about Katya, so anything was fair. She would probably never forgive me.

Katya stood up and stretched. "Aaron was here earlier. He's already nervous about his testimony."

She didn't know that I had been called as a witness for the Crown.

THE FACE OF DEATH

The constable of Marloes, Kerlyn Pugh, had been a friend of Robert's since they played pirates and sailors on the island as children. Kerlyn was a short man, tending to thickness round his middle, but his arms and shoulders still retained the powerful build of a fisherman, which had been his trade for five years. After taking the oath, Kerlyn seated himself in the witness box. His face was slightly flushed, pink patches creeping upwards toward his ginger-colored hair, and I guessed that one branch of his family tree had been Irish.

Kevin Sperry stood up from the barristers' table. "On the morning of the 21st of May of last year, what were you doing?"

Kerlyn explained that he'd been sitting at his desk at eight o'clock, having come in early to finish up some reports from the day before.

"Who came to your office that morning?"

"Katya Denys and Robert Kensley."

"What did they say to you?"

"Robert said there'd been 'a bit of trouble' with Mattheu Vandermeer and that Miss Denys had had to shoot him in self-defense."

"What was your response to this?"

"I told them Vandermeer never struck me as the type for an up-and-downer."

"How long had you known Mattheu Vandermeer?"

"I didn't really know him that well—I mainly knew of him and that he'd bought Skokholm seven years ago."

"How long have you been constable?"

"Six years."

"In that time, constable, did you ever have a complaint against Mattheu Vandermeer for any reason?"

"No, I did not."

"Any reason to believe that he was not who he said he was?"

"No."

"Any evidence whatsoever of violence or drunken behavior?"

"No."

"Constable Pugh, Katya Denys stated in her interview that Mattheu Vandermeer had fired at her with a rifle. Did you find this rifle at the scene of his death?"

"No."

"How about a bullet from a rifle? Was that found?"

"We weren't able to find any bullets, except the ones from the Walther PPK."

The case of the vanishing rifle, I thought. So much for self-defense.

"Would you tell us where you found Mattheu Vandermeer's body?"

Kerlyn explained how he and his deputy, Brynn Carne, had taken the county boat over to Skokholm, following Robert in Vandermeer's motorboat. When they reached the island, instead of putting in at South Haven, Robert had kept going round the inlet called Wreck Cove to Crab Bay. Just past the large boulders off the shore, Robert turned the boat to the north and cut the engine, drifting toward the rocks where Mattheu Vandermeer's body lay. Kerlyn cut his engine also and felt the pull of the current as he and Brynn were swept toward the rocks and their gruesome burden—the body with its eyes staring up blankly, the hue of death on the face, blue against the red rock. Kerlyn shouted to Robert, "I haven't seen Vandermeer in a year or two, but he looks different. What happened to his beard and that long hair?"

Robert stared at Vandermeer's face. "He's only cut his hair and shaved in the last twenty-four hours. He didn't look like this when I left."

Vandermeer's white shirt was bloodstained, and there were three visible bullet wounds, in the left shoulder, the center of the chest, and slightly lower, in the upper abdomen. Kerlyn took out his camera from its waterproof case and snapped photographs of the body from as many angles as he could, then sat back on his heels in the gently rocking boat. "Tide's coming up," he said. "We should get him on board." They managed to position the two boats so that the body was between them, with Vandermeer's head toward the county boat. Robert leaned out into the water and grabbed Vandermeer's legs, lifting them up while Kerlyn and Brynn lifted his torso, all of them feeling the strain of working at such an awkward angle. They managed to get the body into the county boat, and then motored the short distance to South Haven with their engines on half-power. While Brynn drove the boat, Kerlyn stared at Vandermeer's face, as if trying to read there the story of his death. Finally, he unfolded a white blanket and covered the body as they docked.

"What did you say to Robert Kensley at that point?" Kevin Sperry said.

"I asked him what he was doing back on the island."

"What was his response?"

" 'I'm studying the wild rabbit population' is what he said."

"And what did you say to that?"

"Robert had been working as a fisherman for a year. I asked him since when was he a wildlife biologist."

"What was his response?"

"He laughed and said that he'd really come to visit Morwenn, and he had to get past the guardian of the gates somehow."

"Robert Kensley said that he had to get past the guardian of the gates?" Sperry asked.

"That's what he said. I thought it was a strange remark to make, with Vandermeer lying dead behind us in the county boat."

Mark Wickham rose to question the witness. "Constable Pugh," he said, "you stated that you found Mattheu Vandermeer's body on the rocks in Crab Bay, is that correct?"

"Yes."

"In your opinion, how did his body get there?"

"It was clear that he'd fallen from the slope."

"Why?"

"We found bloodstains on the ground where he was shot."

"What would you say is the angle of the slope leading down to Crab Bay?"

"About forty-five degrees."

"Like this?" Mark Wickham held one hand at a forty-five degree angle to the other.

"Yes."

"What do you think would have happened to a rifle dropped on that kind of an incline?"

"It would have rolled down."

"Into the bay?"

"Yes."

"No more questions, M'lord."

* * *

I watched Robert enter the courtroom, wearing a three-piece dark blue suit and a blue silk tie. His shoes were highly polished. Obviously, Lord Kensley had sent money, insisted that Robert buy a proper suit, so that he would not be disgraced. I watched him swear to tell the truth and wondered if there was any way he could do so without incriminating us both.

Kevin Sperry hoisted his heavy body out of the chair, and although I could not see his face, I imagined that his expression was one of barely-suppressed glee. "State your full name for the record."

"Robert Charles Kensley."

"Your place of residence."

"I'm staying temporarily on Skokholm Island."

"Do you have a permanent residence?"

"No, sir, I do not."

"When you arrived on Skokholm Island in April of last year, what name were you using?"

"Thomas Weaver."

"If your name is Robert Kensley, why were you using the name of Thomas Weaver?"

Here we go, I thought. Our lies and deception back to bite us in the arse. Mark had advised Robert to answer Sperry's questions as directly and concisely as possible.

"Mattheu Vandermeer didn't allow visitors to the island, except there was a wildlife biologist he was letting come over to study the wild rabbits. I talked him out of going over there and took his place."

"How were you able to 'talk him out of going'?"

I shook my head and wondered if Robert was in danger of prosecution himself, some sort of "obtaining by deception" charges. He had lied outrageously about Vandermeer to Thomas Weaver, but Vandermeer was certainly not in a position to press charges of slander.

Robert took a deep breath, obviously trying to maintain his composure. "I said some things to him about Vandermeer, which weren't true, and he decided to go back to London."

"So you became Thomas Weaver so you could go back to the island."

"Yes."

"Why did you want to go back there so badly?"

Robert's obsession with the island was something we'd discussed many times, and I knew it had to do with his desire to regain the happiness of his childhood. I also knew he would never disclose this in a courtroom—he was aware that his sentimentality would seem foolish.

"I wanted to visit Morwenn. She had been my nanny when I was a child."

Still too mushy, I thought. All that trouble to visit a nanny—the jury would never believe him. But there was no rational answer to Sperry's question.

"In your interview, you stated that you 'found an Iron Cross in Mattheu Vandermeer's desk drawer.' What reason would you have had to be going through Vandermeer's personal possessions?"

"I was looking for my camera."

"In his desk drawer?" Sperry's voice exuded sarcasm.

"My camera disappeared. I thought he might have taken it."

"What did you do, Mr. Kensley, when you found this Iron Cross?"

"I wrote a letter to my grandfather in London, asking his advice."

"Is it true that your grandfather once owned the island of Skokholm?"

"Yes."

"And you wanted to go back there so badly, you lied about who you were, in order to do so."

Robert, of course, could not deny it. Here it comes, I thought. Fasten your seatbelts, ladies and gentlemen. Sperry's going to crash the car.

"Did you ever consider the possibility that if Vandermeer were a fugitive Nazi and could be charged with some past offense and gotten out of the way, you could have your island back?"

Robert could tell a lie here. Sperry's only asking the

question to put it in the minds of the jurors, and we all know he has no proof.

Robert pulled his shoulders back, but I could see the strain in his face. "No," he said.

"Did you receive a letter from the defendant?"

"I did."

"What did she say in this?"

"That she wanted to investigate Mattheu Vandermeer."

"How did you help her do this, since Vandermeer didn't allow any visitors to the island?"

"I talked Morwenn into pretending that her back was out, so she'd need help with things, so Vandermeer would agree to let her cousin come."

"Katya Denys was Morwenn Madoc's cousin?"

"No."

"But you told him she was?"

"Yes."

"So Morwenn agreed to this deception so that Katya could investigate her employer?"

I crossed my arms. The hole gets deeper by the minute.

"She didn't know. I told her Katya was my girlfriend."

"So you lied, not only to Vandermeer, but also to your former nanny." If Sperry were allowed to pace the floor of the courtroom, he would be strutting like a rooster.

The questions were taking their toll on Robert. His eyes moved round the courtroom, but he wouldn't look at me.

"What name did Miss Denys use, when she came to the island?"

"I introduced her as Katherine Dennis."

"One final question," Sperry said. "Were you present on the island when Vandermeer was killed?"

"No, I was in Marloes."

"What were you doing there?"

"Katya had sent me over to the mainland with a letter. She said it needed to be mailed as soon as possible."

There, we were both cooked, as liars and deceivers of the first order. No one would believe a thing that came out of my mouth, if I decided to testify in my own defense.

Mark Wickham stood up, in an attempt to mitigate the damage. "You mentioned, Mr. Kensley, that Mattheu Vandermeer did not allow visitors to the island. Did that include relatives of Morwenn Madoc, his housekeeper?"

"That's correct."

"Did that strike you as odd?"

"Yes, it did."

"When did your camera go missing?"

"A few hours after I took a snap of Vandermeer."

"Did you ever find the camera?"

"No."

"You stated that Miss Denys wrote to you because she wanted to investigate Mattheu Vandermeer. Was there anything in her behavior or actions that ever made you think she might want revenge, for any reason?"

"No."

"No further questions."

* * *

That evening, after Robert left my cell, I lay on my bunk and studied the ceiling—tired of thinking, tired of trying to decide what to do, tired of existing, blocked into a corner, a place of exile, because of my choices. The only way out was to back up, to return to what I was before, but was it possible to go back and untangle the snarled threads of my life? There was far too much time on my hands in the Welsh prison. I realized that all my decisions had been motivated by reasons that had only to do with myself—even the dialogue with Emil Janisch, the confrontation in the name of my sister—that was for me. What need had Rebekah, no longer in the realm of the living, of revenge or even answers from the man who killed her? It is only the living from whom the truth is veiled. I had come to believe that all would be revealed, answers given to unspoken questions, at the moment of death. Rebekah needed nothing from Emil Janisch. I realized I might be years from that enlightenment, as I looked ahead at the hours of my future.

There were dark mornings when awakening from sleep seemed so cruel. Because I had lost all self-esteem, I couldn't see my value to society, even if by some miracle, I were released. I thought I might be able to survive, if only the sun would come out, and I could watch it move in the small space of my window, remembering how it used to shine on the waters of the ocean.

THE TELLING OF SECRETS

Two days after my testimony, I found Katya lying on her bunk, staring at the ceiling. She turned her head to look at me. "When I went outside today, in the exercise yard just before dusk, I watched a hawk circle in the air. I wondered what it would feel like to float on the air like that. If I could fly," she said, "I could just take off and leave all this behind." She sat up and spread her arms wide to indicate the small space to which she was confined.

I stood against the metal bars of her cell, feeling them dig into my back, and I wondered what had happened. She had seemed calm, almost indifferent, before. "You were doing so well."

"It's easy for you to say that I'm doing well," she said. "You're not trapped here, and you're not inside my head."

She avoided my eyes, fingering the cuff of her white shirt.

"I've admired your courage," I said.

Her voice was bitter. "My courage has always had

more to do with hatred than with bravery—something my mother never would have understood. The courage of Stephania Denys was unselfish—it had to do with taking care of her husband and her children, fulfilling the requirements of her faith. If I had an ounce of any kind of courage, I'd kill myself."

"No, you don't mean that." I looked down at the palms of my hands, where perspiration had broken through. I thought about my mother's suicide in prison. "You don't know how many people you would hurt."

She stood up. "Name five people who would even care if I died."

"Me," I said. "Aaron, of course, and Mark Wickham and all those people you told me about, whose testimony you recorded."

"I'll never see any of those people again."

"Every action," I said, "has its effects."

"What's made you the expert, here?"

"My mother killed herself when I was three months old, so I never knew her. You don't think that's affected me?" I approached Katya and took hold of her hands. "Promise me you won't try to hurt yourself."

"I told you I didn't have the courage to do it. It's just driving me mad, though, to think that I might spend the rest of my life in prison, because I wouldn't let Emil Janisch kill me. I have to sit there in the courtroom, knowing that he should be the one on trial. I have to listen to people like Morwenn who paint a picture of him as a saint, and I know it's not true, but I have nothing that will stand up in court. She portrays both you and me as liars. I know she'd like to see me hang."

"Why don't you testify? Why don't you just tell the truth?"

Katya looked at me like I was an imbecile. "You are so naïve, you know nothing. Why do you think they would believe me?"

"Maybe people have more compassion than you think."

Again, she looked up at the ceiling. "You should try walking in my shoes for a day or two, living with my memories. You and your warm grandfather and your American boarding school."

I turned away from her. She had never been so hostile before, even on the island, and I felt the heat rising in my cheeks. I wanted to say to her that I'd never met anyone with a bigger chip on her shoulder.

She touched my arm. "I'm sorry, Robert. You didn't deserve that. It's just that I'm afraid of the future." I turned around and saw the terror in her eyes as she said, "Here in prison, in the daytime, I feel safe. But at night, I dream they put the noose round my neck and drop the trap door from under my feet."

I had told very few people about the deaths of my parents—it's not something I'm proud of. But the fact that Katya was thinking about suicide frightened me. That evening, I sat beside her, holding her hand, and I told her how my parents had died, as if that would somehow protect her, if I exposed this painful secret. I suppose, also, that her remark about the warm grandfather and the boarding school had stung me, and I wanted to show her that my life had not been as carefree and perfect as she imagined.

I've often wondered if I was in the house when it

happened. Surely, I was. Where else would I have been? My father would have been too surprised to scream when my mother drove the fireplace poker into his chest. But I'm sure the woman in his bed would have screamed bloody murder. Did I hear that? My parents had only married because my mother was pregnant with me, and they were far too young. In January of 1930, my mother found my father in bed with our landlady and went crazy. She stabbed my father, missing the major arteries, but he died six days later from a massive infection. My mother hung herself during that first night in jail, twisting her nylon slip into a noose.

Although I had no complaints about my grandfather and Morwenn as substitute parents, I often wondered what a normal childhood would have been like, with a mother and a father and perhaps a sister or brother. As a child, I loved books about orphans like Oliver Twist and Heidi.

My grandfather had kept this story of my parents from me, hoping to shield me from the stigma of it. When I was six years old, I pulled the newspaper clipping from the back of the family Bible, where someone had preserved it, as if being saved there in the holy book could somehow alter the deed or sanctify it.

I had learned to read at the age of five. At six years of age, I knew how to spell my full name: Robert Charles Kensley. When I saw the name "Charles William Kensley" in the first line of the newspaper article, I took the piece of paper to my grandfather. William sat down heavily in his chair and pulled me close to him for a moment, his hand resting on my head.

Then he smiled and said, "Robert, I know you are a brave boy." I was relieved, because finally I would be allowed to hear the truth about my father and mother. I sat down on the floor at my grandfather's feet. I had been told only that my father was very sick and had died in hospital. Grandfather and Morwenn both told me that my mother died of a broken heart, but I had never believed this.

Grandfather held the newspaper clipping in his hand, covering it with his other hand, and he told me what it said because he knew it by heart. That way he could explain it to me, try to soften the hard edges. How can the fact that your mother killed your father and herself be explained gently?

The clipping disappeared from the Bible. I checked more than once, but I didn't find it until two years later, in Grandfather's desk drawer under a ledger. By that time, I was able to read the entire clipping myself, and I was able to sense, at that tender age, that the whole thing had been such a scandal—that's why my grandfather had left London. As a prominent figure in London, he would have been crucified by the press, except for his own newspaper, *The London Daily Times*, which had printed the sanitized version I found in the Bible.

But I never knew my parents at all, so how can it be such a tragedy? It was like they had never existed. I didn't know what they looked like, how their voices sounded, even what they liked to eat. I wonder if anything from my parents imprinted itself on me in the first months of my life. Katya, at least, has pictures of her family in her mind. Whether this is a blessing or a curse, I don't know.

THE WARSAW GHETTO

The storm has passed—my ranting about killing myself was only to let off steam, but I know it upset Robert. This place can be like a pressure-cooker. With no distractions, I let things build up until I have to explode. I can write things in the journal until I'm exhausted, but there's nothing like a good scream every now and then. Of course, I can't scream here, but I can rant and rave with poor Robert as an audience, and it's almost as good.

I try to imagine whether it would be worse to never know your parents or to have a perfect childhood and then lose everything. I have a lot of time to think, these days, so I consider things from every angle. I flip the question from parents to children. Would it be more painful for a woman who wanted children to be unable to conceive or for a woman who had a child to lose it? The first question, about parents, is more real for me than the second, of which I've had no personal experience.

Robert and I could sit and play an "oh, poor me" game until the end of time. We both have our scars, and I try not to trivialize his experience just because mine seems more dramatic. I know I've made comments to him in the past about this, and I feel awful when I remember. The truth is that although I've lost them all—I can't hug them or talk to them and have them answer back—I still had them for a while. What kind of person would I be without knowing Papa? He was just a quiet carpet-maker who loved books and learning more than life itself, but because of his calm nature, I can sometimes find peace in this solitude. And Mama, so different in personality from Papa, but so good for him, so good for all of us. She was small—barely five feet—but she showed us how to be strong and loving at the same time. Our home was a haven of extended family, good food, music, and books. In our community, everyone seemed happy in his role. Perhaps I saw everything with the starry eyes of a young girl, but I knew that I was truly blessed.

I had once told Robert about this part of my life, the only part I was willing to share at the time. "My life as a child," I'd said to him, "centered round my family. My strongest memories are of the Sabbath." Even now, I can close my eyes and see the candles flickering in the house on Zlota Street and smell the *challah* my mother had just baked. "Sometimes, Mama would start getting ready for the Sabbath as early as Thursday evening. I remember her making the *challah*, which is much like other bread except it's braided. Since no work could be done on the Sabbath, there was much to do on Fridays to get ready. Sometimes, I took the Sabbath chicken to be slaughtered in the kosher way."

"How is that done?" Robert had asked.

"It has to be blessed by the rabbi and the blood drained out. I would also help peel carrots or potatoes or cook lima beans. I loved it when Mama made *tcholent*. I know, what is it? A wonderful dish—potatoes stuffed with meat. It would simmer all Friday night in the oven."

"This is making me hungry. Why don't you cook these things for us?"

"Think about it for a minute, Robert. Those are Jewish dishes. Do you think I want to plant that idea in Vandermeer's head?"

"I see what you mean. Go ahead with your story."

"It's not a story. This was my life for twelve years."

"Tell me more about your Sabbath."

"Long before the first evening star appeared, we would put on our best clothes."

Robert had grinned. "What? No ritual for dressing?"

I lifted my eyebrows. "Fine, if you must know, each of us would take a pan of heated water to some private part of the house and bathe carefully before we dressed."

His face turned red, which made me smile.

"On Friday evening, all the men—my father, my brother Patryk and my grandfather—went to services at the synagogue. Meanwhile, at home, my sister Rebekah and I would watch as Mama, with a scarf over her head, lit the Sabbath eve candles and prayed over them. When the men came back, Mama served the meal. On special occasions, our parlor was the dining room. We had a huge carved table—it was beautiful. Mama put on a spotless white cloth, and she always set out the two *challahs* and a bottle of wine, with a silver goblet at Papa's place.

"After Papa blessed the wine, he would wash his hands

and then bless the *challah.* The first course was fish, and the head, which was a delicacy, was served to my father, but he would share part of it with Patryk. He started this after Patryk's bar mitzvah. You know what a bar mitzvah is?"

"Yes."

"After the fish, I would help Mama carry in chicken soup, along with meat and vegetables. During the meal, we sang table hymns. For dessert, we would have fresh fruit and then tea and some sort of cake. On the high holy days, we had honey cake."

"Why honey cake?"

"Honey cake, to remind us of the sweetness of freedom . . . " I had been unable to finish the sentence, remembering all that happened later and all that had been lost.

Four days before my twelfth birthday, our world turned upside down. My life changed so dramatically, in such a way that I could not have foreseen nor would I have wanted to. In one defining moment, my existence splintered into life before and life after. I'd been sitting in front of the dressing table mirror in my bedroom, trying to inch a comb through the tangles in my shoulder-length hair. When the comb snagged on a knot, I threw it down on the dressing table and began to separate the strands of hair with my fingers. If I'd listened to Mama, I thought, I would have braided my hair last night. Now I'll be late for school. I heard the boom of thunder, and I remember thinking, if it's going to rain, my hair's going to frizz anyway, so there's no point in trying to do anything with it. Pulling the curtain aside, I saw fire and smoke on the outskirts of Warsaw. I couldn't take my eyes away from the flames. A strange, high-pitched sound startled me, just before an explosion that knocked me to the floor. I scrambled up and ran downstairs to the living room, where Mama was already kneeling on the floor in front of the radio, adjusting the black knobs, but all we could hear was crackling and the steady hum of static. Rebekah sat next to Papa on the couch, with her head on his shoulder, and when more bombs exploded, she screamed and put her hands over her ears.

"What will become of us?" Papa said. His voice was thick with fear.

My fifteen-year-old brother, Patryk, stood by the window. "They're German planes, of course," he said. "I can see the markings on the sides."

"I've stored food and water and candles," Mama said, as she stood on tiptoes to close the last set of curtains in the living room. "Patryk, come away from that window. We need to go down into the basement."

The bombing continued for twenty-six days. When the Nazis rolled into Warsaw with their tanks and their troops, they handed out bread to the starving citizens. But living conditions deteriorated rapidly, especially for Jews, as our rights and properties were stripped away one by one.

On Yom Kippur, I stood beside Rebekah in our living room, since we were no longer allowed to attend the synagogue. My eyes were closed, and in my imagination I could taste the *challah* that Mama had baked the day before. I listened to Papa read from the book of Jonah, but with another part of my mind, I searched my memory and my knowledge of history and found nothing for which my people should have to atone.

"Then Jonah prayed unto the Lord his God out of the fish's belly, and said, I cried by reason of mine affliction unto the Lord, and he heard me: out of the belly of hell cried I, and thou heardst my voice . . ."

The front door opened, and Aunt Bella said, "Mikolai." She was flushed and breathing hard.

"Couldn't it wait?" Papa said to her. "We're in the middle of services for Yom Kippur. Why don't you join us?"

"No," she said. "It can't wait. It's too important."

Papa pulled the white prayer shawl off his head.

"The Nazis have made the ghetto official," Bella said. "In two weeks, all Jews must be inside the fenced area, and all Christians outside. No Jews can leave the area without a work pass."

"Why don't the Nazis just call it by its real name?" Patryk said. "It's not a ghetto—it's a prison."

Mama was calm and practical as always. "This should be no great surprise," she said. "Since April, Jews have been made to give both materials and labor to build the ghetto walls."

Now we would become refugees. I looked to Papa for guidance, but he only stared at the wall, stroking his beard, lost in his own thoughts. "We're outside the boundaries, Papa. Where will we go?" He didn't answer me.

"I've already spoken to our parents," Aunt Bella said. "You'll move in with us."

Rebekah started to cry, and I thought she was upset about having to share a room with her cousins.

"I don't want to leave here," Rebekah said. "I love our house."

I hugged her and said, "Just think. Now you can see Grandma Lidia every day."

Mama was already mapping out a plan of action. "We must hire a wagon tomorrow to start moving our things."

I watched Papa's face, knowing that he did not cope well with change. He said nothing, but the despair showed in his eyes.

Patryk's face was flushed, his whole body tensed, as if he wanted to spring into action. "Those thieves," he said. "They're stealing everything from us. Soon, we will have only our lives, and when the time comes, they will take them also."

I was frightened by the thought of being confined to one area of Warsaw, of not being able to come and go as I pleased, although we had lost much of our freedom the day the Nazis marched into the city.

Mama said quietly, "They deliberately chose our holiest day to make this announcement."

"There is one thing they cannot steal," Papa said, and he reached out to touch Patryk's hand. "They can never take our faith." He draped the prayer shawl over his head and motioned for Patryk to sit beside him. Together, they continued the reading of the book of Jonah. I knew that Papa, moving as if in a dream, would be sustained by the ritual, the familiar words that kept him connected to the God of his fathers.

* * *

In the Warsaw Ghetto, we were no longer allowed to own stores, and we could not legally buy goods from non-

Jews. Starvation was rampant, and every morning, bodies were collected by the Jewish Burial Society. Patryk, like other teenagers and children in the ghetto, formed a smuggling operation in order to help feed our extended family, which included our grandparents, our aunt, and her four young children. Because of Patryk's fair coloring, he could pass as Aryan when he removed the armband identifying him as a Jew. He and Teodor and Stefan would scale the wall in the cemetery and drop down into the Aryan sector of Warsaw, where food was available for a price. He would return with his pockets bulging, with cabbages and potatoes and whatever else he'd been able to get.

One evening, when Patryk didn't come back at his usual time, I sat with my parents in the living room, and there was total silence. The only light was a small lamp beside Papa's chair. A book was open in his lap, but for half an hour, his hand lay across the same two pages, and he looked only at the front door and occasionally at Mama, who would not return his gaze.

"He is on his way back now," Mama said. "I know he is." We heard a soft tap on the door, and no one moved. It was as if we hoped to stop time in that instant. If we didn't answer the door, Patryk would be all right, and we could keep waiting for him to come home. Finally, I got up from the sofa and walked to the door. I looked back at my parents, who stood together now in front of the sofa, and I could see the pallor of their faces in the dim light, as my father nodded.

As soon as I opened the door and saw Stefan and Teodor, Patryk's friends in the smuggling ring, I knew he was dead. I motioned for them to come inside, and I closed the door. Teodor held his cap in his hands, and he looked at the clock, at the light, at the window—anything to keep from making eye contact with Mama. He started to say something, but I could barely hear him as I slumped against the front door. He finally said to Mama, "You should sit down."

She fell backwards onto the sofa, crying out Patryk's name in a long wail. I had never seen Mama cry like that, and I sat on the floor, across the room, feeling as if there were no longer any strength in my arms or legs.

"Hush, Stephania," my father said gently. "Let him speak." He motioned for the boys to sit down, and then he touched Mama's face, holding her in his arms as if to protect her from what we knew would follow. Mama sat up with her eyes closed and brushed the tears from her cheeks.

"On our way back from the Aryan sector," Teodor said, "Patryk was ahead of us, the first to go over the wall. I was almost to the top myself when we heard the machine guns. I dropped back into the Aryan cemetery, and Stefan and I hid there for two hours, until we no longer heard German voices. Then we climbed over the wall and found Patryk." Teodor put his hands over his eyes, and Stefan sat with tears streaming down his face. "I'm so sorry," Teodor said. "I'm so sorry."

Mama's scream echoed through the silence of the small room, and she stumbled out. A few seconds later, we heard the sound of violent retching from the bathroom down the hall. I ran to hold Mama's damp forehead over the toilet as she vomited again and again, and I had to bathe her face with cold water to stop her screams when the vomiting was over. From the living room, we heard Papa's deep voice beginning the Kaddish: "Magnified and sanctified be His great name in the world which He created according to his will."

Mama rushed out of the bathroom and said to Papa, "We don't even have a minyan to say the Kaddish."

"Stephania, we have no time to wait until the day comes and the first star appears. I no longer know what will be from day to day." I could see him struggle to remain calm. "This is the time we have, these are the people who are here." And he began again, reaching to touch the shoulder of Teodor, as he motioned to Stefan. As the voices of the two young men blended, following Papa and Grandpa Herzl, in recitation of the Kaddish for Patryk, I stood with my arms round my mother, who wept silently. "And may He establish His kingdom during your life and during your days and during the life of all the house of Israel, speedily and in the near future, and say Amen." Although I knew that my father had re-affirmed his faith in God through repetition of the Kaddish, I did not hear him speak again for a week, except for once.

Two days after Patryk's death, I told Mama I was going to take Patryk's place in the smuggling ring. She was furious. "No, no, you will not do this." She wouldn't look at me. "Mikolai," she said, "tell her, she will not do this thing."

I touched my mother's face. "We have no more food, so you must give me your blessing. I have no choice."

Stephania shook her head. "I cannot lose another child."

"I have to go. I won't sit and watch us all starve." I put on my coat, buttoned it with fingers that would not work properly.

As I opened the door to leave, I heard Papa's voice, and it seemed far away. "Please be careful, my Katya. I have only two children left."

A few weeks later, I came into the house and closed the door. I threw an empty sack on the floor, pulled two more empty sacks out of my baggy trousers and shook out my hair from the knitted cap that had concealed it.

"You should be happy now," I said to Mama. "No more smuggling."

Stephania got up from her chair. "What has happened?"

"They have German guards with police dogs in the cemetery, so we can't get over the wall."

"What will we do?" she said. "Mikolai, did you hear what she said?"

He sighed and looked down at his hands. "What do you want me to do? Can I conjure up bread and vegetables out of the air?"

Stephania said, "I have two pounds of dry beans hidden in the pantry," and then she said very firmly, as if saying this gave it truth, "We will make them last."

"How long can all of us survive on two pounds of beans, Mama?" I knew the question was also the answer.

"I'll make a thin soup, lots of water. Maybe it can last a week or two if we stretch it out. What I would give for just one onion or a carrot!"

That afternoon I sat on the bathroom floor with my eyes closed, my hands over my mouth to keep from screaming. As the faucet dripped erratically in the sink above my head, my empty stomach rumbled, and I saw in my mind the roving bands of street children, emaciated and ragged. I wondered if I would see my fifteenth birthday.

A few days later, I stood in the street with everyone else, reading the proclamation over and over so I could repeat it to my father, who hadn't left the house since Patryk's death. "All Jews qualified for labor are exempt from deportation and may remain in the ghetto; those Jews who were not heretofore included in the labor force may henceforth be included. They will be taken to barracks where they will work." We were all to be deported.

All that was left of my world was now gone, and I hardened myself again. I lived as if I did not inhabit my body. I did not really live in that flesh but stood apart and watched that young woman become a stranger. After we could no longer get food, I had stopped wondering how things could get worse.

One day, I went with Mama and Papa to the common grave where we thought Patryk might have been buried, where the only distinction given to corpses was separation by sex. We left Rebekah with my grandparents and Aunt Bella. When we returned, everyone was gone, and the house was wrecked, with furniture knocked out of place or broken and the precious photograph of Grandma Lidia's mother thrown to the floor with such force that glass shards had ripped the photograph.

My parents ran from room to room, frantic. I slipped into a state of disbelief where I felt only a vague anxiety—surely this was happening to someone else. I followed Mama and Papa as they walked silently over to our neighbor's house. At first, Marysia wouldn't open the door, but then she pulled the three of us inside and locked the door. Her eyes were red and swollen from crying. "They took my father," she said to Papa, "and your parents and Bella's children. All the old people and children from this block." Marysia put her hand to her mouth. "Bella was screaming. She wouldn't let go of the baby, but they hit her in the head and pulled the child from her arms when she fell. With blood on her hands and face, Bella got up and ran to the baby and she went with them."

"What about Rebekah?" I asked her, and I tasted blood from having bitten my tongue.

"They wouldn't let her find her birth certificate to show she was old enough. They said she was too small to work."

Mama slumped against Papa, who put his hand under her elbow and guided her out of Marysia's house. I stayed behind to hug Marysia, and then I heard a baby crying in the other room. "By the grace of God," Marysia said, "he was asleep when the Nazis came. I put him in Mother's wooden trunk, and he stayed asleep and quiet." Her eyes filled with tears. "I don't know how much longer I can keep him hidden.

The spacious home of Grandma Lidia was empty with only the three of us—so quiet, except for Mama's keening for her youngest daughter. She had lost two children now, besides her husband's family, and this time she would not be comforted. When Papa tried to touch her, she screamed and knocked his hands away. I was more frightened than I had ever been in my life, so I stayed busy by straightening the furniture and making piles of damaged items. Mama sobbed and screamed and wailed for half an hour. Papa eventually gave up and withdrew in silence into his own grief. Exhausted from her outburst, Mama lay quietly on the sofa for a while, then got up slowly and walked over to my father, kneeling to kiss his hands. "They are all alive," she said, "and they are together somewhere, looking out for each other." We coped by denying the truth.

After the deportation notice was posted, six thousand Jews were taken on the first day. The smell of fear permeated the ghetto. Rather than sign the death warrants for his people, the head of the Jewish council, Adam Czerniakow, committed suicide.

"We'll get jobs," I told Mama, "in the Toebbens uniform factory. You and I, we'll go tomorrow."

"You need a machine to get a job there," she said. "We have no machines."

"Patryk buried two sewing machines last year. I know where they are—I'll dig them up after dark."

Mama's eyes filled with tears. "Where did he get sewing machines?"

"He was very practical—like you, Mama. He traded for them on the black market."

She started crying, and Papa walked in and asked what was wrong. Mama looked up at him. "Our son buried sewing machines last year. Now Katya and I can get jobs at the factory. But what about you, my darling? Katya, I can't leave your father."

"No," he told her, "you must go, both of you, to get jobs in the factory. I will think of some way to escape the Jew hunters."

When we got home the next day from the uniform factory, we couldn't find Papa. "They've taken your father," Mama said. "They have quotas every day, six thousand more Jews, or they'll be put on the next train themselves."

I walked into my parents' bedroom, the room with the high ceiling on the corner of the house. I never knew what made me open the door to the cupboard. He was hanging from the ceiling of it, and I will never forget how his face looked—swollen, discolored, and grotesque. How could he do such a thing, knowing that Mama and I would find him! I could never forgive what I took to be an act of cowardice, a way to escape deportation. Mama lay in the bedroom with the curtains drawn, on top of the bedspread, for three days, refusing food. She drank small, reluctant sips of water only when I forced her. Mama saw no reason to continue living—it was too soon after Patryk's death and the loss of her daughter and her in-laws. Knowing that it was sinful, I cursed my father—how could he not have known what his death would do to Mama? I stayed with her day and night for fear that she, too, would try to harm herself.

Now Mama made no sound when she cried, but tears ran from the corners of her eyes, and I would find the pillow soaked. One afternoon, she turned to me and reached out to touch my face. "You don't cry for your father," she said, her voice as soft as her hand. I could only stare at the patterns in the carpet—there were no words to express my anger.

NICOLAAS

I couldn't help thinking about what Katya had said. Why the hell had I told her about my mother's suicide? The last thing I wanted to do was give her ideas. That night, I tossed and turned until the sheets were wound about my legs like a mummy's wrappings. What kept coming back to me—slapping me in the face—was Emil Janisch's "confession." It had seemed so credible at the time, how Mattheu Vandermeer had killed the Nazi who killed his pregnant wife. The more I thought about this, the more I cursed my own gullibility. "Vandermeer" had supposedly kept the Iron Cross to remind himself of his guilt. What tosh! No wonder Katya had been so angry with me. Because I grew up in such isolation, I hadn't learned to read people that well. Often, I missed the telltale facial expressions and body language that signaled lying. I tended to be more optimistic than cynical and would, in most instances, give people the benefit of the doubt. Although some people would accuse me of being an accomplished liar myself, I say that I like to entertain people by stretching the truth to make a good story. If I have to lie, I never do it without what I consider a bloody good reason, and I will never lie merely to save face.

I slept only a few hours that night—an hour or an hour and a half at a time. I woke up at 5 a.m. with the thought that I should go to Amsterdam. If I investigated Janisch's lie, perhaps I could discover the truth. If I found something in Amsterdam that would help in Katya's defense, perhaps she would forgive me. I wished to God that I could be worthy of her affection.

* * *

During my first morning in Amsterdam, I spent an hour copying down names and addresses of all the Vandermeers listed in the telephone directory. The first address was near the train station. I knocked on the door of the small, neat house, and a woman answered. She was about sixty-five years old with blue eyes in a round, friendly face. "*Ja*?" she said.

"I am looking for information about a man named Mattheu Vandermeer. He was a minister of the Dutch Reformed church in the early '40's."

The smile faded, and she shook her head. She seemed agitated as she shut the door in my face. It may have been that she didn't speak English.

At the second address, my reception was slightly less chilly when I mentioned Mattheu Vandermeer's name. "Mattheu Vandermeer?" the man asked. He was in his early thirties, heavy-set with a pale, high forehead. "He was a cousin on my father's side of the family. We lost track of him in '44—there was so much going on then. I heard later that he'd been killed."

"Do you know how he died?"

"No, I don't." He paused and looked up at the ceiling, as if searching his memory. "I think his son still lives here, but I don't remember his name."

The third name on my list was Cecilius Vandermeer, who lived on the outskirts of the red-light district. When I asked him if he spoke English, he grinned, revealing nearly toothless gums, and motioned for me to come in, saying, "Yes, yes, please." Cecilius looked to be close on eighty years of age, and he still had a full head of white hair. Cataracts clouded his eyes, but he got round well in his own house. He invited me to sit down at his kitchen table and insisted on serving me coffee. "Yes, I knew Mattheu Vandermeer well. He was a brave and foolish man, getting himself killed like that."

"What happened to him?"

"Nicolaas told me his father went after the Nazi bastard who killed his wife."

I could not believe my good fortune. "He had a son named Nicolaas?"

"Yes."

"Is he still here in Amsterdam?"

"No," he said.

My heart sank, and I was afraid that he might have died.

"He lives on the outskirts of town."

"How far?"

"About thirty miles from here."

* * *

I found Nicolaas and told him about the man who had called himself Mattheu Vandermeer. Nicolaas told me what he knew about his father's death. He was eager to meet the woman who had killed Emil Janisch and had readily agreed to go back to Carmarthen with me. However, my first priority was to convince Morwenn that the man she had loved was not Mattheu Vandermeer, but Emil Janisch. I wanted her to give up the journal that I knew she must have taken.

I took Nicolaas to Morwenn's sister's house in Marloes, and Catrin invited us inside. I introduced him as Mattheu Vandermeer's son.

"I don't understand," Morwenn said.

She looked at me. "Robert, what are you trying to do?"

I could see her doing the calculations in her head. He'd have been about fourteen years old in 1946, when Vandermeer first arrived on Skokholm. Nicolaas sat forward in the chair, his eyes fixed on the clock above Catrin's fireplace. I watched Morwenn studying his face for a resemblance to Mattheu. The coloring was right—the blue eyes and sun-bleached hair—but not the bone structure. This young man with the high cheekbones had a delicate quality in his face that Mattheu Vandermeer lacked.

I said to Nicolaas, "I want you to tell Morwenn what you told me."

"Please, my English is not good." He smiled; his teeth were white and perfectly formed. "My father is the only Vandermeer named Mattheu in Amsterdam. In 1945, he was killed, I think, by a man named Emil Janisch."

Morwenn looked as if the breath had been knocked out of her.

VIEW FROM SPY ROCK

Mark Wickham called back the coroner as the first witness in my defense. Before rising, Mark Wickham took off his reading glasses and rubbed his forehead. "Dr. Thompson, would you please read out the fourth paragraph on page two."

"The victim had an old, well-healed eight-centimeter scar on the left seventh rib. A seven-centimeter scar was noted in the right lower quadrant of the abdomen, suggesting previous removal of the appendix. A scar on the right kneecap of four centimeters. Under the left arm was a small scar, approximately one centimeter by three centimeters."

Richard Thompson looked up from the report and ran one finger between his shirt collar and his generous neck, as if the collar were too tight.

"One more question, Dr. Thompson. How common is the blood type AB?"

"It's the rarest of all four blood types."

"And did you type Mattheu Vandermeer's blood?"

He paged through the autopsy report. "Yes, sir, I did—it was AB."

Mark sat down at the barristers' table. "I have no questions, M'lord."

"Does the Crown want to cross-examine?"

"No, M'lord."

"Then the defense may call its next witness."

Judith Rittmueller was a tall, middle-aged woman, big-boned and solid, who moved with a surprising amount of grace. She smoothed the skirt of her well-cut black skirt with a manicured hand and then touched the tight curls of her permed red hair. In her other hand, she clutched a pair of reading glasses.

Mark Wickham smiled at her. "Thank you for coming down on such short notice, Miss Rittmueller. Can you tell us where you live?"

"Here in Carmarthen." Her voice was faint, much too small for her size.

"Could you speak just a bit louder, please?" Mark said to her.

She smiled.

"How long have you lived here?"

"My family come to Wales in 1921 from Germany. I am twenty years old then."

"So German was your first language?"

"*Ja*, I speak only German first twenty years of my life."

"Miss Rittmueller, were you acquainted with the deceased, known as Mattheu Vandermeer?"

"I know only his name and that he owns the

island."

"Do you know the defendant, Katya Denys?"

"No, I do not."

Mark Wickham walked to the evidence table and returned with a sheet of paper, which he handed to Judith Rittmueller. "In what language is this written?"

I turned round slightly to see if Robert was in the visitors' gallery, but he was not in his usual place.

Judith Rittmueller looked at the page for a moment. "It is German."

"I will need to have you translate the whole page for us." My mouth was dry. How well I knew that page, having read it so many times since I first took it from Janisch's file. Each fact, each number, was burned into my memory.

"Begin now?" Judith Rittmueller asked.

"If you please."

She put on her glasses and opened the file. "Date of record," she read in a clear voice, "eighth of June, 1940. Name: Emil Janisch; Rank: Captain, SS Number 11698." Mark Wickham, at the defense table, jotted down notes as she read. "Height: 179 cm; weight: 77 Kg.; head circumference: 57 cm; hair color: medium brown; eye color: light blue; shoe size: 9; Nazi party membership number: 778784." She glanced up at Mark Wickham, who nodded. "Identifying scars and marks: a scar of eight centimeters parallel to the left seventh rib. Also a scar of 4 cm on right kneecap. Tattoo under left arm with blood type, AB." I crossed my arms. The Nazis' love of detail had been so helpful in the identification process. Too bad Janisch had cut off the bit of skin under his arm with the blood type tattoo—it would have identified him with great precision.

Mark Wickham stood up, holding the sheet of paper with his notes, and nodded again to the witness. "Thank you very much, Miss Rittmueller. I would like to have the court stenographer read back the testimony from the coroner's report, regarding identifying marks and scars."

The stenographer read back the information: "The victim had an old, well-healed eight-centimeter scar on the left seventh rib. A seven-centimeter scar was noted in the right lower quadrant of the abdomen, suggesting previous removal of the appendix. A scar on the right kneecap of four centimeters. Under the left arm was a small scar, approximately one centimeter by three centimeters."

"No further questions."

Judith Rittmueller stepped down.

Mark Wickham then called to the stand Dr. Jakob Finster, an elderly physician with an unusual amount of wavy brown hair for his age, worn much longer than the other men in the courtroom, almost to his shoulders. His eyes were distinctive also—large and prominent, with a unique violet color. I remembered the letter from his office when I was investigating Janisch. Because of confidentiality, they would give no information beyond the fact that he was a plastic surgeon. I leaned forward slightly as Mark Wickham handed Dr. Finster a manila file folder. "In 1945, what kind of operation did you perform on a patient known to you as Mattheu Vandermeer?"

Dr. Finster opened the file and scanned the first page, holding it at arms' length. "I did a rhinoplasty, which is an alteration of the structure of the nose."

"Dr. Finster, does a rhinoplasty change a patient's appearance dramatically?"

"A rhinoplasty has the potential to change a patient's appearance dramatically. It all depends on the degree of surgical alteration."

This was a major change, I thought. Show them the before-and-after photographs.

"In your professional opinion, Doctor, did the surgery you performed on Mattheu Vandermeer's nose in 1945 make a drastic change in his appearance?"

"Yes."

"In what way?"

"Mattheu Vandermeer's nose was originally quite prominent—what could be called 'hawk-nosed.' I removed cartilage below the bridge of the nose so that the angle of the nose fell straight from the bridge to the tip with no outward bend."

Mark Wickham took a small photograph album from the evidence table. "I would like to direct the court's attention to a book of photographs taken by Dr. Finster—before and after photos of his patients." He handed the photograph album to Dr. Finster.

I looked out the window to my right. Did Finster know who Vandermeer really was and why he needed to change his appearance? Surely he did. Why else would Janisch have chosen a German surgeon?

"Are these photographs of patients upon whom you performed plastic surgery?

"Yes."

"How are the photographs labeled?" asked Mark Wickham.

"They have no name visible, in order to protect the confidentiality of my patients. The names are written in pencil on the back of the photograph, but the names cannot be viewed without removing the photograph from its plastic sleeve, since there is another photograph on the other side." Dr. Finster coughed. "I have also received permission from all these patients to display their photographs as needed in court."

"Would you please remove the photographs of Mattheu Vandermeer before and after his rhinoplasty?"

From the album, Dr. Finster removed two photographs, which he handed to the court clerk, who then passed them on to the jury. How could we prove that Mattheu Vandermeer had been Emil Janisch? He was already using his stolen name.

* * *

That evening, back in my cell, I waited for Robert, who always came on Tuesdays and Fridays. Had he forgotten? Was he ill?

I reviewed the day's testimony—the autopsy report and the SS file and Finster's photographs. Was it enough to convince the jury of Vandermeer's true identity? All we had was one matching scar and pictures of Vandermeer's nose job. Not exactly 'a trout in the milk,' as Morwenn would say.

I remembered the day on the island when I first saw the tiny scars on either side of Vandermeer's nose. One morning, after washing the breakfast dishes, I'd gone over to the farmhouse with my scrub brush, some rags, and a bucket of clean water. It was a beautiful day, and I hated the thought of being trapped inside by housework. I needed to wipe over the red floor in the entry and take out the fireplace ashes. I left the bucket and scrub brushes in the entry and entered the living room. Through the window, I saw flag irises beside a small pond. I swept the ashes from the fireplace into a metal dustpan, then emptied it into a box outside the front door, where Morwenn had asked me to save the ashes for the garden soil. I swept the entry floor between the bookcases, then sloshed a bit of water from the bucket and knelt on the floor to wipe it up with a clean rag. The front door opened, and I looked up to see Mattheu Vandermeer in the doorway, his long hair backlit by the sun. He surveyed the floor and stepped onto a patch that I had not yet cleaned. “You’re working much too hard, Katherine. Let’s take a half-holiday, and I’ll show you round the island.”

Still kneeling, I sat back on my heels with the wet rag in my hands and wondered what had prompted this unusual display of friendliness. With a clean corner of the rag, I rubbed at the black stains on my hands from the fireplace ashes, buying time. Did he suspect me? I stood up and walked over to the bucket of clean water where I rinsed my hands and dried them on my apron. No matter where we went on the island, Robert wouldn’t be too far away. I took off my apron and folded it, put it next to the bucket and stepped carefully over the patch of clean floor. Even though my heart was beating faster than normal, my voice was calm when I said to him, “I would like to see your island, Reverend Vandermeer.”

“That’s much too formal. Call me Mattheu.”

“All right.”

“Have you been up to the top of Spy Rock?”

"No, I haven't." I couldn't help being suspicious of the name "Spy Rock." Was this too much of a coincidence, or was I just being paranoid again?

"I'll show you the view from there." From the farmhouse, we walked alongside Morwenn's long, narrow cottage. I knew that Morwenn would see us, if she was sitting on her sofa looking out the window, and she would resent me even more. I wasn't comfortable with the whole situation.

We walked side by side on the path, my hair flying in the breeze, the cries of seabirds all round us. As we turned south, to follow the path toward Spy Rock, Vandermeer pointed out the shearwater burrows in front of the ancient dry stone wall to the left of the path. "Have you heard them at night, calling to their mates?" he said.

"Yes, I stood out here one night and listened for about half an hour, until I got too cold."

We continued on the path through bluebells and sea campion. Pointing to a shearwater carcass, Vandermeer said, "There's one that didn't make it past the greater black-backed gulls." His remark left a bad taste in my mouth. I wondered if there was any way I could avoid climbing to the top of the rock outcropping without arousing his suspicions, but I followed him up the well-worn path on the north face of Spy Rock and tried to keep my mind occupied, while still maintaining caution. As I watched his slender form ahead of me, I pictured Emil Janisch, whom I had seen only in full dress uniform, but who had been at least twenty pounds heavier, which would affect the contours of his face. Mattheu Vandermeer's face, even with the full beard, was more angular and lean, although it was difficult to assess its contours without seeing the line of the jawbone.

When we reached the top of the rock formation, we discovered a congregation of red-legged oystercatchers, mostly silent, and a pack of rowdy seagulls. I felt especially vulnerable, knowing he could turn on me at any moment and push me over the edge. "What's the elevation here?" I asked, and I began a silent chant. I am Morwenn's cousin. I am Morwenn's cousin, as if saying it enough would make it true. My knees felt weak.

"About fifty-four metres, or a hundred and seventy-five feet—that's measured from sea level."

I sat down on a flattened rock, facing South Haven and the cluster of white buildings, with Crab Bay behind us. I could see the landing platform at South Haven and the stone steps coming up from the water. Where the hell was Robert? This was a different vantage point from which to see the island, but I'd enjoy the view more if I weren't so suspicious of my tour guide.

Mattheu Vandermeer pointed out the islands of Skomer and Middleholm north of Skokholm and the mainland of Wales to the right. In that light, his eyes were navy blue, like the deepest parts of the ocean. I had never been that close, physically, to Emil Janisch, so the intricacies of subtle eye colors were irrelevant, and I knew that, but I couldn't keep from looking at his eyes, which drew me in, like those of a cobra.

Unhindered by buildings or trees, the wind was a brutal force at that high point of the island, and I had to keep brushing hair out of my mouth. "Where's Thomas today?" I asked, hoping that my uneasiness would not show.

"I sent him over to the mainland to pick up hardware for the shed." He pointed to the left, "Over there, you can see the path that used to be traveled by a horse pulling a cart. They'd load up at South Haven and haul supplies up to the lighthouse. Right down there, of course, is Crab Bay and to the southeast, which you can't really see from here, is the cove where the *Rebecca Hawkins* was found wrecked in 1928."

I barely heard the last sentence. In the harsh midday light, I'd caught a glimpse of a tiny scar on the side of his nose. I stared at his face. As he turned back toward me, I saw the scar's counterpart on the opposite side of his nose. It was difficult to concentrate on Skokholm's history and geography.

Vandermeer pivoted ninety degrees counterclockwise. "By all rights, North Haven should be way over there," he pointed toward the north with his left hand, "since South Haven is right here, but since there's no haven on the true north of Skokholm, it's a relative north and south."

Why should the scars on his nose disturb me so much? I already knew, but it felt safer to deny it. God help me, does he know who I am? Would Morwenn have betrayed me? Stay calm, and get down off this rock formation. "Where did it get the name Skokholm?" I asked him, trying to keep the tension out of my voice.

"There's a Scandinavian word—*skokkr.*" He spelled it out. "The hulk of a ship."

"Ah," I said and stood up, anxious to get moving again. We walked down from Spy Rock, placing our feet carefully on the path marked by white stones, as gulls overhead scolded with raucous calls, protecting their nests. I followed Vandermeer on the path toward the lighthouse and watched it flash toward us every ten seconds, as regular as the hands of a clock. Usually, I had trouble with my past at night, but on that day of bright sunshine, the lighthouse beam reminded me of the searchlights at Auschwitz. Don't, I told myself. Pretend you are a young carefree Englishwoman, and this man is a sunburned Dutch minister. Just make it through the day, and everything will be all right. I grabbed at clichés to squash down the panic and keep myself breathing.

"Were you interested in birds before you moved here?" I said, hoping that my voice would not betray me.

"No. But it's hard not to become a bird fancier when living amongst such an abundance of species."

I took a slow, deep breath. "What are your favorites?"

"I would have to say the puffins, for sheer entertainment value. And then, it's a close tie between the shearwaters and the storm petrels . . . the shearwaters because of their unique calls in the night and the stormies because of their diminutive size. However, I do have a particular fascination with cormorants." He paused beside the lighthouse, looking out to the ocean, where the Irish ferry passed in the distance.

I thought about the people on the ferry. Surely, they had normal lives, unlike this drama we were playing out. I could leave the island, as soon as Robert got back. I could go back to London and pretend to be an ordinary person. But I would always think about this man and my dream of seeing him on trial.

"You're very quiet," he said to me. "Is something wrong?"

In a fantasy world, I would confront him, here and now, with the truth. But the reality was that the two of us were virtually alone on an island, and if I slipped on the rocks, while looking at the view, it would be nothing more than a tragic accident. A normal person would continue the conversation.

"This is a beautiful place," I said, "but I don't see how you could live here for such a long time. Don't you ever feel the need to be with other people?" Speaking these words, I calmed myself. He stared out at the ocean, and I noticed tiny flecks of yellow in the irises of his eyes, which explained why they sometimes looked green.

"I don't need people much. I am happy with my books, my birds . . . " His voice trailed off. "Your cousin has been a good companion."

He looked at me. "What about you?" he asked. "Could you live in a place like this, windswept and desolate," he gestured at the island, "and yet so beautiful?"

"I'm used to being round more people."

"Well, yes, in London, I guess so," he said. "Now tell me how you're related to Morwenn. I'm assuming it's on your mothers' side because you have different last names."

His congeniality unnerved me, and I didn't want to play that game—that false recitation of Morwenn's family history as my own, because it would be too easy to stumble. My mouth tasted like salt. "Morwenn's mother Cadi and my mother Elen were sisters, two years apart.

My mother went off to London when she was seventeen, to go to university. She met my father there, Melvin Dennis, and they married when she was nineteen. She never came back to Wales, except for the funeral, when Cadi died."

"Is your mother still living?"

Our small talk was evil—it forced me to deny my family. I wanted to scream at him, my mother died in your gas chambers, you bastard, but I was a survivor, and I only smiled as I said, "Yes, she and my father are both in good health. They live in Sheffield, so I see them often. I've two older brothers, both in London, who have their own families." How easily the lies slipped off my tongue. The only bit of truth was when I added, "I have no sisters."

Later that evening, I knocked on Robert's door. After a moment, he opened it with his arms full of rumpled clothing. "Vandermeer said he sent you to buy hardware today," I said. "Did it seem like a legitimate errand?"

Robert motioned me inside and shoved the pile of dirty clothes under his bed.

I leaned against his desk, and Robert sat on the bed. "We couldn't do any more work on the shed without the new hardware. Why do you ask?"

"He wanted to show me round the island today, and I was on pins because you weren't about."

Robert smiled. "Was I to be your knight in shining armor if he got fresh?"

His naiveté, as always, irritated me. "No, Robert. I was more concerned with the very real possibility that he might have found out who I am and why I'm here."

"That would be dangerous only if he were really Emil

Janisch. You've never been sure of that."

"He has scars on either side of his nose—small, perfect scars which suggest very strongly that his nose has been altered. I can't see why an ordinary man—a humble clergyman from Amsterdam—would need to have that done." I paused. "That's why his face looks so different to me. Janisch's nose had an outward curve to it, almost like a beak—very prominent. Vandermeer's nose is perfectly straight. It even changes the appearance of his eyes. And the beard hides his chin." Robert began to chew on his thumbnail, as I said, "The question now is not whether he is Janisch, but what does he suspect, if anything, about me. Would Morwenn say anything to him, even accidentally?"

He rubbed the back of his neck. "I don't think so. She wouldn't deliberately betray you if she believed he was Janisch, which she doesn't. She practically worships Vandermeer and wouldn't want to confess her own part in this scheme of ours."

He got up from the bed and stood in front of me. "When this all started, I never considered how dangerous it might be for you. Maybe you should leave as soon as possible—I could take you back tomorrow morning."

I shook my head. I'd thought about this all afternoon. "I have to find some proof of his identity." My words sounded ridiculous—too brave, too noble—considering the danger.

"Like what?"

"A document. Something with his name on it. The scars described in his file."

"How do you intend to check for those?" he asked,

and there was no humor in his voice.

"I don't know yet." This was the part of my plan that I would not share with Robert.

"Katya, you're so young. You have the whole of your life ahead of you. At what point do you let this all go, and get on with living?"

I walked to his small window and watched the sun drop toward the ocean. When I turned back toward Robert, he was watching me. "You still don't understand, do you?" I knew I wasn't being fair—how could he understand what I'd been through if I'd never told him about it. "The story of my life doesn't make good conversation at the supper table."

Robert took my hands in his. "Katya," he said softly, "I care about you a great deal, and I want to help you, but I need to know who you are. I know you've been shaped by your past. Just give me a glimpse of it—I won't run."

"I always thought you would."

"What?"

"Run."

He shook his head. "Try me."

I wanted to shake him out of his complacency, out of the narrow view that all was right with the world when all was right in *his* world at the moment. "Do you remember," I said, "when I told you a little about my family?"

"Yes."

"Besides my parents and grandparents and brother and sister and the aunt and cousins who lived with us in Warsaw, I also had uncles, aunts, and cousins in other cities in Poland. Out of those thirty-nine family members,

I am the only one left. The only one, Robert. I can't go on with my life as if nothing happened."

"What do you owe to the dead?" With one finger, Robert traced the outline of veins in my hand. "And when will the debt be paid?"

I had no answer.

"Your hand is cold," he said. "Are you all right?"

I told Robert I was fine, which was a lie, because I was on a very small island with a man who used to kill Jews for sport.

AARON

Robert was still not in the courtroom the next day. What was going on? I watched Aaron Levy, with his hand on the Old Testament, swear to tell the truth. He sat down in the witness box, solemn and immaculately groomed in a three-piece light gray suit and charcoal tie.

"Where did you meet Katya Denys?" asked Mark Wickham.

"In Israel."

"What kind of work was she doing at that time?"

"She was a nurse at Mt. Hadassah."

"How long have you known her?"

"Almost five years."

"How would you characterize your relationship to Miss Denys?"

"We have worked together since 1950." Aaron looked down for a moment, then looked directly at me as he said, "In some ways, I regard her as my own daughter."

I felt tears prick the corners of my eyes.

"Where did you and Miss Denys work together?"

"In London."

"Will you describe the nature of your work?"

"We interviewed survivors of the concentration camps. Generally, Katya would conduct the interviews and then transcribe them. I would go over the interviews with a tooth comb, looking for patterns, details."

"How was this information utilized?"

"If a former Nazi came to trial, we could use the files to locate witnesses. We also tracked the locations of certain officers who had eluded capture."

"What information did you have on Emil Janisch?"

"We had a file on him with testimony from numerous witnesses."

"What alerted Katya Denys to the possibility that Emil Janisch might be living on Skokholm Island?"

"She found a letter from Robert Kensley and a sketch that he had made of Mattheu Vandermeer's face."

"When did you arrive in Marloes last year?"

"On the afternoon of the 20th of May."

"Whom did you run into in Marloes?"

"Robert Kensley."

"What did he give you?"

"He had a letter from Katya, for me, that she had asked him to mail."

Mark retrieved a sheet of writing paper from the evidence table. "Is this the letter?" he said, as he handed it to the clerk, who delivered it to Aaron.

Aaron put on his glasses. "Yes, it is."

"How do you know it was written by Katya Denys?"

"I am quite familiar with her handwriting, since I reviewed all of her notes from survivor interviews."

"Will you read it out, please?"

Dear Aaron,

I'm sorry to have left so suddenly, without telling you where I was going, but I knew you would try to talk me out of it, and I needed to do this. I have been on Skokholm since the 1st of May. Your friend's grandson was clever enough to devise a scheme to get me over here. I've been posing as the housekeeper's cousin and helping out with household tasks, which has allowed me opportunities to watch Mattheu Vandermeer and occasionally to go through his papers.

Here is what I have found so far: Mattheu Vandermeer corresponds with a German woman, a Johanna Dengler in Villa General Belgrano, which, as you know, is a gathering place for former Nazis. Secondly, Mattheu Vandermeer may have utilized the services of a plastic surgeon named Dr. Jakob Finster, also German. Third, he has a very healthy bank account in Zurich. I realize all this is circumstantial and proves nothing.

However, I have been translating Vandermeer's journal, which is written in German, and this morning, I ran across passages that convinced me of both his nationality and his loyalty to Hitler. Please help me bring this man to justice. Would you start the ball rolling to get an indictment against him if I can confirm the physical evidence from the SS file of Emil Janisch? I will remain on the island only long enough to do this. Then I will wait for you to contact me in Marloes through General Delivery at the post office. Please, Aaron, do this for me.

Always, Katya

I watched the faces of the jurors; one of the younger

men looked at me for a moment. Did they believe what I'd written to Aaron? I wanted to bite off a hangnail on my thumb but did not dare.

Sperry rose from his seat as Mark Wickham sat down. "Mr. Levy," he said, "did you send Katya Denys to Skokholm Island to investigate Mattheu Vandermeer?"

I knew Mark Wickham had been willing to risk this question from Sperry in order to put Aaron in the witness box. I rocked back and forth in my chair, with a movement so slight it would be imperceptible to anyone else—my attempt to cope with the mounting tension in my body.

"No."

"Did you agree, at any time, to help her in the investigation?"

"No."

Sperry needed to ask no further questions.

* * *

The next witness was Dr. Broderick Crowther, whose eyes were bloodshot and his skin pale. I wondered if he'd been up all night delivering a baby, because he seemed exhausted. His navy-blue suit was at least ten years old—I guessed that he hated to spend money on new clothes. Mark Wickham asked him to describe the bruises on my neck.

Consulting his notes, Dr. Crowther said, "By the time I saw Katya Denys, which was approximately nine hours after her injury, she had large areas of ecchymosis, or bruising, on both sides of her neck, along with considerable swelling, denoting soft-tissue injury." His voice was clear, his tone displayed confidence, as if he was happy that all he had to do was read from those notes.

"Dr. Crowther, have you ever seen a victim of strangulation?"

"Yes."

"When was that?"

He looked up and to the left, as if searching his memory. "On two occasions, during medical school, we observed the wounds of strangulation victims at autopsy."

"Were the wounds of these strangulation victims similar to the bruises and swelling you observed when you examined Katya Denys?"

"The wounds were similar, yes."

"Was it your impression that Katya Denys had been strangled, as she claims?"

"I have no reason to believe that her injuries were caused by anything other than strangulation." He fought back a yawn.

"Will you describe the injury to her right wrist?"

Dr. Crowther read again from his notes: "Obvious fracture of the right ulna, with point tenderness, three-plus swelling, and considerable ecchymosis. Distinct imprint of blunt object. Patient states that she was struck on the arm with a cane or walking stick." As I remembered the intense pain of the injury, I was certain that my wrist, although completely healed, had begun to throb again.

"What was the series of events—was she struck first and then strangled?"

"She said that he broke her arm first and then knocked her to the floor and tried to strangle her." I felt myself shutting down; the terror and pain of the attack was still too fresh in my mind. To distance myself from the proceedings, I studied the back of the bronze statue out on the square below the courtroom window.

"Did she tell you who her assailant was?"

"She said it was Mattheu Vandermeer."

I pulled my attention back from the window. Kevin Sperry turned slightly and glanced at me before he spoke again. "Dr. Crowther," he said, "is it not true that Katya Denys was in a great deal of pain when you examined her on the 21st of May, 1953?"

"Yes."

"Was she favoring the right arm—protecting it from further injury?"

"Yes, she supported the right arm by holding it against her body."

"Considering the amount of pain she was in, do you think she would have been able to use her right hand to, say, open a door, write a letter, pull the trigger of a gun?"

I sat forward, hugging my right arm against my body like a shield

"No, I don't think— " Before his sentence was complete, Broderick Crowther realized his mistake, but it was too late. He had answered automatically, but there was no going back.

"Is it possible that Katya Denys could have injured her arm in a fall instead of being struck, as she claims?"

I leaned forward even farther, almost doubled over, with my elbows digging into my thighs.

Broderick Crowther sighed. "I can't say it's not possible, but there was the distinct imprint of a cane or a stick— "

"No further questions for this witness, M'lord." Kevin

Sperry's booming voice cut off the rest of the doctor's sentence.

I sat up suddenly, and the hard rungs of the chair dug into my vertebrae. Sperry, you are such a bastard.

After the luncheon recess, Judge Mulholland unexpectedly adjourned the court until nine o'clock Monday morning. We would have no session the next day or on Friday. As far as I knew, Mark Wickham was out of witnesses. That left only the closing statements, and as far as I was concerned, we hadn't done much toward proving self-defense. I sent word to Mark Wickham that I needed to see him.

* * *

Robert finally appeared that evening, and when I asked him where he'd been, he smiled and said, "Out of town."

"Did you go back to the island?"

"No." He looked smug but would not elaborate, except to say that he had a surprise for me. No, two surprises, actually, but I'd have to wait. I told him that his secrecy and smugness were exceptionally cruel. When he laughed, I wanted to strangle him. After re-living Janisch's attack and having Sperry imply I'd broken my own arm after I shot Janisch, I was in no mood for humor.

EMIL JANISCH

"The defense calls Nicolaas Vandermeer."

An excited murmur ran through the visitors' gallery, because no one from Carmarthen or Marloes had heard of him. Like the others, I watched the tall, lanky young man with sun-bleached hair walk through the door and stand in front of the court clerk, placing his hand on the Testament to take the oath. Katya turned round and looked at me for a moment, with a question in her eyes.

His accent would mark him as either Dutch or German. I heard the whisperings of those near me, and I tried to imagine what Katya was thinking—what everyone would be thinking—who was this young man? Nicolaas sat forward in the witness box, his eyes fixed on Mark Wickham, and those who knew Vandermeer by sight searched the handsome face for a resemblance.

"State your name, please," said Mark Wickham.

"Nicolaas Vandermeer."

"Your place of residence?"

"Amsterdam."

"How long have you lived there?"

"I was born there and have lived there all my life, either in the city itself or on the outskirts."

"What is your father's name?"

"Mattheu Vandermeer." The buzzing of excited conversations in the visitors' gallery grew in volume until Judge Mulholland intervened. "I will have order in my courtroom," he said.

Mark Wickham continued. "How common was the name 'Mattheu Vandermeer' in Amsterdam in 1945?"

"There are twenty other Vandermeers at that time—all related to me. There is only one with the name of Mattheu—my father."

"Is your father living?"

"He was killed in 1945."

"I know this may be hard for you, Nicolaas, but I'd like for you to describe what happened on the night of January 17th, 1945."

Nicolaas swallowed and looked over toward the window. At last, he focused on Mark Wickham and began speaking in a slow, measured voice. "During the war, my parents hide a Jewish family, the Rosens—a gentleman and his wife and young child—from the Nazis, in the attic of our home, because at that time, in Amsterdam, all Jews are in danger. The Rosens are with us for a year, when we hear a terrible racket outside our door and loud voices shouting for us to open up. We delay for a time to secure the hiding place. The German soldiers break through our door and push past us, my father and I and my mother who is pregnant and only weeks from her time." Nicolaas Vandermeer looked down at his hands, and I was afraid he would not be able to continue, but he looked up at Mark. I noticed Katya rocking back and forth, almost imperceptibly.

"The Germans tear up our house, smash furniture and break windows. 'Jew lover,' one of the officers tell my father, 'where are they? It will be worse for you if you do not turn them over right away.' My father keeps quiet.

"I look at the officer in his splendid SS uniform. His eyes are very light blue, very unusual, and I read the name 'Janisch' on his nameplate. I notice the name because it's not German, and I think it must be Hungarian."

There is absolute silence in the courtroom—I don't hear a single cough or rustle of papers. It's as if we've all stopped breathing. I can't see Katya's face, but she has her hand over her mouth.

Nicolaas Vandermeer's voice cracked with emotion. "I saw Janisch point at my mother, and one of his men slams the butt of a rifle into her belly, and she falls to the floor. My father kneels beside her, screaming 'no, please God, no.'

"Behind me, I hear one of the Germans say, 'Emil, listen.' I turn to see an officer directing Janisch's attention to the ceiling, where we hear banging. The Rosens betray themselves to save us.

"The Nazis find the trap door under a false panel in the ceiling, and they drag the Rosens down the stairs and out of our house. My father still kneels beside my mother, who is unconscious. Emil Janisch kicks my father in the ribs. He tries to get up, but Janisch kicks him again, then motions for two soldiers. They pull my father to his feet and drag him out of the house, as he screams my mother's name. I am there, I am twelve years old, with my hurt mother who bleeds to death while I run to get help."

"Nicolaas, what happened to your father?"

The muscles in his jaw tightened, and he began to blink rapidly, as if to keep back the rage that he must feel. Although I'd heard his story before, I still felt my muscles tense. This couldn't be easy for Nicolaas.

"If you need to take a moment," Mark said to him, "go ahead."

Nicolaas Vandermeer shook his head and swallowed. "My father, they take to Protective Custody Camp at Vught, where he stays six months. He is bitter and broken, and I know he worries about me constantly, although I am with my grandparents. In the last days, in 1945, my father gets away from the camp and comes back to our house, where I find him one night sitting in the room where the Nazis kill my mother. He stands up and hugs me, he's crying. I'm scared because my father never cries. Then he lets me go, turns away from me. 'I will find the Nazi bastard who kill your mother,' he says, 'and I will kill him.'

"My father is a man of God. I never hear him talk like that."

" 'No, Poppa, don't do this. You don't know what you're saying.'

" 'I will not rest until he is dead.' My father makes this pledge, and he finds Emil Janisch five days later, drinking with his comrades in a bar, and he waits until Janisch leaves, by himself. He follows Janisch into a dark alley, and there is a struggle. Emil Janisch wins that fight—of course, he is an officer—they teach him how to kill—fighting a minister. We find my father's body the next morning, and no one ever sees Emil Janisch again in Amsterdam, but I know he is alive, because my father's papers are gone."

I watched Katya put a hand back to massage her neck.

Mark took the photo album from the evidence table and handed it to Nicolaas. "Do you recognize any of the people in this photograph album?"

Nicolaas paged slowly through the photographs, then stopped. "This one." He pointed at a photograph. "This is Emil Janisch."

"Are you sure?"

"How could I forget his face? I see it so often in my nightmares."

"Please remove the photograph of Emil Janisch and read out the name written on the back."

Nicolaas Vandermeer pulled out the picture and turned it over. "It says 'Mattheu Vandermeer, before surgery.' " Nicolaas looked up at Mark Wickham. "He stole my father's name." Mark took the photograph from Nicolaas and passed it to the court clerk, who delivered it to the jurors.

Kevin Sperry had no cross-examination for the witness.

As Nicolaas Vandermeer left the courtroom, he looked directly at Katya with unmistakable admiration, but then she turned round, toward me, and she seemed on the verge of tears.

Judge Mulholland ordered a short recess before the next witness, so I went down the marble stairs to the vestibule, where people waited on benches or stood in clumps or passed in and out of the mullioned doors under the stained glass window. I went outside, even though it was so cold, the air hurt my lungs. I would not stay long—I just needed to stretch my legs. As I walked quickly, turning the collar of my coat up toward my ears, I thought about Nicolaas's testimony. Had the jurors been convinced? There was no reason for Nicolaas Vandermeer to lie. He would have no motive other than to punish the man who killed his parents. If Emil Janisch was dead, he would sympathize with whoever killed him, but if the dead man in this murder trial was not Emil Janisch, Nicolaas would have no reason to help Katya. What more did the jurors need? Nicolaas had picked out Janisch's picture from Finster's collection and found his father's name on the back of the photograph.

What the jurors needed, I thought, was to hear Morwenn Madoc recant her testimony, and that's just what she was about to do.

When the court re-assembled, Nicolaas joined me in the visitors' gallery. "Do you think it was helpful, what I said?" he asked me, and I could see that he was still shaken from re-living those awful memories.

"You've probably saved her life," I said to him, just before Judge Mulholland entered and we were asked to rise.

"The defense calls Morwenn Madoc." This announcement caused almost as much of a stir as when Mark had called Nicolaas. Morwenn entered from the vestibule and made her way to the witness box. She looked different—younger, perhaps?—and she wore a black suit with a white blouse and a small garnet brooch that I'd never seen before. Her black hat was in the latest style and partially shaded her eyes. After Judge Mulholland warned her that she was still under oath, Mark asked her why she had decided to testify for the defense.

Katya didn't turn round this time. She would have been surprised by Morwenn's reversal but not shocked. She would have known that I would take Nicolaas to see Morwenn.

"I had the diary of Emil Janisch translated two days ago." She took a deep breath. "Tis the first time I've been able to say his real name. I've been deaf to things people were saying about his past, thinking there was a mistake—that they were really after someone else." She looked down for a moment, and when she spoke again, her voice was softer, and she glanced at Katya. "That's why I was so angry with Katya Denys. I thought the man I had known could not have done those things."

"How do you know this journal was written by Emil Janisch?"

She put a hand to the back of her neck, to finger the short curls escaping from beneath her hat. "It was the same handwriting—the same as his love notes to me, long ago—and the writing of the lists of building supplies and market lists and all the other lists he made." Morwenn hesitated and looked out the window, as if to collect her thoughts. "His hands that wrote such fine script, that played the violin like an angel—those same hands signed the warrants to kill thousands of people, and he was so proud of what he'd done. It was all there, in that diary, page after page. Not only what he did, but why. There were no excuses—he truly believed what he was doing was honorable. He made himself out to be such a patriot, but he was nothing more than a murderer of children."

"Objection, Your Honor," Sperry said. "The witness is speculating."

Judge Mulholland frowned at Sperry. "Over-ruled."

Outside, the rain had stopped, and I could see fragments of blue sky between the clouds.

"Miss Madoc," said Mark Wickham, "could you locate in the journal some of the passages to which you have referred?"

"The passages are marked," she said, "with slips of paper. The worst one is about three-quarters of the way through." As she left the witness box to sit in the visitors' gallery beside me, Morwenn smiled at Katya.

Judith Rittmueller was called back, and she read to the court one of the passages that Morwenn had indicated: "I have examined my life, and I must conclude that I am not a murderer. Nor am I a mass murderer. I regarded orders from my Fuhrer as a sacred duty. My loyalty, now and always, lies with Germany and its survival."

Fingering the garnet brooch at the neck of her blouse, Morwenn listened to the words of Emil Janisch. She bowed her head, and I took hold of her cool hand and squeezed it.

After court had adjourned for the day, after we had risen for the exit of the judge and the jury, Morwenn said to me, "How could a man change so much—not just the way he looked but his very nature? He was so good at lying, he didn't even have to think about it. He could tell me I was his whole world and then write love letters to that tart in South America." She looked out the window, where the sun had just broken through heavy clouds. A tall man in an overcoat walked across the square, past the bronze statue. "I fell in love with a gentle man who played the violin, who held shearwaters in his hands when they were too tired to fly, who spent hours watching and writing about the birds he loved. Was this a lie too? Was our life together a lie? I've no idea what parts were real, but the truth of Emil Janisch is in that journal. He had no need to lie when writing in his own book." Her eyes were moist. "I have to live with the fact that the man I loved was responsible for the deaths of innocent men, women, and children—and had no remorse."

"Morwenn," I said to her, and I put my hand under her chin and tipped her face up. She was crying now. "Don't blame yourself. You didn't know who he was. He lied to you from the very beginning." I hugged her and whispered in her ear, "I'm so proud of you."

AUSCHWITZ

As I was led down the stairs from the prisoners' dock, one thing continued to puzzle me—how Emil Janisch could take the name of his victim. But then, the Nazis took everything from their victims and used it for their own purposes—like the hair of corpses to make socks for Nazi soldiers or to stiffen their uniform collars. Even the artificial limbs and braces from Jewish victims were sent to the front for German soldiers. For their own children, the Nazis took the tiny garments from murdered Jewish babies. With surgical precision, they could separate useless emotions like guilt or sentimentality from the objects, or perhaps they never experienced these inconvenient emotions in the first place.

Later that evening, Mark and Robert came to my cell to revel in the day's victory. They had bought a bouquet of flowers, divided it in half, and they each presented their share of the flowers simultaneously, as a joke. Robert and Mark both looked extremely pleased with themselves, and I hated to put their knickers in a twist, but there was something that needed to be said. "I want to testify about what happened the night Janisch died."

"I can't let you do that," Mark said. "Why would you want to, in the first place? After Nicolaas's testimony, and Morwenn's, you're in good shape."

"Now that the jurors know what kind of person he was," Robert said, "they'll believe he was capable of killing you."

"Yes, but our case for self-defense is still weak," I said to Mark. "The rifle he tried to kill me with was never found. And Sperry made my injuries look like they could have been self-inflicted. I could tell them what really happened."

"You might incriminate yourself," Mark said.

"Why are you doing this?" Robert said. "Now that things are looking good, are you afraid there'll be a happy ending?"

I glared at him.

"Okay, I'll keep my mouth shut," he said. "Mark, you're her barrister. You handle this."

I sat on the edge of the bunk with my ankles crossed, staring at my hands, not at Robert, as he spoke to me. He leaned back against the bars of the cell, and Mark pulled the one chair up so that he was facing me.

"I've had a lot of time to think," I said.

Robert, staring past me, chewed on his thumbnail.

"Katya," Mark said.

"No, please let me finish. I need to get this off my chest—what happened that night. "

I slid off the bunk and backed up into the small space beside the sink. "I can't say that I never thought about killing Emil Janisch—I thought about it more than once." I put my hands to my cheeks, which would soon burst into flames. "Emil Janisch died because I went to the island in pursuit of him. Pure and simple." I looked past Mark to Robert, who was staring at a spot just above my head. He wouldn't look at me.

Mark stood up and turned away from me. When he turned back, I could see that he was trying to stay calm. "Your agenda goes way beyond proving self-defense, doesn't it?"

I stepped away from the wall. "If I don't testify, the jury could assume I'm guilty of murder. Now that we've proven Janisch wasn't an innocent man, they'll talk about my motive for killing him. What have I got to lose? I'm tired of this whole charade. Janisch is the one who should be on trial, not me." I shrugged my shoulders. "I can't lie any more. "

Robert seemed to come out of his trance. He came over to me and touched my arm. "You don't need to do this," he said. "No one's asking you to lie."

"Do either one of you believe that the court could sentence me to anything worse than Auschwitz or Bergen-Belsen?

Robert's sigh was exaggerated. "You survived those places, but you know the penalty for murder."

"You're both being fatalistic," Mark said, and he pushed himself away from the bars of my cell.

"Realistic," I said quietly.

"Is the possibility of freedom, and happiness, so foreign to you?" Robert said to me, and I heard the frustration in his voice.

"Look," I said, "I've never told anyone the whole story, not even Aaron. At this point, keeping my mouth shut feels like lying. I want people to understand why I had to confront Janisch. I've had to hide my feelings since I was twelve years old, since the Nazis took over my country. I won't do it any longer." I turned toward the sink and gripped its edges, leaning my weight on my arms and looking up, as if to look in the mirror, but there was only a blank white wall. I pivoted slowly to face Robert and Mark. "I had to hide my feelings so I could survive the camps. I had to do it on the island, so I could deal with Janisch. I'm tired of lying to myself and to everyone else. I just want to stand up there in the witness box and let them hear what kind of man Emil Janisch really was. And then people will understand why I had to do this—I had no choice. I could either try to identify Janisch, or drive myself crazy for the rest of my life, knowing that he might be living somewhere, free of guilt, laughing at the world and defying us to find him." I slumped onto the edge of the bunk with my hands clenched between my knees. The tension in the cell was like a leopard pacing back and forth, ready to spring when its cage door was opened.

Robert put his hand on my shoulder and squeezed it gently. "I don't know," he said. "Maybe she should testify, Mark."

Mark sat in the chair again, staring at the two of us but obviously lost in thought.

"I know you're thinking in terms of winning the case and seeing Katya acquitted," Robert said, "but she's trying to tell us it doesn't matter. The truth seems to be more important to her than avoiding prison."

Mark crossed his arms and said to Robert. "If she wanted to hang herself, would you kick the chair away?"

Robert glared at him.

"I've had to sit through this whole trial and hear Emil Janisch portrayed, for the most part, as Mattheu Vandermeer the saint," Katya said. "I just want to set the record straight. Scars and blood types and words in a lost journal—that's all those jurors have heard. They can't even begin to imagine what Emil Janisch was like, except for Nicolaas's testimony."

Mark stood up and turned away from us for a moment to compose himself, staring out into the empty hallway between the cells. "This goes against everything I was taught," he said as he turned back. "We're not supposed to let our clients incriminate themselves. I can't let you jeopardize your freedom." Leaning against the bars of the cell, he closed his eyes and pressed his fingertips against his eyelids.

"What good is freedom if I have no soul?"

"Good God," Mark said. "Let me get you out of jail, and then you can go and find your soul."

I ignored him. "These things inside me—they're tearing me apart." I clenched my fists in my lap.

"I can't let you incriminate yourself."

I looked down at my hands.

"Katya, did you go to the island with the intention of killing Emil Janisch?"

"No."

"Why did you take the gun?"

"I was a survivor; I didn't want to be in the position of victim again."

"So you knew this man you pursued could be violent?"

"Of course."

"You knew you might have to use the gun to defend yourself."

"I hoped it wouldn't be necessary."

Mark took a deep breath. "If you decide to testify, these are the kinds of questions Sperry will ask you."

I held up my hands. "Mark, I don't have anything to hide."

He sighed. "It's too risky."

The expression on his face showed that he realized the irony of his remark too late.

"Life is a risk," I said, and I controlled my voice. "No one is guaranteed they'll wake up in the morning."

"Are you suicidal, Katya?" said Mark. His face flushed. "Because if you want to lose this case, if you want to be in prison for a very long time, go ahead and tell the jury what you just told us." He tipped his head back to ease the tension, and I heard the ligaments crack in his neck.

I stood up. "Don't you see, Mark? There were so many lies: the ten pounds of bread and marmalade and sugar promised to those who reported voluntarily for 'resettlement;' the train tickets sold to Greeks who found, too late, that their final destination was Auschwitz; the sales to Jews of farms that did not exist; the 'showers' at Auschwitz for people newly-arrived from the train, where poison gas came out instead of water; the people removed from the villages surrounding Auschwitz so there would be no witnesses." I knew my voice was louder, but I pronounced each word with care. "People living lies—Vandermeer on the island, even Robert and I on the island, obtaining by deception to accomplish our goals." I could feel the color rising in my cheeks. "This is where the deception ends."

I could almost hear Mark's unspoken thoughts—God in Heaven, what a stubborn woman.

"I have to tell my story."

"This is crazy." Mark ran his hand over his hair.

"You can't keep me from testifying. When the judge asks me if I have anything to say, believe me, I'll say yes."

"We're talking about a court of law," Mark said slowly, his voice firm, "not a psychoanalysis session. Let me get you acquitted, then we can deal with your angst."

"No, I want the jury to know exactly what Janisch did. If that provides a motive for murder in the first—well, so be it. Emil Janisch died because I went to the island without thinking beyond the moment of identification—that's all I could see." Mark Wickham shook his head and called for the warder to let him out of my cell. He would not look at me, but Robert had a wistful smile, as if he were both proud of and frightened by my determination.

As he left, Mark said to me through the bars, "You may think you're being noble, but you've gone back to your role of victim."

A victim, Mark had said. How strange. I had never seen myself as one. I had always thought of myself as a rescuer, especially when it came to Rebekah.

"Do you see me as a victim?" I asked Robert. Why did it matter so much?

"No, I don't."

* * *

After Robert left that evening, I thought about what Mark had said. In my mind, I'd never been a victim. Maybe that's why I'd never identified with other survivors.

I remembered one of the turning points of my life. One event had touched off the next and the next, like a collapsing line of dominoes. I had been in Auschwitz for three months when I heard there was to be a selection. I had worked part of the time in the factory and part of the time outside doing manual labor. Since the factory was closing, we would be put on outside details again. We knew how dangerous those work details could be—we had seen women beaten to death by kapos for no reason.

I heard rumors that the selection was for a good job, with better food and better living conditions. I tried to make myself as presentable as possible, although, looking back, I saw how futile this was. I had no hair to groom, but I wore a kerchief to protect my scalp from the sun. I washed out the kerchief and flattened it carefully to dry. My uniform was that of a dead Russian soldier, and I still wore his blood on my jacket since we could not wash our clothes, having nothing else to put on.

Just before the selection, I jumped up and down, running in place to make my face look flushed and healthy. Because there was no iron in our diets, we were all anemic, but it was possible to fake the flush of health for a few minutes.

God smiled on me, and I was chosen. We were taken to a barracks in the other part of the camp—to the medical block, where the bunks were less crowded. We were given clean clothes and more generous food rations. Because we were kept inside, in "quarantine," we enjoyed three days of rest and relaxation.

On the fourth day, we were taken outside and lined up in rows—this was something to which we were accustomed. We stood for such a long time, and the sun was hot, but we were used to that, also. I stood in a row near the back of the group, which consisted of one hundred women. When our two female guards began to argue, one of my fellow prisoners, in the row in front of me, was snatched out of line by another woman. I did not turn round to see where they went, but the thought occurred to me, at that moment, that our "special detail" could be marked for death.

I should have known it was too good to be true, and I began to plot my escape, knowing that it would be necessary to keep my eyes and ears open and to learn as much as possible about my surroundings. In the evenings, we were not locked in the barracks but were allowed freedom within a certain area. We could visit the latrine or socialize with other prisoners outside in the prison yard. I used this opportunity to explore.

I had been on the "special detail" for almost a week before I saw the children. They were housed in the barracks next to ours, and I'd been told they were undergoing medical tests. They never came outside, but I saw their faces, every now and then, in the windows—as gaunt as the children of the ghetto, with the same blank eyes. Early one morning, I thought I saw a face, just for an instant, that looked like Rebekah's.

One evening, I saw the children's guards outside, and when they turned their backs, I slipped into the barracks. The small bodies ravaged by medical experiments convinced me there was no God. Some of the children, those with a bit of spirit left in them, approached me, staring at the ragged stranger. I searched their faces—there were so many, all with hollowed cheeks and sallow skin. Rebekah was not among them.

I began a silent tour of the barracks, the mobile children trailing behind me like the wake of a boat. Curled on bunks were emaciated children, drawn up into balls to protect themselves from the world. Some of those who had not retreated completely followed me with their eyes as I passed.

I found my sister in a bunk in the far corner of the barracks, lying on her back with her hands at her sides, her brown eyes open, staring at the ceiling. I almost walked past, but then I recognized the eyes, now sunk deeply into the white face with its skin stretched so tightly. She was nothing but bones, fragile as a bird, and as I gathered Rebekah into my arms, I was afraid that she would crumble and disappear. She stared at me as if I were a stranger. Rebekah did not speak even though I said her name over and over, with the terrifying thought that perhaps Rebekah was so damaged, she didn't recognize me.

Finally, I saw tears slip out of the corners of Rebekah's eyes. She continued to stare up at the ceiling, and her mouth was working as if she wanted to talk. I held her cold hand, remembering the tiny warm fingers that had gripped mine when she was a baby. Finally, Rebekah turned her head and looked at me and squeezed my hand. How could I explain to her that I couldn't stay?

I could only promise her that I'd come back, that I'd get us out of this mess, this dangerous web spun by Josef Mengele.

* * *

The first and most important step in my plan was to get Rebekah, so weak from near-starvation, strong enough to walk by herself. I shared my bread rations with her as often as I could. Once a day, in the evening, I managed to slip into Rebekah's barracks and feed her bits of bread and tell her how we'd go and find Mama when the war was over. Living conditions were sometimes better on the medical ward, but that was only when one could avoid the experiments. I did not wish to become a walking zombie like so many of Mengele's subjects.

In a few days, Rebekah seemed stronger, and we began to practice walking. I knew the only way we'd survive would be to get uniforms and get back to my old barracks—our current clothing would identify us as Mengele's subjects. I also knew that prisoners marched toward the crematoria did not come back; they would have been forced to take off their uniforms and put them in piles before they were killed. If only I could get there, I could steal uniforms for Rebekah and myself, but it was not possible. The crematoria were too far away—a separate universe with a special set of workers, the *Sonderkommando*, who had no contact with other prisoners.

I'd have to find the uniforms we'd taken off when we first came to the medical ward. We'd put them in piles—everything went into piles—and I tried to remember who took them away, seeing their faces in my mind but unable to put names with the faces. I found one of the women, and she showed me the corner of the building where the uniforms were stacked. For this, I had to give the woman my evening ration of bread. It took me an hour to find my old uniform and another hour to find Rebekah's, because the numbers on uniforms had to match the arm tattoo. I tied the two uniforms under my shapeless dress.

That evening, I went to see Rebekah, who was sitting up on her bunk. I hid the uniforms under Rebekah's mattress and explained that we must leave the medical barracks and go to another one that was safer. I told her that she must put on her uniform the next morning and stay covered with her blanket. I would come to her later, and we would take a walk.

Waiting for the moment, I slipped out of line at roll call after I was counted and ran to Rebekah's barrack, where I found her waiting. Quickly, I changed into my uniform and took Rebekah's hand. Two sisters in Birkenau, caught in Josef Mengele's web. We began to walk. That morning, there was only coffee, and we were weak. The wind so strong we had to fight to stay upright. Even with the cold wind, sweat poured down my sides. In ten minutes, walking across camp, past guards, as if we had been ordered to do so, we reached my old barracks and then slipped, grateful for our lives, into Hilda's work group. My palms were bleeding from having dug my nails into them. I never told Rebekah that we could have been shot on sight, but she knew.

Rebekah became my sole reason for living, and I clung to the idea of Rebekah's survival as if to the mane of a stallion racing toward the edge of a cliff. There was no room for despair. Rebekah was my innocent self, which I had lost in the Warsaw Ghetto, where the SS troops had looted homes, beaten people and shot them without provocation. Jews were required to move off the sidewalks if SS were present. As a twelve-year-old, I had seen old men beaten until they could never stand again, just because they couldn't get off the sidewalk fast enough, and I continued my ritual of being hardened—blood in the streets no longer frightened me. I forced myself to look until I became immune to the sight of it. But when Rebekah was with me, I had covered her eyes.

In Auschwitz, I had to make sure we got on Hilda's crew. At the end of the day, I watched to make sure Rebekah ate, and then we had the short space of darkness before we got up to do it all over again. I guarded her as she slept. If she screamed from nightmares, I would wake her into the genuine nightmare of our existence.

What kept me going was the dream of finding our mother when the war was over, of guiding Rebekah into Mama's arms and saying to her, 'Look, Mama, I've found Rebekah, who was lost.' In that moment would be the greatest happiness of my life.

The workday began at 4 a.m. with roll call, which could last for hours. We did various kinds of work in the camp, but it was always tedious and backbreaking. The day's experience depended on which particular kapo, or prisoner-guard, was in command of that work detail. I learned to avoid the kapos with green triangles on their uniforms, because they were in prison for murder. These kapos were especially sadistic and would often beat three or four women to death in the course of a normal workday.

Others, like Hilda, would use their whips only when the SS were about. Rebekah and I tried to get in Hilda's line every day, for although she still worked us hard, no one ever died on her work crew.

We would get a twenty-minute break for a lunch of thin soup. Supper was a ration of bread, dry and tasteless, seldom more than a crust handed to us on our way into the block after evening roll call. Rebekah and I began to save half our rations, so we would have something to eat in the morning. Often, the amount and quality of the rations reflected the extent of German victories. When we started getting small pieces of cheese with the evening's bread, we knew the Germans had reached Holland. When things were going badly for the Germans, the soup was often not much more than water, with a pitiful number of vegetables on the bottom of the kettle. Somehow, waiting in line longer did not give a better chance of getting bits of vegetables. No matter how long we waited, the vegetables always seemed to go to someone else. Sometimes, in the evenings, I would sneak out of the block and scour the grounds outside, looking for bits of potato or anything else edible, and I always gave half to Rebekah, no matter how small the morsel.

Bread was another key to survival, not only for its sustenance, but also because it could be traded for other items that were needed. When Rebekah cut her hand badly on the bricks we were moving, I traded my evening bread to get a bit of salve for her wound.

Jewelry, also, had a high value in barter. Many of the women in camp managed to hide some bit of jewelry, a ring perhaps, or a charm with sentimental value, and when necessary, these items could be hidden under the tongue. One day, Rebekah had spoken a few words, casually and without thinking, to a young man in an adjoining work-detail, an act expressly forbidden by the SS guards. I was terrified, because I'd heard that our guard, Maria Grebe, had threatened to report Rebekah to the head supervisor, which could cost Rebekah her life. I returned to my bunk in the block to find Rebekah weeping, and I held her hands, which were cold and clammy. 'Don't worry,' said Roiske, one of our block mates. 'We've bought Maria off with a collection of jewelry. She's agreed not to report Rebekah.' I hugged Roiske and kissed her, so grateful for the gift of my sister's life that I was unable to speak.

If I had allowed myself to cry in Auschwitz, I would never have been able to stop. It was better to shut down all emotions, to let the body function on its own, with only enough consciousness present to avoid mistakes. It was necessary to be on the alert at all times—to find the kapos less likely to beat their charges, to look out for bits of food on the ground after evening roll call, to find the safest work details. I realized from the first day that I could not let myself have memories of home or family as they were in the past. To indulge in sorrow would undermine my attempt to survive. And my sole purpose was to survive so I could save Rebekah, because the future was the only place in my mind where there was hope.

At night, we lay on a crowded bunk, usually sharing a space meant for one person with five or six others. Since there were no pillows, we arranged ourselves on the slanted bunks with our heads at the high end, and sometimes the bunks would break during the night or one of the women would die. Twice, I woke up next to a corpse.

Though exhausted from the day's labor, I often lay awake, listening to Rebekah's breathing, unable to sleep through the moans and weeping of the other women. Our bunk was next to the tiny window, and the searchlights flashed through it, bathing everyone in an eerie light. On most nights, I would doze off for a few minutes, to be awakened by the sound of machine-gun fire, screams, or the sickening crackle of the electric fence that meant one more prisoner had escaped the hell known as Auschwitz. Then I would pray silently the words of my faith: 'The needs of thy people are many and they are unable to express their wants. May it be Thy will, O Lord our God and God of our fathers, to give each and every one of us his daily sustenance and to everyone whatever he lacks.' At that point, God had ceased to answer my prayers, but the repetition of familiar words helped keep my mind off other matters.

TESTAMENT

I swore by Almighty God that the evidence I would give was the truth, the whole truth, and nothing but the truth. Mark Wickham asked me to tell the court what happened on the night of Mattheu Vandermeer's death.

At midnight, I had slipped outside into the light of the full moon and walked carefully to the main house, because I was not wearing shoes. I thought about what I planned to do and wondered if Robert was asleep. Taking a deep breath, I pushed on the door, grateful that I'd had the chance to oil the hinges earlier. The painted stones were slick and cool under my feet. I crept through the entryway and squeezed the door handle, lifting the latch with no sound, thinking so far so good, because there was no light from under Vandermeer's door. I prayed he was a sound sleeper.

Switching on a small flashlight to locate *Brown's Commentary*, I slid the two large volumes out, one at a time, holding the space between the other books. I had my hand on the journal when I turned slightly to look down at the bottom of Vandermeer's door, less than three feet away, and watched in terror as the space beneath it lit up. I froze, not daring to breathe, and prayed for a few extra moments to escape. Shoving the journal into my coat pocket, I replaced the volumes without making any noise, then charged toward the door, which I had left open. I pulled it shut just as I heard the creak of Vandermeer's bedroom door swinging open.

I dashed out of the farmhouse and back to the relative safety of my room. Half-expecting to hear an angry Vandermeer behind me, demanding his stolen journal, I sat on the bed, out of breath, my feet stinging from the rocks on the path. He would discover the loss only if he reviewed his old journals in the middle of the night. That possibility, which I could not discount, made me anxious to get started.

The propane wall lamp hissed into life when I lit it with a taper, and I sat as close to it as possible and flipped through the gilt-edged pages of the stolen journal. When I reached the part I had translated a few days earlier, I translated another three lines, and there was no doubt in my mind about Vandermeer's identity when I read the lines together, whispering them to myself in the green light of the propane lamp. I sealed the envelope of my letter to Aaron and placed it in the inner pocket of my coat, along with my Walther pistol.

I stepped outside and stood for several minutes in the dark, trying to catch my breath. When I knocked on the door of Robert's hut, he opened it, fully dressed and alert, so I knew he had not been asleep. "Come in," he said, and although his expression was pleasant, he didn't invite me to sit down.

I handed him the letter after he closed the door. "This is for Aaron Levy, and it needs to be posted as soon as possible. Will you do that for me tomorrow?" I twisted my arm to see my watch in the dim light of his propane lamp. "I guess it's today. I'm sorry for coming so late." I knew I was taking a risk by giving Robert the letter, but there was no other way to contact Aaron.

"I'll take it, of course, but the spy games are over, Katya."

"I agree," I said. "The games are over."

"I've already told Reverend Vandermeer that I'll be leaving on Friday. When I take your letter today, I'll make arrangements for Clyde to collect me." Robert crossed his arms and leaned against the bedroom wall. "You can either leave with me on Friday or come along, with your things, when I post the letter today. It's up to you."

The games were finished, but my mission was not. "I think I'll wait and go on Friday," I said, casually. "Just a few loose ends to tie up. I'd like to square things with Morwenn before I go." I hated lying to Robert, going behind his back, but he was now a liability. Once a source of both irritation and amazement, his innocence now endangered me. Yes, the games are over, and I must keep Robert Kensley out of it.

* * *

About one o'clock in the afternoon, Robert took Vandermeer's boat to the mainland with my letter for Aaron Levy, but he had not yet returned. A storm had come up just after he left, which would have made the crossing from Martinshaven quite hazardous. An hour and a half after supper, I went back to the Wheelhouse kitchen and poured the contents of two pentobarbitone capsules into Vandermeer's coffee. I prayed the coffee would disguise the taste, that I had waited long enough for his stomach to be empty. I clutched the thermos close to my body as I ran through the rain.

When I knocked twice on Vandermeer's door, he called out for me to come in, and I was surprised that he was not playing the violin. Instead, he sat in an armchair with a book in his lap. "You didn't need to go to all that trouble, bringing my coffee over in the rain. But I appreciate the thought. Won't you stay and have some with me?"

This unusual attempt at conversation surprised me, and I wondered if it was because he knew I was leaving. I shook my head. "I can't drink coffee in the evening; I'd never get any sleep."

"Sometimes I have that problem too," he said, "but I enjoy the taste of it. Won't you have some sherry, then?"

I panicked, realizing he might not drink the coffee. No, I'll insist. I hesitated for a moment, not wanting to seem too eager. "All right."

As he poured the sherry into a small glass, I unscrewed the top of the thermos and poured the dark coffee into a blue ceramic mug, which I held out to him. "The least you can do is drink this, since I brought it all the way over here." I smiled and looked into his eyes, extending the cup to him.

"Thank you," Vandermeer said. He took a sip of the coffee and put it down. "You know, Robert is unlikely to make it back tonight. He says that the two of you will be leaving on Friday, since Morwenn's back has improved." He smiled at me. "I think I shall miss you, in spite of the fact that you can't cook and you spend too much time dusting."

God in heaven, I thought. I froze a smile onto my face and prayed it would look genuine. He was staring at me, but I remained silent, hoping he would drink his coffee if I didn't distract him with conversation. Drink it, you bastard, gulp it down, I yelled in my mind, as I took the smallest possible sips of sherry.

"In a way," he said, "I regret not getting to know you better." He picked up the blue mug.

Put it to your lips, I thought, as if I could move his hand with the power of my mind. "Perhaps I will come back some time to visit," I said, and I leaned back, crossing my arms against the seduction in Vandermeer's voice, which made my stomach clench with nausea. I watched as he drank his coffee.

He set down the mug and stood up, smiling at me as he crossed the room to sit next to me on the couch. "You have beautiful eyes," he said, and I glanced at the coffee table, trying to see how much remained in the mug. "And lovely skin." As he touched my face, I flinched and shut my eyes tightly. How soon will the pentobarbitone work? What if the caffeine works against it? God help me.

As I watched Vandermeer pull back to look at me, I realized fully how alone and vulnerable I was in that room with him. My face must have shown my anxiety. "Don't be afraid," he said. "It's been so long since I've been near a woman. Do you know that I have been celibate for eight years?" He closed his eyes for a moment.

Close to panic, I couldn't bear the thought of his touching me, and I struggled to calm my impulse to run by focusing my thoughts elsewhere. I wondered about Morwenn, certain there had been something between the two of them. Looking back at Vandermeer, I thought, why shouldn't I expect you to lie about being celibate? Your life is a lie. And what calmed me was the old familiar hatred. As long as the well-worn anger burned inside, my resolve was firm.

"Eight years like a goddamn priest!" His voice was now husky, his speech already slurred by the drug. My fingernails dug into my palms. "A man," he said, "and that is what I am, should not live—what was I going to say?—I know it was clever." He smiled, and his eyelids drooped. "Strange feeling. Mouth's dry." His face was close to mine.

I closed my eyes and felt his warm breath, coffee-flavored, against my cheek. His hand was on the back of my head, pulling me toward him, and I was certain my palms would be bloody when I opened my hands. His very closeness inspired revulsion, but I was calm in the midst of it, because I could hide my emotions better than anyone. Hadn't it kept me alive?

How could I have let him keep such a hold on me for so many years? He was only a man. There, with him, I could not even call up the terror that his memory used to bring me. He was only a heavy-breathing, desperate man, full of lust and pentobarbitone.

"Hold on," I said, "I shan't be a moment. Why don't you finish my sherry while I'm gone? That should help your dry mouth." I slipped from his embrace and bolted out the door. I stood outside, under the shelter of the porch, to catch my breath and collect my thoughts. The drug needs more time to work; how long did the pharmacist say it would take?

I took several deep breaths and walked back into the living room with a calm, almost lethal, resolve, but my heart refused to slow its wild dance. I found him lying back on the couch with his arm over his eyes. "Mattheu," I said sharply, praying I hadn't given him too much of the drug.

"Very, very sleepy," he mumbled, and I breathed a sigh of relief.

"I'll help you to bed," I said to him, as I pulled him to his feet. He managed to stagger into his bedroom, leaning heavily against me, then fell like an unstrung puppet onto the wooden bed and sprawled on his back, grinning at a private joke with his eyes squeezed shut. When his breathing became deep and regular, I waited a few more minutes, watching his chest rise and fall. With a match, I lit a taper, which I touched to the mantle of the propane lamp. It hissed gently and gave off a faint greenish glow. Vandermeer's eyelids fluttered. Concerned that he might wake up, I turned off the gas and blew out the flame.

In the fading light from the small window, my fingers found the buttons of his shirt, unfastened them, and pulled the shirt out of his trousers. From the pocket of my coat, I withdrew the small flashlight and snapped it on, focusing the beam on his bare ribcage, looking for a scar of eight centimeters on the seventh rib. It was there—an uneven slash of white on his pale skin. He stirred in his sleep, threw one arm above his head and tried to turn over, but fell back with a loud groan.

I snapped off the flashlight and stepped away from the bed until his breathing became a light snore. As gently as I could, I pulled the shirt away from his left underarm area and shone the light there, trying to keep my hand from shaking. What if there's just a scar? What if Janisch had Dr. Finster remove the tattoo at the time of the other surgery—the one to alter his nose?

The scar was just below his left armpit. I had counted on the blood type tattoo as one of the most important bits of evidence against him. I was afraid he would be too clever to leave it; so many Nazis cut their own tattoos off with pocketknives. Yet the zenith of his power had been as a Nazi; I had hoped he would keep the proof of it, like he kept the Iron Cross.

With Janisch's altered appearance, he couldn't be identified in court by witnesses, but the tattoo was crucial. The documents—the journal, the letters from Johanna—his lawyers could claim I planted them myself. I had, after all, gained admission to the island under false pretenses. What were his chances for justice? What if he tried to make a run for South America? My thoughts raced from possibility to possibility. I knew I had to capture him that night, before he slipped away again, into a hiding place where I could never find him. This was my only chance.

I slipped a loop of gauze round each wrist and tied them to the sides of the slatted headboard. After removing Vandermeer's shoes, I tied his ankles together, watching his chest rise and fall, his breathing still deep and noisy, with an occasional snore. He would not wake now if I lit the propane lamp.

With scissors, I clipped off his hair an inch from the scalp, the sun-bleached strands soon lying in careless piles on either side of his head, which I lifted up to snip the hair at the back. I needed to see him neatly barbered and shaved, as he had been in Auschwitz. I had taken Robert's razor, and I lathered soap in the washbasin and smoothed it on Janisch's beard. As I shaved off his mustache, the deep cleft between his nose and upper lip was revealed, such a memorable feature of Janisch's face. I tried the razor on the beard, but it was too heavy and too long, and he began to roll his head from side to side, moaning. I stepped back with the razor in my hand, my heart beating faster. His eyes remained closed. When he again became quiet, I clipped his beard with scissors, close to the skin, then shaved it, which revealed the distinctive chin. I studied his face and wondered how he could sleep at night with so much blood on his hands. I thought of Rebekah, of her blood, as I put the razor on the nightstand, took the pistol from my coat pocket, and sat down in the chair at the foot of the bed to wait, listening for changes in his breathing.

* * *

I watched as Janisch's eyes opened slowly, then shut again, the tranquilizer still dulling his brain. He pulled up his knees, tried to turn over, and struggled against the restraints at his wrists. His ice-blue eyes now wide with fear in the dim light, Janisch lifted his head and looked round the room, and I knew he could see me out of the corner of his eye. He cursed in German. "*Verdammt! Verdammt noch mal*!" He let his feet, bound at the ankles by gauze, slide down so that his legs were straight again, and his head fell back against the pillow.

I stepped forward to the edge of his bed, moving into his line of vision, as I aimed the gun at his chest. The terror in his eyes pleased me. "This should not be such a surprise to you," I said. "Didn't you know someone would find you eventually?"

"Who are you?" A vein stood out on his forehead, now beaded with sweat.

Still holding the gun in my right hand, I put my tattooed left forearm in front of his face. "A souvenir from Auschwitz. You remember that place?"

Janisch's pupils were dilated, and he stared at the gun.

"A Walther PPK," I said. "Did you have one like it?"

He was mute, staring at the ceiling.

"I survived your camp, Janisch, but thousands of others did not. I am here today on their behalf."

"I am not a murderer."

"How dare you say that!"

"I was given the Iron Cross for my work in liquidating the Warsaw Ghetto."

"Liquidating." I drew the word out, emphasizing each syllable. "Such an innocent word for the killing of children and old women. It takes such courage to shoot them."

He glared at me with a new kind of hatred in his eyes. "You dare mock me? I was following orders from the Fuhrer."

"How many people died in your gas chambers at Auschwitz? Do you have a number? No, you can't even say because those figures numb the mind. The average person can't even comprehend such evil." Adrenaline shot through my body, making my heart gallop. I licked my lips, and my saliva tasted salty. "For a moment, let's forget the thousands of deaths you supervised and focus on one single death, without the formality of a selection—something totally random, an afterthought, a whim." I watched his face. "Does anything come to mind?"

He stared at the ceiling and gave no sign of having heard my question.

"You shot a young girl in cold blood as we carried baskets of wet laundry. Don't you consider that murder?"

He looked over at me with obvious contempt. "I was ordered to kill Jews. They were a threat to Germany's survival." He spit out his words through clenched teeth, "I am a patriot."

"With a hero's medal for killing children in the Ghetto." I paused. "Tell me, did your precious Fuhrer order you to dash the heads of Jewish babies against the walls in order to save bullets? Or was that your own clever idea so you'd have more bullets left for target practice on prisoners?"

"I was ordered to carry out the extermination as efficiently as possible."

"Orders, orders," I said. "Your filthy mouth spews Nazi propaganda like bile. Tell me some truth about yourself, and maybe I won't kill you. Why did you shoot that young girl who was carrying the laundry?"

"I don't remember her."

"I remember her," I said. "I see her face every moment of my life. She was my sister."

"I don't remember."

"There were three of us on laundry detail: Rebekah,

our friend Halina, and myself. My hands were wet from the laundry, but at least they were inside the gloves that our supervisor had allowed us. I remember thinking how ridiculous it was to be hanging out clothing in such bad weather. It was so damp, the clothes would never dry, even with that brisk wind that stung our faces.

"I had taken the heaviest load of wet laundry—the wool blankets that had to be washed every single week. Halina and Rebekah had divided up the shirts and towels, the socks and the underwear. I listened to the crunch of their boots on the gravel behind me, and I heard Rebekah say something to Halina, but I couldn't hear exactly what she said because the noise from the wind was too loud.

"My mouth was dry, and my back hurt from bending over the laundry sink for so long. I was daydreaming when the zing of a bullet startled me, and I turned to see who was shooting so close to us. I saw Rebekah fall to the ground, but I thought she was just frightened. Then I saw that her eyes had rolled back in her head, and there was blood on the front of her jacket. I dropped to my knees in the gravel and ripped open the jacket to see mangled flesh—a death wound. I grabbed a towel from Halina's basket and pressed it to Rebekah's chest, but the towel turned red so quickly. I didn't want to look into her face, but I couldn't help it. I was terrified by how pale her skin was and the trickle of blood that ran from one corner of her mouth.

"Then I touched her cheek—it was still warm, but I knew she was gone." My throat was tight. "By the time I looked up, you had already handed your rifle to an aide and you were putting on those white gloves of yours—

still unsoiled by grease or dirt or blood. I heard you say to your fellow officers, 'Look, they were trying to escape,' and I saw the smirk on your face when one of the officers replied, 'Emil, those are the girls who hang out the laundry every day.' You dismissed this fact with a careless wave of your hand and turned to go, the officers following you like puppies. Later I remembered what the officer had said—so careless, like a game, 'Emil, you are so full of nonsense.'

"I was frozen like stone, and I stayed there in the gravel, sitting back on my heels, as I watched you walk away. With my arms limp and helpless at my sides, I whispered under my breath, "Shoot me, you bastard," thinking to myself, I'm sorry, Mama, it should have been me. I couldn't save her. I couldn't save our Rebekah.

"At that moment, I wanted to tear you apart with my bare hands, and I could easily have gouged your eyes out. I wanted to set you on fire and listen to you beg for mercy. But I could do none of those things. Halina pulled me to my feet, pulled me away from Rebekah, and like a robot, I picked up the basket of laundry and stumbled toward the drying place, not seeing anything through my tears, not even waiting for Halina who stayed behind to gather up the wet things Rebekah had dropped." I dipped my head down and the muscles in my neck were so tight, I thought I would scream.

"I could easily have strangled you at that moment, but I pegged out your damn Nazi blankets, believing I could infuse the wool with such hatred that anyone who slept beneath the blanket would have nightmares forever. I knew Rebekah's body would already have been taken to the crematorium, and I could not go there in my mind, so I daydreamed of magical powers that would set a blanket on fire in the middle of the night, incinerating the person beneath it, waking him from sleep by pain so unbearable that death would be a release. I repeated, again and again, the words of a prayer to keep from screaming. I was like a woman in labor, giving birth in secret, whose screams would endanger everyone close to her, who bites on a stick or a rag and suffers the agony in silence."

The metal of the gun felt cold against the palm of my hand. "How could you shoot a fourteen-year-old girl with less thought than if you'd stepped on a cockroach?"

Janisch stared at the ceiling, his pale eyes unblinking.

"Before the Nazi gods took hold of you, Emil, when you were just a child—did you kill small animals for fun?"

"My mouth is so dry. Give me some water, please."

I hesitated, weighing the potential danger. More than anything else, I wanted him to keep talking. There was a carafe of spring water on his bedside table, and I managed to pour water from it into a glass with my left hand. I put the glass of water to his lips, and he lifted his head slightly to drink. He swallowed twice, a trickle of water running from the left corner of his mouth. I moved the gun close to his chest with my right hand, so he could feel the pressure of it.

"I was a good child, not some monster," he said, turning his head to look at me. "I try to follow the rules." His pupils were large, with only a tiny rim of blue circling them. "I am very sensitive child: I jump at loud noises. My father, he tries to cure me of this by slapping me if I cry for any reason. To make me tough, to turn me into a man, he says, he takes me to the execution of a murderer when I am only ten. Would you do that to a child?" He turned back to stare at the ceiling.

Your memory is short, I thought. What about all the children who saw their own parents die at your hand? And the parents who watched their children die? Not wanting to interrupt him, I kept silent, saying only, "Please continue."

"My father is loyal to Germany, even though it is not where he is born. He is Hungarian, an ignorant man who hopes to better himself and his family by being a 'good citizen.' When the *Hitlerjugend*, the German youth party, is organized, I am one of the first to be signed up, and I am never consulted in the matter. But I am proud to do as my father wishes, to serve Germany." Janisch swallowed and took a deep breath. "May I have more water?"

I remembered the constant thirst in the camps, but gave him another sip of water. "From the very beginning," he said, "I enjoy the structure of the organization and do well because I have discipline. I work hard and join the National Socialist party in '40. I become an officer in the SS and work in the liquidation of the Warsaw Ghetto, a filthy Jew-breeding slum. Hitler gives me the Iron Cross for that, and I am made under-Commandant at Auschwitz. Then my father is proud; he respects me."

I took a step back from the bed, still aiming the gun at his heart. "In 1944," I said, "you went missing from Auschwitz."

"They transfer me to Amsterdam after an attempt

on my life. A filthy Jew ruins my career in one moment."

"In Amsterdam you took the identity of Mattheu Vandermeer and were able to escape to the British Isles."

"Yes."

"I had hoped to hear something like remorse for what you did."

"Oh, I have regrets."

"Yes?"

He turned to look at me. "You are very beautiful, Katherine." He stared at the ceiling again. "Are you Jewish?"

"Yes, but my name is Katya."

"That's Russian."

"I was named after my Russian grandmother. I am Polish."

"A Pole, then, as well as a Yid?" He strained against the gauze holding down his arms, and his face reddened. "Two strikes against you." But then he curled his thin lips into a smile. "My biggest regret, Katya, is that we did not have time to complete the extermination."

His remark was like a slap in the face, and I was certain that I could not hate anyone more than I hated him at that moment. I lifted the Walther PPK, positioning its heavy muzzle against Janisch's left temple. I watched his eyes, navy-blue now by that dim light, as they stared unblinking at the ceiling. A crack of lightning illuminated the room for an instant, and his whole body jerked, as if he were convulsing. I saw my own face in his mirror on the wall to the right of the bed, and it was almost unrecognizable, my features like a pale mask. All that I felt was the blackness roiling inside, the hatred that had festered since Patryk's death, the desire for revenge that had fueled my own survival.

I saw Rebekah fall to the ground—how many times had she fallen, over and over again, in my imagination. This man, the pale and trembling coward tied to the bed, had shot Rebekah, and he couldn't even remember doing it. My finger tensed on the trigger. It was the moment for which I had waited nine long years. I watched Janisch's face, the clenched jaw, the sweat running down the side of his forehead into his ravaged hair. He blinked rapidly. "You can't do it," he said, in a voice made hoarse by fear.

I pulled the gun away from his head. "No, I'm not like you." I remembered Janisch's lie about the Iron Cross burning Vandermeer's palm when he became aware of his guilt as a murderer, and I was certain that guilt would not burn like fire but would instead weigh down my spirit like a boulder until the end of my life. Through the ringing in my ears, I tried to block the sound of young voices that chanted in my head—avenge us, for we are too young to die, avenge us, for we are too young . . .

Janisch's eyes were shut tightly, as I walked out of his bedroom, and out of his front door into the rain. Behind me, I didn't see his eyes shoot open, nor did I see the slow and deliberate movements of his right arm as he ripped at the gauze restraint by rubbing it repeatedly against a loose nail in the bed frame.

Gusts of wind drove rain into my face and eyes, as I walked carefully down the path to Crab Bay. I had come too close to killing him, and this unnerved me. I thought about flinging the gun into the ocean, but my role as a survivor would not let me do that. In spite of the steep angle of the slope down to the hide, I was willing to risk a fall just to have shelter from the rain and wind, some place to sit still for a moment to sort things out, to make some sense of the voices and thoughts whirling out of control, as erratic and disturbing as the lightning which continued to flash.

I turned the handle of the door and stooped to enter, climbed over the narrow wooden bench and put the gun on the ledge below the viewing slits. Since the rain was blowing in from the bay, I opened the side window to my right, where I glimpsed the full moon when the clouds drifted away for a moment. I thought of the monster, now such a small pathetic monster, still tied to the bed in the farmhouse. In his room, I'd had the power of life and death in my hands and found I could not be his executioner. I was afraid of what I had almost done.

I engaged the safety and left the gun on the ledge. Emil Janisch had won again. I heard voices that seemed to rebuke me, and I put my head in my hands. There was no way out, no way to win. I couldn't kill him; I might not be able to get him extradited, and I couldn't bear the thought of his freedom, his life in paradise without guilt or remorse. I wept, as the heavens seemed to weep, without hope, and I rested my forehead on the ledge, conscious of the gun near my temple. My sobs were deep and painful, and I allowed myself to scream, as if I were releasing years of agony with the sound. Anyone with me would have been frightened by the intensity of my grief, but I was alone and had never felt more isolated in my life. When there were no more tears left, I sat up and opened the viewing slit of the hide. A bright sliver of the full moon was visible behind the clouds, and the rain had stopped. We could go to the mainland and leave Janisch on the island. Even if he got loose, how could he leave without a boat? He'd be a prisoner until I could get a warrant for his arrest.

As I opened the door of the hide, I noticed a rabbit burrow in front of me, covered with sea campion. I placed the gun in it and climbed from the hide to the path above, shivering in the damp cold. I walked back up to the farmhouse from Crab Bay, passing Morwenn's room on the way. I'll let Morwenn sleep a while longer—first, I'll check on Janisch. I pressed the handle of the latch on the front door, and it made a loud metallic clank, but there was no longer any need to be quiet. I pushed the door open, and from the shadows of the alcove, a dark form leaped out at me, and there was pain in my right arm—a numbing, paralyzing pain, as if the jaws of a wolf had clamped onto me. When I clutched my arm, the strong hands of death circled my throat. A fall backwards, my head struck the floor and his knee in my stomach held me down. No air—let me breathe—I pulled at his hands. I opened my eyes and in the pale moonlight from the door, I could see Janisch's terrible face above me.

Hoping to strike something tender, I kicked upward with my right foot, aiming for his groin. My hands slid away from those crushing my throat, and darkness began to take over my world. No, I will not die, not now, not here, I will not die! My fingers groped blindly, reaching upwards to grasp the sides of his head, and I jabbed both thumbs into the soft globes of his eyeballs. I heard his scream, and it seemed far away. I was, at last, able to fill my lungs with air, although each breath stabbed my throat like a knife. I rolled onto my side and heard Janisch moaning, a few feet away. Run Katya, said the voice inside me. Don't let him finally kill you.

I struggled to sit up, and when Janisch tried to stand, I scrambled to my feet, slipping on the wet floor, stumbling, almost falling, with the sound of Janisch's moans and curses behind me. I ran out through the open front door and alongside Morwenn's cottage, on the slight chance that Morwenn might be awake and see us run past. I knew that Morwenn would most likely be asleep, and the sound of feet running on grass outside would not wake her. Aware of the uneven ground beneath my feet and the danger of injury, I ran toward the flashing beam at the far end of the island. I knew the man behind me would kill me without hesitation, and my only hope was to get the gun I left in the hide at Crab Bay.

As I veered off the main path to go down to the hide, slowing my pace because of the incline of the slope, I realized that the clouds had passed from the face of the moon, and I wondered if Janisch had seen me go down. Gun in the burrow—I rehearsed the sequence as I made my way down the slope, praying for sure footing. I could not afford to fall there. Grab gun with right hand—my wrist is killing me—I've never shot with my left hand. Reaching in with my left hand, I retrieved the gun from the rabbit burrow. I placed my feet in a wide stance and held the gun in my right hand, supported by my left. I glanced behind me at the moon shining on Crab Bay. I wondered if I would be able to see Janisch, or if I would be the one lit up by the moon, like the shearwater visible to the gulls before the moment of its death.

I waited, but still he did not come. The gun felt heavy; I had practiced using my index finger to pull the trigger, which sent currents of pain through my wrist, but it would not matter—as long as I could pull the trigger. Now the moon hung, round and silver, above the rock formation to the west; soon it would pass from view. How long until dawn, I wondered. Could I wait there until Robert returned? I thought of waiting at South Haven. Was the sky lighter now? I listened to the roar of the ocean below and behind me, as I shifted the weight of the gun to my left hand and tried to flex the muscles of my right hand, which was swollen and numb. It would be so tempting to go inside the small shelter, to be protected from the wind, from the biting cold of it, but I could not risk being trapped there. I was so tired. I stood with my back against the hide, my feet spread apart for balance. I was afraid to put down the gun, even though the weight of it was painful.

He appeared at the top of the slope, his white shirt half-buttoned and flapping against his skin, his breathing labored from running. He took a few halting steps down the incline and stopped. Time seemed to stop also, and then it whirled round and raced backward through all my nightmares, because Janisch had just lifted the rifle to his shoulder, and my legs were paralyzed. He was unsteady on his feet, and I managed to back round the hide, as the bullet zinged past.

My heart pounded in my chest, and each breath seemed to rip the inside of my throat, but I walked out from behind the wooden structure, holding the pistol with my finger on the trigger, my wrist supported by my left hand. Janisch was fifteen feet above me, the rifle tight against his jaw, his eye in the sights, ready to fire again. I braced my feet again and aimed for his heart, knowing that a head shot was too risky. As I squeezed the trigger, the pain in my wrist almost took my breath away.

I had aimed too high, and the bullet entered his left shoulder, but he dropped the rifle, which rolled down the slope beyond his reach. His face twisted with anger and pain, Janisch lurched down the slope towards me, and I fired again. The second shot hit him squarely in the center of his chest and he stopped short, staggered backward for an instant, and started to fall forward just as my third shot opened a major artery in his chest. Blood pumped onto the white shirt.

He fell, rolling now, propelled by the immutable laws of gravity toward the rocks and turbulent waves of Crab Bay. As he went over the edge, a bird diving without wings toward the ocean, there was no scream, only the gentle rush of waves upon the rocks. No bird calls broke the heavy silence, no angel chorus sang to greet the departed soul, and I found no joy in the moment of Janisch's death.

Still holding the pistol, I walked down carefully, below the hide, as far as I dared to go. He was on the rocks, just above the water, his head at an odd angle to his shoulders, his eyes open, as if staring at the sky. One hand trailed in the water, and there were no white gloves to put on, but his white shirt glowed in the moonlight where it was not stained dark with blood. My hands were so cold and swollen, it was as if the weapon had become part of me, but I pried it from my numbed right hand. Unwilling to bear the weight of it any longer, I dropped the gun, and it clattered onto the rocks.

It was almost more than I could handle to climb up from Crab Bay. I was numb with fatigue from the sleepless night and from the import of what had just occurred. As I reached the top of the slope and stepped onto the path that led toward the buildings, there were pink streaks in the sky, and I knew it would not be long until dawn. My wrist throbbed, and I felt as if I were trying to walk through icy water up to my shoulders. In spite of the cold, I stood for a moment with my eyes closed, listening to the muted sounds of the wind.

THE VERDICT

During parts of Katya's testimony, Nicolaas Vandermeer, sitting on my left, wept openly. Morwenn, on my other side, pulled a handkerchief from her pocketbook, but made no sound. Aaron, on the other side of Nicolaas, remained as impassive as a stone, as far as I could tell. What Katya had testified about—an evil beyond most people's comprehension—would come as no surprise to him.

At the end of her testimony, Katya looked dazed. Her face, normally pale, was more so, and her eyes couldn't seem to focus. She finally looked over at Mark, who had sat down during her testimony. As he stood up, Mark Wickham said quietly, "I have no more questions, M'lord."

Kevin Sperry looked at Katya for what seemed like half a minute. "Did Emil Janisch shoot your sister in cold blood?"

"Yes."

"Did you hate him?"

"Yes, of course."

"Did you ever think about killing him?"

"Yes."

"Did you take a gun to the island?"

"I did."

"Why?"

"In case I had to defend myself."

"So you knew this man could be dangerous?"

"Yes."

"No further questions."

Judge Mulholland ignored the light buzz of conversation among the spectators. As Katya was escorted back to prisoners' dock by the guard, I studied the faces of the jurors. They were, as they had been throughout most of the trial, carefully impassive, although one of the older women looked as if she might have been crying at some point. That part about Katya's sister had gotten to me, too. She'd never told me exactly what happened to Rebekah, but I could see why she hated Janisch so much. Would she pay the price, now, for this confession? She was directly in front of me in the prisoners' dock with her head down, probably looking at her hands or twisting the braided silver ring on her finger. So now, it was done, and I wondered if she had a sense of peace in her heart. Mark Wickham was less than serene—he sat at the barristers' table with his head in his hands, his white bench wig knocked slightly out of place.

As Kevin Sperry stood to make his closing statement, I couldn't see his face. "I have been deeply moved by the defendant's testimony. And I ask you, how does one cope with such a loss and with the knowledge of such evil?"

He paused, looking down at the floor. "But I must remind you of the purpose of the law, which is to preserve order in our society. We can, in a sense, look at the law as being more important than justice, which is sometimes unattainable. If we disregard the law, or if we try to amend it to accommodate special circumstances, we open the doors to anarchy.

"I submit to you that the defendant, Katya Denys, went to Skokholm to kill Emil Janisch, as evidenced by the gun in her possession, her indisputable motive, and the pentobarbitone sodium in the victim's bloodstream. Katya Denys does not deny killing Emil Janisch. What further proof do we need?" Sperry turned toward Katya, glanced at her for a moment but did not make eye contact.

"We do not dispute that Emil Janisch was a cruel man, and we do not condone his actions. But we must defend the most basic principle of our legal system—that murder, for any reason whatsoever, is against the laws of God and man."

I could imagine Katya sitting with her hands outstretched in her lap, palms up, weighing Janisch's guilt against her own, both hands tense and heavy.

Sperry hesitated, then looked directly at the jury. "You must view the actions of Katya Denys in light of the truth. Emil's Janisch's death was carefully planned. Miss Denys had motive, means, and opportunity to kill Emil Janisch, and that is what she did. I serve the law, ladies and gentlemen of the jury, as you have been charged to do, and it is your duty to find the defendant guilty of murder."

As Mark Wickham stood up to address the jury, I

could see small beads of perspiration on his upper lip. He bent his head for a moment, his fist to his mouth. "My learned colleague may have given you the impression that the law cannot be discussed or interpreted, that it is a holy and sacred thing, written in stone. But I submit to you the idea that the law is quite complex, made up of numerous statutes and previous legal decisions, all meant to preserve both the ideals of public safety and moral justice. There are times when these aims are incompatible, and one is achieved at the expense of the other. The statutes may be too simple or they may be too complex, and it becomes necessary to debate the true meaning of the law. In a civilized society, the spirit of the law is just as valid as the letter of the law—that is why we have jurors and a trial by our peers."

I could see Katya pulling back from Mark's words, obviously tired of sitting in that sturdy wooden chair with the eyes of a hundred people on the back of her neck. She seemed to be studying the Great Seal of Britain, depicted in a huge painting to the left of Judge Mulholland.

"The sixth Commandment states 'Thou shalt not kill,' but we pin medals on the chests of those soldiers who kill for their country. That Commandment, even as God's law, is subject to interpretation. The law itself, words frozen on paper, cannot serve justice if it is interpreted without regard to other factors. The duty of this court is to aim for the ideal of justice within the framework of the law. Consider what true justice for Katya Denys would be—the restoration of her family and the wasted years of their lives. How can we mitigate the torture, the starvation, the backbreaking physical labor, the humiliations? We cannot. All we could do in this courtroom is to add further punishment to my client."

Several of the jurors on the front row glanced at Katya, and I wondered what they were thinking. Mark Wickham's words had to fight their way through the ringing in my ears. Did Katya want to look out of the tall windows to her right—after months of imprisonment—just to watch the people down below on the square? It would seem like indifference on her part, so she would at least pretend to listen to her barrister.

Mark Wickham cleared his throat. "I submit to you that the goal of Katya Denys was to have Emil Janisch answer for his actions in a courtroom. Her intention, as shown by the letter written to Aaron Levy, made this very clear. On this basis, you must reject the Crown's request for a conviction on the count of murder.

"I would also ask you to bear in mind that there were mitigating circumstances—the necessity of self-defense. Katya Denys would have become another victim if she had not defended herself. I also ask you to consider the circumstances which led to Katya's obsession with Emil Janisch and why she could not ignore his existence—why she was willing to risk her life to reveal the truth about him." I watched Mark as he sat down, and I knew he was emotionally drained. Katya had not made it easy for him to defend her case. I listened to the expectant silence of the courtroom, tried to imagine the thoughts inside the jurors' heads.

I watched the judge in his black robe and bench wig, in his heavily-carved chair of authority and tried to remember that he was only a man. I studied his face, trying to read the nuances in the tilt of his head, the look of his eyes under the bushy brows, and the lines of his mouth. The words from that mouth would determine Katya's future, and mine. Judge Mulholland took off his glasses and rubbed his eyes. "The injustices done to Katya Denys and her family," he said, "began in a time and place where men with the wave of a hand played judge, jury, and executioner to millions of innocent people. But the crime in question, the death of Emil Janisch, occurred in a time and place governed by British law, by which Katya Denys must be judged." Katya must be exhausted. Would she be relieved, now that the ordeal was almost over? As she turned to go down the stairs and back to her cell, she looked up and smiled at me, and the bravery of that gesture broke my heart.

I watched Aaron Levy approach the barristers' table in the center of the courtroom. "Might I have a word with you?" he said to Mark.

Mark nodded toward the door. "Let's get out of here." He had already removed his bench wig, which he stuffed into his briefcase between stacks of papers and folders. He tore off his black robe and tossed it to his law clerk, along with the briefcase. I saw them start down the curved staircase that led to the vestibule of the courthouse.

I left Nicolaas with Morwenn, and with legs that felt like lead, I went down the stairs and across the black and white marble floor of the vestibule. Mark and Aaron were nowhere in sight. Outside, the sky was dark and heavy with clouds, and the mid-February chill bit through the fabric of my overcoat. I looked at the groups of people near the courthouse and still didn't see either Aaron or Mark. I walked down a narrow street lined by shops, some empty, some with only meager displays of merchandise. A damp cold made me shiver, as I contemplated Katya's future. I found myself in Nott Square and sat down under the statue of the general, with my hands shoved into my pockets to try and keep them warm. I looked up as Aaron and Mark approached.

"You look like hell," Mark said to me.

"Knowing Judge Mulholland's reputation, what do you think the sentence might be if she were convicted?" I said.

"Why are you assuming she'll be convicted?" Aaron said. In the sunlight, his face looked ten years older than when the trial had begun.

"Life in prison is a possibility," Mark said. "I thought I could work the oracle."

I knew the meaning of the term, but I wanted him to elaborate. "What do you mean?"

"I'd had some success—with the other two cases."

"This was a special circumstance, Mark," Aaron said. "You can't blame yourself."

"I wanted to save her."

"You may have saved her life."

"For what, though? What kind of life will she have in prison?"

"Why did she insist on testifying?" I said to no one in particular. "What would be accomplished by locking her up? She'll never do this again."

Aaron walked over to the plaque below the statue and read aloud the inscription: " 'The noble army of martyrs praise thee. Near this spot suffered for the truth, Saturday, March 30th, 1555. Dr. Robert Ferrar, Bishop of St. David's. We shall by God's grace light such a candle in England as shall never be put out.' " Aaron paused. "Did Dr. Ferrar become the candle?"

I'd asked a shopkeeper the same question two weeks earlier. "He refused to renounce his beliefs," I said, "and was burned at the stake by whatever religious group had just taken power."

"Good God," Aaron said, and he took a seat on the bench next to Mark.

Mark leaned toward me. "It was important to Katya to take responsibility for her actions. You heard her speech that night in the jail cell, and you also heard me try to change her mind." Mark paused. "As I recall, you were in favor of her testifying, Robert, and at the time, you seemed to understand why she wanted to do it. Why the change of heart?"

"I don't know." I stood up and walked over to the statue. "If I could take her place, I'd do it. I'd spend the whole of my life in prison just to let her go free."

"She pulled the trigger, Robert," Aaron said, tapping out a cigarette. "Not you." He cupped his hands against the wind to light it.

I couldn't believe Aaron wasn't being more supportive. "You think she deserves to be locked up?" I said to him.

"Of course not. But she did walk into the tiger's cage, with full knowledge of its history." Aaron snapped his cigarette lighter shut, studying my face. "Are you in love with her?"

I looked off into the distance, shifting my weight from

one foot to the other, then crossed my arms. "Yes," I said quietly, "I am."

"Have you told her how you feel?" Aaron asked.

"No."

"Why not?"

"I don't feel I'm worthy of her."

"Rubbish," Mark said, standing up so that he was face to face with me. "You're just afraid of commitment. You've never been able to stick with anything in your life."

"You're wrong. I just never found anything—or anyone—I cared to commit to."

"This is quite convenient for you, isn't it?" Mark said. "A commitment without commitment. You fall in love with a girl who'll be in prison for at least a good portion of her life, and you're footloose and fancy-free."

I could feel my face burning. "If they put her away, it's your fault." I wanted nothing more than to clock him one, but Aaron stood up and stepped between us.

"No more violence," Aaron said. "It won't solve anything." He moved forward to run his fingertips over the rough stone of the plaque, over the words carved into it near the top: " . . . the noble army of martyrs . . . " Mark and I faced each other in a hostile silence. "Look at this," Aaron said to us, gesturing at the plaque. "Robert Ferrar, burned at the stake—a senseless death. And Katya— " Aaron looked down. I could see him fighting the emotion. "It was so important to her to tell the truth about Emil Janisch, she was willing to set herself on fire." Aaron Levy, man of stone, had just broken.

* * *

After the jury had deliberated for three days, Mark

Wickham began to have hope. "With your unusual testimony," he told Katya and me as he entered her cell, "it's likely that some of the jurors want to convict you and some want to give you a medal. Let's hope there are more of the latter."

Katya, dressed in her usual white shirt and khaki trousers, sat beside me on the bunk with her knees pulled up to her chest, her feet bare. "Murder," she said softly. " How ironic for me to be convicted. Think about how many innocent people were killed by the Nazis, most of whom got off scot-free. I kill one Nazi in self-defense, and I face the gallows or life in prison."

"Katya," Mark said to her, "you set the stage for it."

* * *

On the fifth day, the jury reached a verdict. I was driven from the prison, then escorted up into the defendants' box from the holding area, and I watched as the jury filed in. Although several jurors looked over at the judge or at the portraits on the wall behind him, not a single one looked to the right, in my direction, and I took this as a bad sign. I glanced at the ridiculous clock beneath the balcony, with its hands frozen forever at five minutes past one. Rebekah had told me about a *trompe l'oeil* train station in Treblinka, complete with a painted clock that always showed the same time.

The court clerk asked the foreman to rise. "To my next question," she said, "I would like you to answer 'yes' or 'no.' Have you reached a verdict in which you are all in agreement?"

"Yes." The foreman's voice was confident.

I saw Chanele standing on the platform in Auschwitz

just before she was to be executed, and I wondered if I could be as brave as she was.

"In respect to count one, do you find the defendant, Katya Alina Denys, guilty or not guilty?" In spite of myself, in spite of my anger towards God and all my doubts, I began to pray silently, Hear, O Israel, the Lord our God is one ...

The foreman said "not guilty," and the words, so unexpected, and the sound of his deep voice startled me out of my trance. From the visitors' gallery behind me there was a small yelp from Robert. I tried to imagine the expression on Aaron's face.

"You find the defendant, Katya Alina Denys, not guilty on the charge of murder, and this is a verdict in which you are all in agreement." I closed my eyes, then opened them and looked at my hands, turned them over again and again, to see both sides. No tremors, no perspiration on the palms.

I stood up and turned to face the visitors' gallery and saw Robert caught in the mass of people, trying to move toward me. I walked to the edge of the prisoners' dock, with knees like jelly and a lump in my throat and reached down to him, but even by leaning over the rail of the dock, I was too high to reach his hand. I felt a gentle touch on my shoulder and turned to see my guard motion toward the door of the dock. He held it open for me.

I walked down the steps to where Robert was waiting. He opened his arms, and I entered his embrace, standing with my cheek pressed against his shoulder. I opened my eyes to see Aaron, Morwenn, and Nicolaas, all smiling at me and talking at the same time. I embraced Aaron and Morwenn. Nicolaas had a shy smile that revealed the dimple on the right side of his mouth. “I cannot tell you how much I admire you,” he said.

As I shook his hand, I smiled and said, “Don’t praise me, Nicolaas. I’m not a hero.”

“You have courage,” he said.

All I could think about was what Robert had whispered in my ear a few minutes earlier—come back to the island with me. I could go to an island at the edge of the world to pursue a dangerous man, but I was afraid of committing to a relationship.

After everyone had drifted away except Robert, we went down to the vestibule and sat on a bench. One part of me wanted to go with him, but it was the foolish, impulsive part. I said to him as gently as I could, “You can understand, can’t you, why I need to be completely free for a while?”

He was silent.

“I need to get back to work, to try and live a normal life. There may be a position for me at Providence Hospital in London.”

His eyes reminded me of a scolded puppy. “You could come out to visit, couldn’t you?”

I turned and hugged him so he wouldn’t see the tears in my eyes, and then I said, “Give me some time, love. I need to be on my own for a bit.” I kissed him lightly on the lips, then walked through the door under the stained glass windows and stepped into the diluted sunlight of Carmarthen.

THE ISLAND

In March, I began my work as a registered nurse on the surgical floor at Providence. My previous experience had been in psychiatric nursing, but I found I enjoyed the challenge of a new field, and I learned the names and functions of all the surgical instruments, as well as the preferences of the various surgeons.

In the evenings, I still wrote in the green spiral notebook, but now the entries were about my new life in London, my work in the hospital, and the people I had met. I enjoyed the anonymity of London. There had been limited publicity about the trial, thanks to Lord Kensley.

After so many years of life as a struggle to survive physically and emotionally, I was learning to cherish the plain vanilla days and gentle solitude in which I now lived. There was a patch of dark earth outside my flat, and when I cleared away the winter debris, I found the new green shoots of spring bulbs. On certain gray London mornings, I imagined that I heard waves breaking on the rocks of Skokholm and seagulls calling. And then I thought of Robert and the way he would stand outside and peer in at me as I stood at the kitchen sink of the Wheelhouse, his dark eyes full of mischief and his hair ruffled by the wind.

I began to receive letters from Morwenn, which delighted me, since what I regretted most about Janisch's death was its effect on the woman who loved him.

Dear Katya,

I'm spending entire days outdoors now that the weather is nice. We have so few really perfect days here. This morning, I scattered vegetable peelings—the ends of carrots and chips of potato skins—on the ground under the sycamore and elderberry bushes in the courtyard. One of the brown rabbits has new babies, and I try to save scraps for her.

I tried to read the book that Robert brought me, but I find it difficult to concentrate these days. My baby is now a young man in search of himself, and it frightens me because I know that I will lose him soon. From the first moment that Lord Kensley put him in my arms, he has been mine, because there was no other mother to claim him. I often wonder what my life would have been like if I'd not been hired as Robert's nanny, if I hadn't moved from Marloes to Skokholm. I was separated from Robert by the war when he was only nine years old. He held onto my arm, crying, but his grandfather pulled him away from me and told him to be "a brave little soldier."

Robert wrote to me faithfully for three years, but then the letters began to come farther and farther apart, until finally there were no more. It hurt me deeply, but I learned never to expect much from anyone. I know it must have been hard for him to lose two mothers by the age of nine. He always seemed happy, though. He reminded me of a little elf, always in motion, always just on the edge of trouble.

I know that Robert no longer needs me. His ties are to the island more than to me. I'm a symbol to him, I think, of a once-happy life. But I will be easily left behind when the larger world calls him. And it will call—I sense in Robert the restlessness of youth. He will tire of the birds and the rabbits and the wind and the gulls, and he will leave me again. Then it may be time for me to rejoin the larger world also, at least to move back to the mainland. I think of you often and pray for your continued good health. I wish we could have met under different circumstances. Perhaps we might have been friends.

Sincerely,
Morwenn Madoc

* * *

Aaron and I met for supper once a week; sometimes William Kensley would invite us to his flat. I enjoyed the intellectual stimulation of their conversations, both men well-read and deep thinkers, willing to debate issues of politics or philosophy in the spirit of learning from each other. William, in spite of his age and failing health, still went to the offices of his newspaper every morning except Sunday. Aaron had begun an account of his experiences during the war. I knew that he still kept track of major figures like Eichmann, because I'd seen the papers in his apartment one evening, when we returned for a forgotten umbrella, but he never discussed this with me.

Aaron was concerned that I had no interest in going out with young men my own age. "I can't relate to them," I had told him. "I'm just not interested in going out and having fun. It's hard for me to let go."

Aaron would shake his head and smile at me. "Someday," he said, "you will feel differently. I'm sure of it. You're a beautiful young woman with years ahead of you. Let yourself be happy."

* * *

One day, I received a letter from Robert, post-marked in Marloes. I slid my index finger under the flap of the envelope, realizing I had missed him more than I cared to admit.

Dear Katya,

As hard as I try, I have been unable to get you off my mind. I keep wondering how you're faring in London, and how your new job is going. Grandfather did pass along to me that you are enjoying your work at Providence. I've almost wished that I needed surgery, so I could wake up and see your beautiful face, and know that I was in the presence of an angel.

Morwenn seems to be healing well. I've encouraged her to think about moving back to Marloes, to be with her sister and her family, but she's so stubborn. I think she wants to stay on Skokholm until she dies.

I know that I won't be here forever. After all was said and done, when my dream of living on Skokholm had been fulfilled, I found myself very much alone. Somehow the birds and the animals were always enough when I was a child, but I guess I've finally grown up. I sometimes dream that you might join me here one day, but I know that's asking a lot.

I think we could be good for each other. I know your quiet strength could help settle me down and maybe I would be good for you, as well. I'd like to teach you how to laugh again.

You're the best thing that ever happened to me, and I would like to picture a future with you in it. Here or there or anywhere—it doesn't matter.

I know I've often behaved like a fool, and I haven't always taken the most logical path. But I know now what's worth having, and that's love.

I held the letter and looked up at the Henry Moret print on my wall, a painting of the ocean done in shades of green and blue with orange-winged sailboats in the bay, which had always reminded me of Skokholm. Tears streamed down my face, but I didn't wipe them away. It had been so long since I'd shed tears of joy.

I had supper with Aaron and Lord Kensley the next day. "I've received a letter from Robert," I told them, looking down at my hands. "He's asked me to go back to the island, but I'm not sure I can."

I glanced at Aaron for his reaction, then at William. "Could I be on that island without remembering Janisch every time I walked past Crab Bay? And what about his grave next to the farmhouse?" There were yellow roses on Lord Kensley's dining room table, and I took a deep breath of their rich fragrance to purge my memory of Janisch's face.

Lord Kensley cleared his throat. "I would think," he said, "that my grandson would know better than to ask you to go back there."

"He's naïve," I said. "Because he loves the island so much—he wants to share it with me. He doesn't realize how hard it would be for me to go back there."

"Why doesn't he come to London?" Aaron said. "He could find work here. Surely it would be easier than trying to survive, hand-to-mouth, on the island."

"Robert has always felt," said William, "that earning a living in a conventional manner required him to give up his individuality. He doesn't want to be a 'drone.' "

"He's living his dream," I said. "I couldn't ask him to give that up."

* * *

With the spring banking holiday at the end of May, I had a long weekend. I considered going to Skokholm for a visit, but I wasn't sure I could handle it. I wanted to see Robert, but was it too soon to face the island and its memories?

I washed a few dishes, vacuumed the tiny carpet of my living room, and sorted out my dirty clothes into laundry baskets. Then I sat on the sofa and picked up the novel I had bought the week before, *'Twixt Land and Sea* by Joseph Conrad. I twirled a strand of hair round my finger as I read. When I realized I'd read the same paragraph three times, I tossed the book on the coffee table, standing up to look out at grey row houses across the street. I tried to imagine what Robert might be doing at that moment. I walked back to the coffee table, picked up his letter, and sat down in my rocking chair, calming myself with its steady motion. As I read the letter again, and as I rocked, I felt the movement of the boat swaying back and forth just after Robert cut the engine, preparing to land on Skokholm that first time. I remembered the deep silence of the island, with only the light songs and chattering of birds.

At the time, I had been focused on the man with long hair standing next to the boat dock. He would not be there if I went back. But would his spirit seep like cold damp air under doorways and slip into my morning dreams to wake me in a cold sweat?

I walked into the bathroom and looked at myself in the mirror. My eyes always seemed to fascinate other people, who would comment on their unusual light color. Now they were the faded green of a Russian olive leaf. I ran my fingertips over the silk of my blouse, feeling the muscles of my upper arm under the smooth fabric. I brushed back my hair, which now fell in waves to my shoulders. As I reached for a lipstick, I wondered if Robert had truly grown up. Lately, at odd moments, I'd found myself thinking about children, and I saw two of them playing on the island, a boy with Robert's dark hair and my own blue-green eyes and a little girl in a red dress with brown eyes like Rebekah's. These daydreams told me that I had made an agreement with life.

* * *

In my seat on the train from London, I thought about Robert standing in the Wheelhouse courtyard. He loved to chat with Morwenn as she pegged tea towels onto the washing line, where the white towels would flap like the wings of frantic birds in the constant wind. They would sit for hours and hours with mugs of hot tea, recalling the events of happier days. Morwenn didn't seem old enough to have been Robert's nanny. I had to remind myself that she was only sixteen when she was hired to care for the infant Robert.

I looked out the train window. London's sky was still grey-brown, and everything looked dingy, except for the green of shrubs that bloomed between the train tracks and the houses. There was only a hint of blue sky in the west and the faint glow of sunshine. A huge field of yellow caught my attention. Between the rows of houses in brick and stucco, there were open fields grazed by Shetland ponies or a few scattered sheep. As we passed Reading, the first town outside London, there was a lone pig in a patch of straw beside a thatch-roofed cottage, small bodies of water, lots of shrubbery, and the first cow, which was black and white. Large green fields were more common now, all deep green except for the occasional bright yellow, which I decided must be alfalfa. There were more single houses, with long narrow backyards and lines of clothes hung out to dry, although blocks of apartments still clumped beside the train tracks.

In Swindon, a church spire, tall and pointed, stood out against sky that was finally blue, and there were more cows in fields divided by hedges of varying heights and composition and horses in flower-strewn meadows. An hour and three quarters out of London, a small sign proclaimed "Welcome to Wales" just before a lovely old church with a graveyard round it. Some of the buildings in Wales were rather different, especially the churches, which seemed to have had a common architect, with the same shade of grey-brown stone and square towers.

Soon, we passed Newport, whose Welsh name was one of my favorites—Casnewydd. A few minutes later, we were in Cardiff. When I saw a beautiful stone cottage surrounded by red tulips, next to a stone church, I wished I had brought a camera—the scene would have made a lovely painting. Near Bridgend, it was overcast again, and young boys in dark green uniforms stood holding British flags. It looked like some sort of ceremony—Boy Scouts, perhaps? Now there were sheep everywhere in fields divided by hedgerows, with scattered single houses. The other stations flew by—Swansea, Pembrey and Burry Port, Kidwelly—even the English names were fascinating. When we reached Ferryside, I looked out at the ocean, where the towers of a castle gleamed in the distance.

When we passed the sign for Carmarthen, I leaned forward in my seat, feeling a small rush of adrenaline. I was in prison there, but I knew such a small part of it—just the space between the prison and the Guildhall. It might not be a bad place to visit, if I could get into the old palace or find the area where Merlin the Enchanter was said to have been born. When the train stopped in the Carmarthen station, I leaned back in my seat with my eyes closed, listening to the low voices of other passengers settling themselves in the seats near me.

Soon we were in Whitland—Hendy-gwyn in Welsh—where the houses were identical—two-story white saltboxes, each with a grey roof and two red brick chimneys. Near the Clarebeston Road station, flocks of sheep grazed near gnarled old trees. We passed Haverfordwest and the ruins of a very old stone building.

Lulled by the peaceful rhythm of the train, I drifted off to sleep for a few minutes and woke up when the train stopped at Milford Haven. I looked out the window and thought about how surprised Robert would be to see me. It was too late to go over that evening, but surely I could find someone to take me over the following noon. The tides would not be right until then.

* * *

The distant outline of Skokholm grew larger and more distinct as Clyde Prosser's boat approached the island. I had tied a purple silk scarf over my hair to keep the wind from blowing it in my eyes, and as I held tightly to the knot of the scarf, I pressed a cold knuckle against my chin and realized that my hands were like ice. I lifted my heels, rising on my toes to stretch out the tension in my legs, aware of my heart beating faster than normal. I wondered how much of it was excitement about seeing Robert and how much was fear of old memories. I refused to let my time with Robert be spoiled by thoughts of Emil Janisch, who had stolen so much from me. There had to be a way to put his memory in the drawer and slam it shut. I focused on the glossy black shapes of puffins floating on the ocean just off the shore of the island, bobbing up and down with their ridiculous orange beaks.

As we approached South Haven, Clyde said to me, "Do you want me to come back on a certain day? You'll have no way t' get hold of me otherwise."

"Could you collect me on Monday?" I said. "I'll have to catch the afternoon train back to London." When we reached the landing platform, Clyde steadied my arm as I climbed out of the boat, and then he handed me the duffel bag.

"I'll see thee on Monday," he said, as he started the engine.

I had expected to see Robert there at South Haven. Although he didn't know I was coming, he would have heard the engine as the boat approached Skokholm. There was no one in sight, and for a moment, I wondered what would happen if they were both gone, Robert and

Morwenn, and I had to stay alone on the island for two days. Vandermeer's ghost flew out of its drawer. My palms grew moist, as I stood on the landing platform breathing deeply, my heart out of control.

Nonsense—this is ridiculous. I picked up my duffel bag and climbed the steps of South Haven, with the sunlight warm on my face. Bluebells and red sea campion formed masses of blue and pink in the meadow just above the steep path from the harbor.

As the wind blew the soft edges of the scarf against my face, I walked toward the Wheelhouse, where I thought I might find either Morwenn or Robert or the two of them. Relieved by the smell of freshly-baked bread, I dropped my duffel in the courtyard and opened the Wheelhouse door to find the long polished table bare except for a small vase of yellow flag irises. I took off my scarf and walked into the kitchen where Morwenn, with her back turned, was stacking cans on the pantry shelf.

"Morwenn?" I said softly.

She spun round, clearly startled, but she laughed when she saw me and opened her arms wide. "What are you doing here?" Morwenn said. "We'd no idea you were coming!"

"It was a last minute thing, Morwenn. I'm sorry I couldn't give you more warning . . . Where's Robert?"

"Oh, my Lord," said Morwenn, pushing a dark strand of hair out of her face. "You've just missed him. He left here yesterday—on his way to London."

"London? Is William all right?"

"Yes, he's fine. It's something else entirely." Morwenn smiled. "Why don't you sit down, and I'll make us some tea." She put the kettle on the stove and lit the fire. "Robert thought he might have a go at being a press man, for his grandfather's newspaper."

"A press man? A job in the city? I thought he'd live on the island 'til pigs fly." I sat down at the kitchen table, my legs tingling. "When did he leave?"

"Yesterday morning, just before noon. He wanted to surprise you."

"He's the one who'll be surprised," I said, "when I'm not there—especially when he finds out where I've gone."

Morwenn poured hot water into the teapot and carried it to the table. As she sat down, she smoothed her skirt, as if trying to collect her thoughts. "He needs more than this island can give him. It was lovely when he was a small boy, but now he needs to make something of himself." She ran her finger along the tablecloth. "If he wanted to stay here forever, I'd have been worried."

"Yes, but it was his dream to make a go of living here."

"A child's fantasy. Not meant to be lived out."

We sat in silence for a moment, watching the gulls outside, and I thought that maybe Robert had grown up after all. "Can you imagine him wearing a suit and tie?"

Morwenn laughed. "He's probably wandering the streets of London right now, barefoot in a brand-new suit, with his tie loosened, and one new shoe in each hand."

"I wouldn't be surprised," I said.

"I can't believe he just left," Morwenn said, pouring tea into my cup and then her own. "The two of you passed—how does that saying go?—like 'ships in the night.'"

"I can't say that I'm not disappointed—I have missed

him—but I'm glad you're still here." I hesitated, staring down into the teacup. "How have you been?" I didn't want to say, how is it without Vandermeer. I didn't want to say his name, as if a dead man still had the power to hurt us.

"I've not been lonely with Robert here. But now that he's gone, I don't know how it will be." Morwenn put down her teacup and looked at me. "How are you doing, love? Have you forgiven Vandermeer—I can't call him that other name—for what he did to your sister?"

There, it's out in the open. How often had I heard about forgiveness, usually from people with little knowledge of evil. "Should I forgive a man who took everything from me? My sister's life was more precious than my own. I would have died for her, if it came to that." I'd had so much time to think about this question. "Besides, in my faith, Rebekah is the only one who could forgive Janisch."

Morwenn looked at me, and her smile seemed tentative, reluctant. "So he remains unforgiven?"

I traced the outlines of my upper lip with my index finger. "Look at everything he did—and you don't even know most of it—and the fact that he had no remorse." I picked up the teacup, held it in both hands. "What about you, Morwenn? How do you feel now about him?"

"I've said I'm angry with him for deceiving me, but I think I'm really angry about what he was. I feel tainted. I know you tried to tell me, but I couldn't face it. I was angry with you for such a long time." Morwenn sighed. "It's going to take a lot more time before I can even think of him without wanting to spit his name out of my mouth like bile. But you have so much more to forgive than I do.

I was only deceived by him." She stared out of the window, her hands wrapped round the cup, but then she looked back at me. "Do you know what I regret most?" Morwenn's face was somber.

I leaned toward her. "What's that?"

"I wish I hadn't buried him in the garden. I have to think about the bastard every time I walk by there."

We laughed until tears rolled down our faces, and the muscles in my stomach hurt. I touched Morwenn's hand and said, "Isn't it funny that we both love Robert so much, and we hated Vandermeer, but for such different reasons?"

"Tell me honestly," Morwenn said, "do you know what to do with your hatred now?"

"I've had a litany all these years—all the remembered wrongs—and I know I have to move beyond that." Suddenly, I was tired, as if the universe were bearing down on the top of my head. I closed my eyes for a moment. "Anyway, what purpose does my anger serve? It doesn't change what he was or what he did.

"Perhaps," Morwenn said, "I'll be able to deal with it someday, too."

"What will you do now?"

"Catrin wants me to move back to Marloes and live with her and her husband. Most of the children are grown now—she's got plenty of room."

"How would you feel about that?"

Morwenn shook her head and smiled, but her eyes began to water. She looked out the window. "I don't want to leave, but I'm getting too old to live alone."

"Morwenn, you're not old at all."